The Bone Key

MARY RAJOTTE

The Bone Key
by Mary Rajotte
published by Quill & Crow Publishing House

This book is a work of fiction. All incidents, dialogue, and characters, except for some well-known historical and public figures, are either products of the author's imagination or used in a fictitious manner. Any resemblance to actual persons, living or dead, or actual events is purely coincidental. Although real-life historical or public figures do appear throughout the story, these situations, incidents, and dialogues concerning them are fictional and are not intended to depict actual events nor change the fictional nature of the work.

Copyright © 2024 Mary Rajotte

All rights reserved. Published in the United States by Quill & Crow Publishing House, Ohio. No portion of this book may be reproduced in any form without permission from the publisher, except as permitted by U.S. copyright law.

Edited by Lisa Morris and Tiffany Putenis

Cover Design by Fay Lane

Printed in the United States of America

ISBN: 978-1-958228-59-3

ISBN: 978-1-958228-57-9 (ebook)

Publisher's Website: quillandcrowpublishinghouse.com

To Mom,
For your unconditional love. I can still hear the joy in your voice when I shared the news that my book was going to be published. If only you were here to hold a copy in your hands.

And my Pa,
I did it! I wish you were here to celebrate with me, and to see how I'm continuing Grandma's legacy.

You are both in my heart, always and forever.
♥

CHAPTER 1

Nightfall

The autumn equinox arrives when the last hint of sunlight fades into dusk behind the imposing stone manor of La Maison des Arbres. An indistinct melody weaves around me like a golden thread of whispered expectation, coaxing me into the circle with my fellow witches of L'Assemblée de la Terre, the earth assembly of our coven. We gather around a long table hewn from rough cedar, not just for our seasonal observance but for the rite every witch in our coven must endure to prove his or her devotion. Before us, a lone witch kneels in the grass, waiting for the ritual to begin.

As the drums become more pronounced, chiming castanets signal the arrival of the High Priestess—my mother, Èvelyne Leclair. Silhouetted against the gothic glass doors of La Maison, she looks out across the grounds of the estate. Her hair shimmers like gold silk, spilling from behind her mask, over her shoulders, and down the back of her gray flannel poncho. When she turns, the drapery of her seafoam dress swishes around her, skimming the floor. My pride swells to see her so powerful and garnering so much respect from the others. I hope to one day command such respect, not only as a witch but as her daughter.

When I was a young girl learning the ways of the Craft, my mother taught me to put on a brave face for life's challenges. My father, a powerful witch and folk healer, warned me the world would provoke me with danger and temptations I could only imagine. Older now, I have seen these things firsthand, only now realizing my truest test was having the courage to be myself.

Months ago, I removed the mask I'd been hiding behind—fashioned from clay and feathers, given to me by our coven elders—and shoved it into a cupboard with no intention of wearing it again anytime soon. But tonight, we welcome the changing of the seasons, and a hint of a thought, an ominous foreboding lingers in the back of my mind. It is more than enough to will me back here, mask in hand, to be with my coven.

Crafted from wood the same way the First Witch of our coven made hers, each mask is unique to its clan. Long-eared. Snowy. Horned. And the great gray. So many of our northern owls stand represented in esteemed ritual masks. Some are the same as mine, decorated with white feathers taken from the elders, while some have a spray of darker speckles across the top. From beneath the plumage, a black beak protrudes between eyes also lined in black. Snowy owls may be among the most common, but each one of us is proud of our origins.

In the distance, a horn signals the start of the ceremony. At the back of the house, a procession of half a dozen male witches appears, wearing their masks and gray-feathered hoods that drape across their shoulders. Carrying smoldering bundles of sage, they move in unison, making their way around the circle, using feathers to waft the smoke up and around those in attendance.

Two male witches dressed similarly to the others wear oversized black gloves, the fingers of which end in sharp talons. Standing on opposite sides of the back door, each lifts a hand for Èvelyne as she exits the mansion.

The gauzy feathers of her snowy owl cape billow in the air as she proceeds down the stone path toward the circle. A flash of amber in her eyes when she catches my gaze reminds me of our last conversation months ago. Taking a leave from the coven wasn't exactly a way to get in her good graces. Maybe coming here will be enough of an olive branch to smooth things over...even if I'm not sure I want to come back for good.

Her hand extends slightly as she draws near, as though she wants to take mine in hers like we are two planets meant to be in orbit. But she continues past, only nodding her acknowledgment. Another hand slips into mine, and when I turn, a tall redhead has moved into the circle beside me.

"I knew you would come!" Gwen says, squeezing my hand.

When we touch, our rings clink together and we both smile, and from beneath her mask, her green eyes flash gold. Where her pinkie finger used to be, she wears a silver jointed finger covering attached to a bangle at her wrist. I compare it to mine—a trinket not only to replace the missing appendage but to celebrate the act of devotion to our coven. It's something we used to joke about: how we are like magpies, drawn to shiny things.

"I get practicing on your own and needing your own space," she says. "But casting a circle by yourself? Today of all days? I couldn't bear to think of you at your place alone."

"You make me sound like some pathetic hermit."

She throws her head back and lets out one of those musical laughs like wind chimes. Maybe coming back wasn't such a bad idea. If anything, I've missed Gwen: she's the little sister I never had. Life has been dull without her, that's for sure. Her enthusiasm for our Gift reminds me of myself when my mother first introduced me to the Craft when I was in grade school. It's nice to have a younger witch to share that same bond with.

"I didn't mean it like that. I'm just glad you're here."

Around us, the wind rises and whispers through the trees, bringing with it the smell of burnt wood and dying leaves. The fading sunset highlights the maples surrounding the estate, already starting their shift from green to red. The musky scent of ash intermingles with sweet, earthen grass and exhaling moss, awakening something deep within me—something that has been with me since birth. A connection I had tried to ignore, but one that's unbreakable.

Moving before the group, Èvelyne faces us, and the drumbeat ceases. She stands before the rough-hewn table adorned with everything needed for the ritual. The small brass bell she bought in a shop in San Diego. A double-edged athamé, its blade set into a bone handle my father brought back after visiting family in Mexico. A sand-filled saucer and cones of incense wait in the center of a ring of candles of various colors made in the garden house at the back of the estate. Spicy cinnamon sticks sit stacked next to a goblet filled with myrrh. A plain silver chalice sits empty. Another filled with water. A third bejeweled one sits atop a brass stand.

To start the ceremony, Èvelyne takes the altar bell in one hand, ringing it three times. The lilting knell brings past celebrations rushing back to me. The thrill of initiation ceremonies. The solemnity of funerals for our fellow owls. The allure of the changing seasons. Each made that much more meaningful because they were experienced with the other members of L'Assemblée de la Terre over these last fifteen years.

Pointing to the ground at due north, Èvelyne moves clockwise around the circle, stopping at the east, south, and west points before moving back to where she started.

"I draw this circle in the name of Lorenza de Salazar, the First Witch of our coven. For the sacrifices she made centuries ago to conjure and create this Gift."

Facing the forest to the north of the estate, she stands with her arms extended in front of her, palms up.

"As Autumn brings balance to night and day, let us find that same harmony within ourselves. May we live our lives peacefully and in tune with Goddess Earth. Let there be poise in all we do. May we know our inner light and our inner darkness. May we continue to receive the blessings from our ancestors so we may honor them with our devotion. As I will it, so shall it be."

Warmth envelopes me, rising from within and spreading across my chest and shoulders. I can't help but feel emotional. Standing here—in this place, with my coven—feels right, no matter how much I've been resisting it. Maybe I've been away too long.

"Lady Autumn," Èvelyne says, facing us, "Queen of the Harvest. Our northern sisters and brothers of Assemblée des Chouettes, the owl coven, honor you on this blessed Mabon. We, L'Assemblée de la Terre, thank you for these rewards. As the Wheel of the Year turns, it brings us to and from each season, from one to another. What *was* has come and gone. What *will be* stands before us."

Approaching the altar, Èvelyne reaches for an earthen bowl filled with salt. She lifts it in front of her.

"Blessed Guardian of the North, Spirit of Earth, we summon and stir you." The ground cools and sighs, shifting as the countryside settles into darkness as the moon rises overhead. "We ask you to bless our sacred space with your presence and protection. Grant us your endurance and strength."

She takes a pinch of salt, pours it onto the altar, and then takes the cone of incense from the dish. After she lights it, she waves the curling smoke around herself before returning it to its place.

"Blessed Guardian of the East, Spirit of Air." As she speaks, the leaves stir on the rising breeze. "We summon and stir you. We ask you to bless our sacred space with your presence and protection. Grant us your creativity and intuition."

Next, she takes a long match from the altar and lights the wick of the tall red pillar candle before her.

"Blessed Guardian of the South, Spirit of Fire, we summon and stir you." Flames lick the sky as the bonfire stokes and reaches skyward with each breath. "We ask you to bless our sacred space with your presence and protection. Grant us your passion and energy."

Last, she lifts the pitcher and pours water into a silver chalice, saying, "Blessed Guardian of the West, Spirit of Water, we summon and stir you. We ask you to bless our sacred space with your presence and protection. Grant us your empathy and emotion."

At the center of the table, an earthen bowl sits atop a wooden pedestal with bone legs that have talons on each end. Beside it, a clear vial with a copper stopper sits in a metal stand, half-full of vibrant purple liquid. Shimmering, it throws a dizzying glare on Èvelyne's face, setting her face aglow. She takes it in both hands and lifts it skyward.

"Blessed Guardians. We honor our sister, Lorenza. As we await the replenishment of the Sacred Tree, we thank her for all she endured."

Turning back, Èvelyne dips her hands in reverence to a tall clay statue of a slender woman in the center of the table. Her hair is a tangle of wild dark feathers framing her face. Her wide-set eyes offset a pointed beak, and massive wings spread in a majestic arc behind her. Around her neck, a time-tarnished sliver of bone hangs suspended from a necklace made from dried vines.

"With this Sacred Nectar, we take in the ancient Gift from our sister, the First Witch, who gave of herself to provide her future generations with such wondrous abilities."

She holds the vial out to us in her cupped palms.

"As we prepare ourselves for the Opening of the Flower," Èvelyne continues, "I call upon the one within you who has the devotion to stand by my side. Who will help me lead L'Assemblée de la Terre as we strive to experience our Gift to its fullest?"

I feel the pull toward the altar, but I can't move. My head pounds. My throat goes dry, and my hands turn clammy. Beneath the mask, my face itches and sweats. It's everything I want—the only thing I have ever wanted. To earn my place as one of those in the coven to receive the highest honor.

To transform. To fly. To serve by my mother's side. My body tenses in anticipation, the want so deep it courses through me like wildfire.

Gwen elbows me in the side, but I stay planted where I stand. How can I ever be like my mother? How can I ever be as powerful, as regal as she? I haven't advanced enough to fly yet. How can I be her right hand when I can't follow where she leads?

With a backward glance, Olivia Bennett, a witch I've known since high school, steps toward my mother. Beside me, Gwen leans in.

"*You* should be the one up there," she whispers.

I'm thankful that my mask hides the flash of embarrassment on my cheeks. Around me, I sense the quiet shifting of feathers, and when I try to meet the gazes of my brothers and sisters, they look away, trying to fathom why I have not stepped into the role my mother has been grooming me for since childhood—the role I was born into. Her Maiden, her right hand, her assistant, confidante, the one to whom she will instill all her secrets and rites so one day she too will head a coven of her own.

"Gracious Goddess." Olivia's voice shatters my thoughts. She stands next to Èvelyne and leads the ceremony as her assistant. "We open our hearts, our souls, our minds to you. Please consecrate our altar and our tools. Please grant us your guidance and protection. Welcome, Goddess, and blessed be."

Olivia lifts the bowl of salt, offering it to Èvelyne, who takes a pinch and mixes it in the water. She lifts the blade, sprinkling it with water before she holds it between both palms and passes it through the coils of smoke rising from the incense.

"I bless and consecrate this blade, in the name of Mother Goddess and Father God, in the presence of the Powers of Earth, Air, Fire, and Water. May this athamé aid this coven in worship, in the celebration of our Holy Days, and work our will. Blessed Be."

As she places it down on the altar before she reaches for the next item, my vision darkens. Is it the heat? The cold? The pressure of being back here when so much expectation for the coming year hangs in the air like incense smoke?

"Now," Èvelyne says, "we welcome our sister Lillian Blanchet to L'Assemblée de la Terre and receive her offering in devotion to this sisterhood."

She turns to Lillian, still kneeling before the oak table. In front of her,

Èvelyne lays a white cloth, upon which Lillian places her hand, palm down. Taking the blade, Olivia offers it to Èvelyne, who holds it over Lillian's hand.

"Do you, Lillian Blanchet, join our family with the courage and conviction needed to uphold our sacred rites?"

"I do, High Priestess," Lillian says. "With perfect love and perfect trust."

Nodding, Èvelyne moves the blade until it presses the blade against Lillian's hand above the top knuckle of her little finger. Lillian's body tenses. Her gaze darts to the group and then back, but she makes no noise. Poising a small hammer above the blade, Èvelyne raises her hand, and then, with three swift thwacks, she sends the blade between the joints, slicing the skin, severing Lillian's tendons. She cries out, slumping forward as blood spurts from the wound, spilling out in a wave. Èvelyne covers her hand with a fresh cloth, which quickly stains red. Next to her, Olivia holds out a small stone plate, upon which Èvelyne places the severed digit before she takes a poultice soaked in yarrow-steeped water and, peeling back the cloth, washes Lillian's wound. Covering her hand with a gauze dressing, she reaches for Lillian's other hand and coaxes her to rise. The acolyte teeters as she stands but quickly regains her footing. Raising her hand, she places her palm flat against her chest and curtsies to Èvelyne before one of the escorts takes her away to tend to her hand, along with her severed finger.

I graze my fingertips along a similar segment of bone, about an inch long, that dangles from a simple cord around my neck. Every member of the coven has one. Carved from a pinkie finger bone, it is a sacrifice of devotion to the coven made at our own initiation. An embedded talon extends from one end. The other end, carved and hollowed out, allows sound to travel through and serves as our calling whistle until we gain the ability to transform into our bird selves and make the call on our own.

Even though I've seen the ceremony done many times and even taken part in it myself when I joined the coven in high school, the sight leaves my skin chilled and covered in gooseflesh. There is a weight to the surrounding air, but it's something more than mere ceremony. It's an omen calling to me, just out of reach. I ignore it, watching as Èvelyne prepares for the next and most important observance.

Having been tended to, Lillian returns to the circle and faces my mother, once again kneeling before her. Taking the vial, Èvelyne holds it in her cupped hands, allowing the vibrant shimmering Elixir to dazzle and dance before her.

"Let this Elixir, given to us from our sister Lorenza, be the magic with which you see, the music you hear, and the wind that shall take you to new heights."

Opening the stopper and cupping one hand under Lillian's chin, Èvelyne deposits a drop of the glowing Elixir on her tongue. When she stands to face the group, Lillian looks as she always has. But soon, the shift begins. Her face widens, her eyes becoming deep-set. Her hair blanches and then shrinks, each strand sprouting into individual feathers. Her body contracts, becoming more stout, shifting from human to owl form.

"Welcome, sister Lillian," Èvelyne says, her voice rising. "May you cherish this Gift, and may it serve you for your lifetime as a member of Assemblée des Chouettes."

Lillian fluffs out her feathers, stretching her wings in a glorious display. My arms tense at the sight. Oh, how I long to do the same. To feel that change in myself. To see what they see through owl eyes. It is all I have ever wanted, and I won't stop until I gain the ability for myself.

I lift my bone whistle to my lips as the others do and blow, avoiding the shame I feel for being unable to shift. To the outside world, there is no sound. But to us, a distinctive signal plays from each whistle. With the call, a shadow in the periphery of my vision glowers in our direction. I blink a few times, hoping it's only the intensity of the rite. But my sight only grows darker. A vision. One I can't fight.

Something moves in the corner of my eye. At first I think it is Gwen, sensing the tension in my body, my hand squeezing hers more tightly, but the darkness encroaches. It spreads like two black wings. A black moth flutters into my view until it hovers over the coven, an ill omen haunting every witch in the circle. Shadows seep in from my periphery like spilled ink, staining everything in front of me.

Someone will die, just like the last time I saw them.

I tear my hand from Gwen's and cover my eyes as though it will stop the vision from haunting me. The moths don't belong here. They never come this far north. I feel them flapping against me, and at first, their wings are soft like velvet. Then they prickle and sting, flitting against my hands and arms, scratching my scalp with their tiny clawed feet. The sound of their collective flight is a high-pitched screech that makes my eardrums burn, and the scene before me plunges into darkness. Like coming in from the outside to a darkened room, my eyes adjust. I'm not at La Maison any longer. I've traveled through time and space, returning to the place where I first saw the black witch moths, and my entire world was shattered.

In the mountains of California, a vibrant hacienda sits in the middle of lush greenery with the desert as its backdrop. A garden of sunflowers and Mexican honeysuckle burgeons beyond the amber-hued stone house. Sun-baked sand warms my feet. I'm dressed in a ruffled sundress, and I'm so proud of my pretty dress that I spin until I'm dizzy.

My father, Alejandro, comes toward me. His long dark hair frames his thin face, and his eyes glimmer as he smooths down my pigtails before handing me a stick. He turns me around, slips a length of fabric over my eyes, and ties it behind my head.

"Ok, *mija*. I will spin you once for every year you have lived. Then, you take the stick and swing. *Sí?*"

Taking me by both shoulders, he spins me around, counting along with the others.

"One...two...three...four...five. *Andale*, Valeria!"

I charge forward when a scream stops me. My father clamps his hand around my arm and wrenches me away. I stumble. He picks me up and runs, clutching me so tight to him that I ache.

"Valeria!" my mother shouts. "Alejandro, come!"

I try to tear off the blindfold, but my *papá* holds it there.

"No, *mami!* No!"

He trips. We hit the ground hard. I fall on my side, gasping as the wind is knocked out of me. The blindfold shifts. My father, his eyes wide, mouth hanging open, falls beside me. Blood blooms across his chest. Something thin sticks out of him. Feathers and metal—an arrow. A small pendant dangles from the end, the letter L engraved into it. A dog or some animal beneath it.

A cloud of moths hovers overhead before they spin wildly and careen toward the treeline. Lost in the gloom, a figure stands near the trees. A tall, slender woman, one I've never seen before, watches. As the moths twirl around her, she reaches her hand out to me, but the moths overtake her, covering her like a dark veil until she disintegrates into nothingness.

Above me, a low-pitched screech calls from the tree. Black feathers extend outward in an arch as an owl swoops down from the branch and lands beside me. It lets out a long call and stretches its dark wings like a shield to envelop me. I squeeze my eyes closed as it knocks me down.

The owl sits with one foot planted on my back to keep me protected. But I turn my face in the other direction. Next to me, my *papá* lays in the grass. His eyes are heavy-lidded and glassy, the color shifted to bright orange—his owl eyes.

I scramble to my feet and race toward a large garden at the side of the house. Tearing flowers from the dirt, I rush back as an arrow flies past my head. When I trip and skin my knees, I cry out, but I crawl forward on my elbows, the flowers still clutched in my hand. When I get back to where my *papá* is still on the ground, I lay the flowers around him. On one hand, he wears a tarnished copper ring in the shape of an owl. I take that and pry it from his finger, laying it on top of the blossoms. Tears stream down my face, but I swipe them away, patting the saltiness into my palms. I kneel over him, reciting the words I have heard him whisper a million times. I don't understand most of them, but I do it anyway, hoping from the very bottom of my soul they mean something. That if they were important to him, they might help, they might bring him back to me. But when nothing happens, when he doesn't move, doesn't breathe, I know the truth. He is gone.

I scream out and collapse to the ground next to his body. The moment I feel it beneath me, the memory dissipates.

I'm back at La Maison where the smokiness of the ceremony rouses me. I gasp and spin around. The owls from my memory have dissipated, but the weight of the guilt for not being able to help my father, not being able to save him, hangs over me like a shroud. I'm back in the circle with Gwen standing next to me.

"Valeria? What is it? What's wrong?"

I skitter away from her and crouch in the grass, gasping at the memory. The metallic smell of blood lingers the way it did that day. I clamp my hands over my ears, trying to stop the echoing loop of remembered screams, of rasping last breaths from those around me. I shake so violently that every muscle in my body aches.

A hand on my shoulder startles me. I open my eyes to a circle of faces looming over me. Owl masks, feathers quivering in the moonlight. Their eyes become like marbles, catching and refracting light. I back away from them, scraping my palms across the frost-sharp grass.

Behind me, Èvelyne lifts the bone whistle hanging at her throat and plays an undulating song. A beckoning. At her call, the Elders in the group let out a collective cry, and all at once, they change, the High Priestess changing with them. Her skin shifts, her fine hair blooms into feathers. Her bones narrow and shorten, her fingers elongating, stretching into wings, toes into talons.

Flapping her wings, she lifts up, taking flight with the others, who congregate in a hypnotic orbit in the sky over the estate. Some swoop in a circular formation, spinning, and dive bombing. Others fly silently or cry out in glee. They come together in a blur of down and feathers, intertwining in jubilant flight. I squeeze my hands into fists at the pang of longing that stirs in me. Witches younger than I am have already tapped into their abilities and surpassed me, earning the right to our coven's most coveted Gifts—transformation and flight. Practicing on my own may have helped me to forget that I can't fly, but being back here brings it into stark focus. I don't measure up. Until I can fly, I won't be able to.

The flurry of activity provokes a veil of darkness. Growing, it drips like melted black wax, a shadowy curtain obscuring everyone overhead. As I'm about to call out a warning, the blackness explodes like a powder keg, breaking into a cloud of moths. Gwen, still standing beside me, yanks on my arm, but I can't see her. The moths twist and turn, hovering over her face until they smother her. When I swipe my hand through the moths, the swarm disperses before coming at me, covering me with their prickling wings and bristly legs, the sound of their flight loud in my ears. Scrambling backward, I swat them away, but that only sends them streaming toward Gwen, teeming over her body, in her hair, her mouth. She reaches out, the moths flitting wildly as she tries to grab me. I stagger away from her and race to the treeline without looking back.

CHAPTER 2

Hunted

The wind lashes like barbed incisors, darting through the gaps between the trees as I crash through branches and stumble over gnarled roots to distance myself from La Maison. Leaves flicker in slow motion in my peripheral vision, shadows encroaching like the swarm of moths, taunting me. The wind—cool and biting—is from their mottled wings, beating, reverberating from red maple to stark white birch, throwing off my sense of direction, so I lose my way in the forests I've known since childhood.

Something flies so close, it grazes my cheek. I fling it away, but it comes back again. I swipe at it and clasp my hands over my head, barrelling blind through the thicket, my boots squelching in the soft carpet of twigs and earthy-scented lichen.

I trip and land on my stomach, thankful for the velvety moss that breaks my fall. I freeze. The flitting has stopped. The moths are gone. They were only a hallucination.

Behind me, a twig snaps, alerting me to a faint presence lingering above the trilling grasshoppers and the rustling of squirrels and rabbits burrowing for impending winter.

The air shushes around me and by the time I look up, Gwen has caught up to me. Her red hair cascades around her like fig tree tendrils in a *cenote* I visited when I was young. I wish I were there, floating in the blue water below. Instead, I lay here, drowning in darkness.

"What happened back there?" Gwen asks. "Something's wrong. I saw it on your face."

I sit up and flick dried thistles from my skirt. "You and everyone else."

"Who cares what anybody thinks."

"My mother."

"Well, yeah," Gwen says, holding out one hand to haul me up to my feet. "She is High Priestess. Kind of a job requirement."

"All I wanted was to get through the ceremony. The last thing I needed was another hallucination. In front of everyone. Again." I pick up a handful of leaves and toss them in the air. "I should have never come. I need to get the hell out of here."

Gwen crouches beside me, her black eyes studying me before they shift back to their usual green. The indigo of her aura surrounds her, cool and inviting.

All I want is what they have. The freedom of flight. The pride that comes with being able to shift. To feel like I belong in the coven I have been a member of for fifteen years. But, even after all this time, it feels further away than ever before.

"What you need is a cleansing," she says, holding out a hand to haul me up from the damp moss.

"No, what I need is a stiff drink," I say, bracing my aching back.

I brush past her and start for the house, noticing the faint wavering curtain of protection around the estate doesn't seem to stretch as far as usual. She's on me in two steps. I'm thankful she came to check on me. At least someone did. But Gwen isn't one to give up after a quick conversation.

"You came all the way out here, Val."

"Yeah. Because you chastised me until I gave in."

She tilts her head back and laughs. "True. But you're just as stubborn as I am. If you didn't want to come, you wouldn't have. Am I right?"

She gets in front of me and cranes her neck from one side to the other, knowing it will get under my skin. As much as I prefer to wallow, I can't help but smirk. She's so much like I was when I first joined the coven. Strong-willed. Excited by the prospect of growing in the Craft. But Gwen's youthful optimism outshines my hesitation.

"See?" She laughs. "I knew you weren't just a big-city bitch. I knew there was a super-cool witch under there somewhere."

"All right," I say, reaching forward and shoving her back. "I get it."

"Good. So tell me what's really going on."

"It's nothing," I say, brushing off her question as I keep moving, seeing the faint glimmer of the bonfire through the trees up ahead. But she grabs me by the arm.

"Enough. This is me. You don't have to put up a front. I know you."

She's holding onto my bicep, studying my face. All I want is to look away. To avoid her gaze. There's mischief in her eyes, like a little sister teasing me into admitting things I'd rather forget.

"I know you're hurting," she says. "You want to be your own witch. To have space to be yourself without all the rules and politics and yes, the ever-watchful eye of the High Priestess. But I feel it."

"What?"

"Yearning. Loneliness. You need to let all of that go. It's like a weight holding you down. What is it? You can tell me, you know."

The more she says, the more the tension in my neck and shoulders pulls taut. This is what I've been ignoring these past six months.

"Whenever I do a spell," I say, "I feel so grounded my thoughts can barely process. When I try to tap into my Craft, something you all make look so easy, I feel…less than. Like I'll never progress. Like I'll always be average. Stuck here in the same place I've been for years. Left behind."

"It isn't a competition, Val. We're your coven. Not rivals. We're here to help one another."

"Yeah? Tell that to Olivia. Did you see her face when she went up to call the corners?"

"Olivia's a catty witch. You're older and wiser."

"Gee, thanks."

We both laugh this time.

"What I mean is you have experience she doesn't. You can work with that. Use everything you've seen, everything you know, and put it into your magic."

"I've been doing that, but it isn't getting me anywhere."

"Maybe you're too focused on the end result. Not on the journey. I know it's hard not to be, especially with everyone feeling the pressure of the trip to Mexico for the Elixir. You need a cleansing. Now."

We've come to a clearing. Pine needles cover the ground in an amber-hued carpet. Damp soil gives off its nightly perfume. Gwen pulls off her glimmering shawl and fans it out, laying it over the detritus like a blanket.

I sit and lay my satchel across my lap as Gwen kneels beside me. She sweeps dried leaves from a downed tree lying parallel to us. I rifle through my bag and produce a wooden cigar box. Pressing my palm to the top, the wood under my hand warms. It was a present from my father on my fifth birthday. The day my entire life changed.

On the top, carved into the rowan wood, is the insignia of the four sister covens, each symbolized by a feather. They come together to form the head and wings of an owl. Two quills extend from the bottom to form talons. I had the same design tattooed on my back the minute I turned eighteen.

Opening the box, I remove a black candle and my narrow tube of waterproof matches. Next to those, I lay out a short bundle of sage and the ornate pocket mirror I bought the summer Gwen joined the coven.

My mother had asked me to show her the ropes, so I took her into the city to a small shop on St. Sulpice. Leaves swept in a tiny torrent in the courtyard of Notre Dame Basilica as the noon bells chimed. We spent a good half hour pouring over everything, picking out incense and trinkets. Our tastes were so similar, we picked out the same things and didn't realize it until afterward when we compared them over cappuccinos at a café down the street. That was the day I realized I had abilities to share, and I wanted to pass them along to Gwen. Even then, five years younger than me and relatively new to the Craft, she showed such promise. That promise is why, even though I'm older than her, she's a higher degree in our coven.

"Tell me what happened earlier. What's blocking you? Why have you stayed away for so long?"

I hesitate, but I can't hold on to the fear anymore.

"The black witch moths. I saw a swarm tonight."

"During the ceremony?"

I nod, clasping my hands. My fingers are freezing, and my rings clink together coldly.

"Do you still see them a lot?"

"Not since the last time."

Six months ago, the coven gathered for another celebration. Imbolc, the stirring of seeds and buried intentions at springtime. We spent the day setting out ice lanterns, and when we finished, they dotted the grounds with a golden glow, interspersed with evergreens piled for burning. Pristine white snowdrops intertwined in massive wreaths of cheerful daffodils and forsythia waiting to adorn the halls of La Maison. Tucked into the blooms, a tiny carved sheep, a swan, corn husk dollies, and beads of garnet and ruby lingered like whispered secrets. Around us, the carpet of snow softened and subdued the landscape, with nothing more than cracking branches as our symphony. But, along with the promise of spring, old rivalries readied themselves to spring forth anew.

Olivia was in my face as usual, berating me for not being around enough. For not showing as much devotion to the coven as everyone else—as her. She had been saying those same things to me for years. I chalked it up to her jealousy over having the High Priestess as my mother, but as we grew older and advanced in the coven, Olivia seemed to make it her mission to one-up me in front of my mother.

At the height of the argument, the moths came. Sweeping down from the treetops like falling leaves, they dripped like ink stains down her face and seeped into the ground around her, tainting the grass and blooms and choking out the promise of new life. I turned away, hoping to erase the dark omen from my mind. But she took it as my backing down and cackled at my weakness. When I turned back, she looked like someone had dipped her in black candle wax, her face melting away, revealing her charred bones beneath. I spun away from her again and stalked off just in time for a large branch to fall, narrowly missing her. When I looked back to investigate the noise, I saw her sprawled on the ground, glaring at me as though I brought the branch down on purpose. From then on, our rivalry became much more intense, with Olivia making her animosity for me clear.

At that moment, I felt the shame of hesitation, the stain of my indecision. But what I sensed was the moths warning me with their presence. That something catastrophic would one day happen to her, to us. The weight of me being the blame for the threat to our coven, that the moths were another omen like the one on the day I lost my father, was too much to bear. Leaving them behind was the only way I could protect my sisters and brothers from the curse I must endure.

THE BONE KEY

∽

"Was it the same this time?" Gwen asks, bringing me back from another dark memory.

"No. There was more than one."

"A swarm? Like your dad? No wonder you flipped out."

I squeeze my eyes closed, but the darkness only reminds me of that smothering sense of blackness. The moths and that dark woman had haunted me since that day in California. I was never sure where they came from or why they came to me, but they did. And only when someone I cared about was in danger.

Gwen tilts her head to one side, watching me closely, so I turn my back to her. I may have perfected keeping my face stoic, but my eyes give me away every time.

"Is this the first time you've seen them since then?"

I open my eyes, and she's studying me again. Reading me in a way no one else can.

"That's it. That's why you've kept away from us," she says. "You saw them before and you think it's related to someone in the coven. Who?"

I shake my head. "I don't know."

But I do. Or at least I think I do. I'm still not sure what the vision meant, and I'm not ready to share it with anyone until I do. Not even Gwen.

"What do you mean?" her voice gets higher. Her pupils dilate, eyes flashing in the darkness.

"It's never clear. They don't settle on only one person. They're just... there. Like a swarm of locusts." I keep my gaze from meeting hers so she won't be able to read my thoughts like usual.

"That's terrifying," she says, moving closer. "Good thing it's only a vision."

But it isn't. It has never been a simple vision. They're an omen, one I can never forget.

A quick flash comes to me of a ranch house down south. In San Diego that day—after the attack—owls were splayed across the grass. Beside me, my father lay still, the light gone from his yellow-orange eyes. And just in the periphery of my vision, that black cloud of moths swirled like a mourning veil, watching me curl up beside my *papá,* gone for good.

A cry chokes in my throat at the memory, and Gwen clutches my arm. I shake my head and brush away the tears from the corners of my eyes. I can't let these memories run my life any longer.

"It's a good thing you came home then," Gwen says. "Mabon is the perfect time to do a cleansing. To get rid of this darkness hanging over you."

I nod and return to the task at hand. Maybe in honoring the darkness of the season, I can stave off the shadows seeping their way back into my life.

From the wooden box, I remove a cone of incense and, taking a match from the case, light it. On my belt, a simple cord hangs free; at the end of it dangles a snowy owl feather tipped with black. I use it to sweep the smoke away from me, sending it in tendrils that curlicue into the sky and get lost in darkness.

Holding my arms out in front of me, I trace a clockwise circle in the surrounding air.

"I cast this sacred circle and close it to those who wish to do me harm. Only my love may enter it. Only my love may leave its field. As I will it, so shall it be."

Around us, a faint glimmering trail of purple and silver encloses us in an orb that hovers over the ground.

Taking another matchstick from the tube, I light the candle. When the wick flickers, I tilt it, allowing the melted wax to drip on a knot in the log. When there is enough, I wedge the candle into the small hole and push the drippings around the base until it stands.

"Hekate, Goddess of the Full Moon," I say. "We welcome you into our circle of power. Give me the strength to accept them, and show me how to cast them away. Hekate, Queen of the Night, I call to you."

I take the gilt-edged pocket mirror and hold it out.

"Let this object reveal my deepest shadows."

I close my eyes. Inhale with focus and breathe out again. My pulse slows. My mind clears. As we sit in silence, I ignore the nagging thoughts as they try to seep in. I imagine the snow that day before everything went dark. The pure beauty of it, the crisp air. That tingling sensation across my skin after a brisk winter walk. The earth slows. The whisper of winter shushes through the air. My thoughts are quiet. But something stirs. A stolen breath sounds from the shadows.

I open my eyes, my gaze flicking to the mirror. Reflected at me are two eyes, but they aren't mine or Gwen's.

A branch snaps.

Something shifts.

Metal slinks. The image shadows. The reflection goes black.

In the trees, in the darkness, a second pair of eyes appears ten yards away. Animal eyes, glimmering gold. Then another pair just behind it. The deep, low growl of a coyote sounds as an arrow whizzes past my head, hitting the tree next to me.

Gwen is up a split second before me. Around her, the moths surge in from all sides. They swim around us, pinging off the circle of protection. Unaware, Gwen takes two steps, but we remain in the circle. By the time I am on my feet, everything is moving at half speed.

Gwen steps a toe outside the circle. I grab her by the arm, desperate to stop her. But she has already broken the seal, and the swarm rushes toward her. I follow, trying to pull her back, but the force from outside the circle of protection yanks her away from me, leaving me inside it. The moths rush for the place where she exited. Still throwing themselves at me, they bounce off the circle and then come rushing back, over and over again. But as Gwen moves, they pursue her.

I burst through the shield, refusing to let her go alone. The change in atmosphere tingles across my scalp. The moment I am free from the circle's protection, the moths batter me. I swipe them away, trying to clear the hallucination so I can track Gwen, but when I wave my hand through the swarm, they connect with my hand, leaving faint wing-beats of dust behind. This time, they're real.

From the shadows, coyotes growl and fabric swishes as an arrow is nocked.

An arm pulls back.

Multiple sets of eyes on us. Six. Eight. A dozen.

The arrow launches, this time aimed directly at me. I swipe my arm through the air. A dull hit before it deflects to the grass.

The squelch of a rubber-soled shoe in mud advances. Sweat beads on warm skin. Heartbeats race: too many, much too close.

To the west, the woods are thicker, extending to the river. Better cover.

To the east, a clearing. La Maison. The coven. More help. But it puts them in danger.

When Gwen bounds forward, everything moves into hyperspeed. She is up and off, her skirt dropping to the forest floor. Her skin turns to snow white, her hair shrinking into downy feathers. With a shriek, she takes off, up, up, flying high into the trees.

I lunge to stop her somehow, but just as she reaches a high branch, a bending stave groans.

The tension-fraught plucking of a sinuous bowstring.

The *shhht* from the fletches slicing through the air.

The thick, wet sound of stone as it penetrates flesh and feather.

Gwen lets out a shrill cry and crashes through branches, landing with a muffled thud in the brush. I fall on my belly. Footsteps advance like thunder hammering the earth.

I crawl through bramble and dirt, skinning my knees on the thorns. I get to Gwen and find her on her side, crimson staining her pristine feathers, her aura fading from indigo to a sick, murky navy. Blood percolates from the holes in her half-opened beak with each quick, raspy breath.

I cup my hand over the wound, trying not to disturb the arrow and its obsidian tip embedded into her chest. My hand trembles over a tiny metal charm dangling from the end. I've seen it before. A shield, a coyote, and criss-crossed swords with an L in the center: the same insignia from that horrible day when these same animals, these hunters, Los Cazadores, took my father from me.

Footsteps draw nearer.

I crawl forward and, using my athamé, carve two crossed spears, a symbol of protection, into the nearest gnarled tree. Within the crosses, I add a V and a G representing each of us. I slice the fleshy part of my palm and press the bloody wound to the carving so our sisters and brothers will find it, find us.

Gwen breathes in deep, then tries to call out, but the sound is trapped, thick and wet in her throat.

"Shh, be still."

She tries again, but she is too weak.

I fumble at my neck, leaving bloody fingerprints on my frigid skin. But I find it. I pull out the cord, put the bone whistle to my lips, and blow.

The sound comes out all wrong. It's weak and too faint for human ears to hear. But to our coven, it is a cascading set of notes. Only this time they are discordant and choppy, a plea for help.

I lick my lips and clear my throat, suddenly dry when I need it most. Gwen was right. I've been so focused on advancing that I've been neglecting the abilities I already have. But what if they're still not enough to get us out of this? Whistle to my lips, I try again. Concentrate. Concentrate.

I fumble through the tune, a personal warning signal only my fellow coven can hear. A beat...two...and then...I think I hear something, but shouting from a few yards away drowns it out.

I play the discordant melody once more and then crouch over Gwen. Tearing off my shawl, I throw it down, then gather her wings and lay her in the center of the length of fabric.

They're coming.

I clutch her to my chest and push myself up.

Something small whizzes past my head. I spin to find darts sunk into the symbol I'd just carved. The bark fizzles from the poisoned tips.

Instead of heading for the faint glow of La Maison, I tear through the trees, using the light of the full moon to find my way, drawing danger away from the house.

My inability to fly is the last thing on my mind.

All I want is for us to survive.

CHAPTER 3

Rally Point

The forest grows thick with menacing thorny branches the further we travel from La Maison. Overhead, treetops bristled by the cold bend toward one another, blocking out the tumultuous night sky. Lingering in the tree line, I wait. Long, dry grass rustles with impatience. The hint of charred firewood gives weight to the air. With Gwen cradled in my arms, wheezing, I don't move until the clouds part and the north star appears. I have my compass bearing. I know where to go.

Criss-crossing through the rugged back-country of ash and maple, I race to give us a fighting chance. The lingering energy of Los Cazadores fades, like echoing words dying away. For an hour, I take the longest route I can afford, allowing the power ingrained in the soil to will me toward my coven's place of safety. When that first lingering silhouette appears in the forest, with its peaked roof and lichen-dusted wooden shutters, its enchanted darkness, and its familiar aura, the tension in my shoulders melts.

The windows are dark ahead, an intricate veil of ivy and vines camouflaging the cabin's rough-hewn logs. Crouched in the darkness amidst a copse of elder trees and set against the looming hillside behind it, the safehouse awaits.

I clutch Gwen to my chest, listening to her labored breathing before I advance. Lingering on the edge of the property, I raise a hand. Energy pulsates in an invisible orb around the building and its grounds. But I wait.

On the other side, I sense movement.

Footsteps.

Not on grass or gravel. On wood.

Floorboards creak.

Hushed voices whisper.

Someone is inside the cabin.

My first instinct is to run. But when I raise my hand, palm out, energy pulsates ahead of me. No one, save someone from our coven, could find this place. I cradle Gwen, trying not to squeeze too hard, and lift my whistle. I let out a quick lament, a call for help.

From inside, a response. A short lilting trill. My mother.

I draw a symbol with my fingertip in the air. With a murmur, the wind stirs, and a small gap forms in the energy field. Only then do I notice my mother's guards standing a few feet inside the protective bubble, hidden until now. One steps toward me and holds out his hands to take Gwen from me. She lets out a weak screech, and I hesitate but hand her over with care as the other guard lets out a shrill call. The door to the cabin opens, and my mother is silhouetted in the doorway, the pale firelight setting her blonde hair aglow like a halo.

Panicked alarm pangs in my temples. Will she accept me back or blame me for leaving La Maison and getting Gwen injured? Will they take her from me? Or turn me out for how I left the protected grounds and put the entire coven at risk of an attack from Los Cazadores? All this time, I've wanted nothing more than to be a solitary witch. Now, I only want them to accept me so I'm not out here alone in the dark, in the frigid night, at risk of being torn apart.

I stagger forward, fighting to stay upright. The last few steps to the front door are two too many. Almost unable to find the strength to take those last steps, I fall; someone catches me and brings me inside.

The old scent of flowery candles permeates the stale room. Pools of hardened wax decorate the surfaces of the tabletops, and mounds of incense ash on the mantle dissipate in the air like stardust from the draft of the door opening. Dried herbs hang in bundles affixed to the beams. In various nooks and crannies, hand-carved soapstone owls of various shapes sit propped, some on window ledges and others between dusty tomes like miniature watchmen. Over the fireplace, a massive oil painting shimmers in the firelight, and our sister, the winged owl witch lives. Her chest rises and falls. Her feathers stir. Her eyes follow wherever I go. For centuries, she has watched, and she watches us now.

"Take her to the back," Èvelyne says.

But I refuse to go, instead dragging my weary bones toward Gwen, who has been placed on a bed.

Behind me, my mother barks orders in trilling French. Water runs in the kitchen for handwashing and filling a laver for cleaning Gwen's wounds. The scent of incense and burnt ash prickles my nostrils. I edge closer to Gwen, but when my mother casts a withering glance in my direction, I don't dare move.

She returns to the table where she and Andres Beauchêne stand. Normally, my mother and Andres do not travel together in times of crisis. That way, if something should happen to one, the other will still be able to protect the coven. But I imagine when Èvelyne came, Andres didn't want it to seem like he was sitting idly at the estate while she protected the coven.

"The Elixir," he says, his body so rigid his movements are stilted and jerky as he speaks.

"Somehow, they know it is almost time for us to get it," Èvelyne says. "As much as we would like to believe it, Los Cazadores are not useless."

"But why?" Andres says. "And why now? We have been at peace for years. Why should The López clan attack us now? To what purpose?"

López. The name makes every cell of my body flood with hatred. The family who has persecuted us for years. The same Hunter clan who carried out the ambush that took my *papá* from us. I don't know how my mother can sit so calmly at the mention of them.

"Somehow, they have discovered the truth about the Elixir and know we are at our weakest now as we wait for our stores to replenish," she says, her blue eyes flashing with determination. "More importantly, they have broken our pact; there is peace no longer. They have taken the first strike; I will not allow them another. We need to send the Messengers. Now. Before any of our other brothers and sisters set out to La Maison."

"Some of them will already be on their way, Èvelyne. Which is why we must warn them. Call them. Text them if you must. Before they show up and realize Los Cazadores have returned. For all we know, they have attacked our sister houses."

"I won't risk some Hunter reading a careless text, Andres. We do things the way we always have done. The way I, as our High Priestess, deem fit."

Guilt pangs in my head, my chest, my heart. The tension in the room swirls around me. It's almost too much to bear. There's a faint rasping from the back of the house—Gwen.

I find Olivia standing over Gwen, who lies on her back with her feathers spread around her like a wilted fan. Dried blood discolors each tip.

Taking deep cleansing breaths, Olivia centers herself before starting the healing ritual. Palms down, hovering just above Gwen's head, she passes her hands over her feathered chest. Gwen gurgles, her chest rising and falling in an erratic rhythm. As Olivia continues, she sweeps the suffering within Gwen's tiny body down until she has traced her entire length. After shaking her hands to cast off the negative energy, Olivia moves back to Gwen's head and repeats the process. When she comes to Gwen's wound, the spot where blood mats her feathers together, she concentrates, focusing her will. She cups her hands and closes her eyes, directing her strength there. She stands that way for some time until she can ease the arrow from Gwen's body. Blood spurts from the wound.

I've always been in awe of Olivia's ability to heal. She may not make life easy for me, but I can't ignore her talent. My hands go cold as I realize...if I had kept up with my practice or had the tools I needed, I may have been able to heal Gwen sooner. Instead, I had to trek through the forest for hours before getting her help.

The cabin is silent, and I notice Èvelyne and Andres are watching Olivia's work. Rather than the palpable weight of panic, the ambiance changes to one of concentration and calm. Reflected firelight from the hearth shifts from overwhelming orange to serene white.

As Olivia continues to heal Gwen, she moves her hands in ever-growing circles until she covers Gwen's entire body. When she finishes, she produces two rough crystals: one stark white, the other greenish black.

"I call upon the power of the full moon's light," she chants. "Heed my call. Charge this quartz with your energy so it may protect our sister, Gwen. And may your endless power forever charge this golden obsidian. Thank you, Sister Moon, for your energy."

She places the crystals on Gwen's chest, one beside the next, before she lifts the top edge of the duvet and tucks it under Gwen's chin.

Finished, Olivia clasps her hands in silent reflection. I ease my way closer. Gwen's eyes are half-open. Can she see me? Does she blame me for what she's endured?

Olivia notices my approach. Her gaze is like amber fireworks. She grasps me by the arm before I can move. "You have a lot of nerve."

"Is she okay?"

She pulls me aside. "Get the hell out of here, Valeria."

"I'm not going anywhere," I say, trying to push past her again. "Not until I know if she'll be all right."

"Fine," she says, shoving a crystal into my hand. "If you won't leave, the least you can do is help."

I hold the crystal over Gwen's chest but pull back for a moment. What if I make things worse? What if I'm too weak from the trek to do anything to save her?

"Val? Let's go! She needs our power. Both of us."

I'm stuck in the same spot. I don't want to hurt her more than I already have.

"Are you kidding me?" Olivia says. "Haven't you built up your backbone yet?"

"Enough," Èvelyne says behind me.

I can't even bear to face her.

"If it wasn't for her, High Priestess," Olivia says, "Gwen would have had her portion of the Elixir at the ceremony. Instead, she chased Val beyond our protective veil like she was a teenager having a hissy fit."

That moment in the woods outside La Maison when the protective veil felt so far away, further than usual, flashes in my mind.

"If it were not for her, Gwen might have died in the forest," Èvelyne says.

Olivia's mouth drops open. "But—"

"We will not debate who did what or whose fault this is. All members of Assemblée de la Terre, of our Assemblée des Chouettes clan, are at risk. Now that we know Los Cazadores continue to search for us, we can only look at this as a narrow escape. Now, we must act."

Olivia shakes her head. "Meaning what?"

"A patrol team is already out, sweeping the area, both here and around La Maison. When we get the all-clear, we will head back there and bunker down."

Èvelyne steps toward me, her hand grazing my elbow. "Has anyone looked at you?"

"I'm fine," I say with a shake of my head.

"You were exposed for hours. At the very least, you need rest."

"I'm fine, Mother. I'll rest later."

"If you're sure," she says.

I finally turn toward her. "I am."

"Then come with me. Please."

She edges me away from Gwen to where Andres waits. Èvelyne pulls a chair out and gestures for me to take a place at the table. I can feel the oppressive pressure of Olivia seething from the other side of the room.

"Tell us what happened," Èvelyne says, taking a seat beside me. "You had some trouble during the ceremony, yes?"

"I had a vision."

"Of the Hunters?"

"No. The black witch moths."

Èvelyne crosses her hands one over the other the way she does when she braces herself for bad news. The fingers on her right hand stroke the ring she has worn for thirty years—the ring my father gave to her during their handfasting ceremony. A half-heart in tarnished copper forms the eye and beak of a snowy owl. My mother wears the other half—my father's half—on a delicate chain around her neck.

"Was your vision clear?"

"No, but it was different than usual. There was more than one moth. It was a swarm that surrounded everyone at the ceremony. It covered all of La Maison."

Just saying it makes me feel sick. One moth is bad enough. But after the raid, I can't help but worry my vision is only a premonition of something worse, something we haven't even fathomed yet. The moths have only ever come to me when something bad is about to happen. The first time they came was the worst day of my life. Now I can't help but wonder what could be worse than watching my father take his last breath.

My mother is obviously thinking the same thing. The way she spins her ring in silence, the way she clasps one hand over the other as though it will give her some of my father's residual energy and protection, speaks volumes.

I'd hoped she would be marginally impressed with my decision to take Gwen to the safe house. That she would see my choice to remove Gwen from harm's way would protect the rest of the coven, a choice her Maiden would have made. But I'm no Maiden. I chose not to step forward when she needed one. And now the person who hates me most stands at my mother's right hand.

I push my chair back and stand, moving toward the fireplace, letting their chatter fall away. Behind me, Olivia continues to try to cleanse and heal Gwen. A cloud of lavender, sweet grass, and yarrow smoke wafts around her. She ignores me when I sit on the edge of the bed and clasp Gwen's hand. Her disdain is an invisible force between us, but she doesn't chase me away.

"The question remains," Andres says. "After all this time, they send their coyotes to find us and attack us now? How can they know?"

"Los Cazadores have been hunting our kind for centuries. Studied our movements, our abilities. It only makes sense they would try to find the source of our powers so they can ambush us at our most vulnerable."

"Someone must have told them."

"Only our sister and brother witches know of the source. For one of our own to divulge this?"

"It would be the ultimate betrayal," Andres says.

"No matter how careful we have been over the years, it was inevitable Los Cazadores would notice our patterns. Even after changing our meeting place, after hiding our places of refuge, it's not enough to prevent them from finding us. Or tracking us with their coyote hunters. This is not simply about taking what we need as a coven to sustain our Gift. It's the way they systematically hunt us. How they seek it out to take it as their own. Centuries of bloodshed, and we finally find peace. Now they throw it all away to take what isn't theirs."

"That doesn't make me feel any better," Andres says. "About any of this."

"Good," Èvelyne says, her eyes flashing bright yellow. "This is a wake-up call. For all of us, myself included. Awaiting the Opening of the Flower is important, now more than ever. If we don't make it in time, the sacred plant will die, and our Elixir will be gone forever."

"How do we know they haven't already found it? Destroyed it? How do we know this will not be the end of our Gift? Of our vitality?"

"You cannot think that way. None of us can. We are stronger than this."

"This is a danger for us all, Èvelyne."

"You think I don't know this?"

I smile. This is why she is the High Priestess, why no one has taken her role from her in the years she has held it.

"We're getting ahead of ourselves here," she says. "Seekers from all four houses are guarding the tree, waiting for the moment it blooms."

"We need more," Andres says. "More of us protecting the source so we can move as soon as it reveals itself."

Èvelyne's furrowed brow is enough to show she isn't exactly thrilled by someone else dictating what course of action we should take, but she doesn't say so. She and Andres have led our coven together for years, but he has never hidden his desire to have sole control.

"When I convene with our sisters and brothers, I will ask that L'Assemblée du Sud send out more Seekers," she says.

"Is that doing enough? We should be down there already, working alongside our Mexican brethren. It would be better than sitting here, waiting for another attack."

Before Èvelyne can answer, a harsh screech followed by a faster and repeated raspy call sounds outside. It filters down the chimney and swirls around the room.

My mother and Andres jump up. Andres unbolts the door while Èvelyne moves in front of the bed, blocking us from whatever lies outside. When it swings open, the guards step aside, and Will, one of our coven's best Seekers, enters. His thick blonde hair is tousled, his round face flushed. He and his fellow patrollers make sure we are safe when we venture away from the grounds of La Maison. Seeing him is a weight off my shoulders. At least I will finally have someone on my side.

"What is it?" Èvelyne asks.

"We've patrolled the area around the La Maison, High Priestess," he says, taking a deep breath. "Ten miles in either direction."

"And?"

He glances at me quickly with his bright yellow eyes, then at Gwen before turning his attention back to Èvelyne. "Everything looks clear. But on our way here, we spotted a pack. They're advancing. Fast."

His warning stirs something lingering behind him no one else notices.

Èvelyne crosses her arms over her chest. "How many?"

"Half a dozen."

The shadow wavers like tiny wings awakening.

"Alone? Or with their Guides."

"For now. But there was one Tracker with them. The others can't be far away."

All it takes is one flick of Èvelyne's wrist. All at once, everyone jumps into action. I reach for Gwen, but Olivia crouches over her, furiously repeating an incantation.

"We have to go, Olivia."

She ignores me, but that doesn't stop the shadowy moths from spilling across the floor and crawling up her legs until they creep around her mouth, muddling her words.

"Los Cazadores," I say. "They're coming."

While Olivia continues the chant, intensifying her magic, I notice Gwen's chest isn't moving. Her half-lidded eyes are closed now. I take a step toward her, but Olivia snaps to attention, her head whipping to one side, flinging the moths away. They dissipate in the air.

"Don't you dare," she says, her voice cracking. "This is your fault. *Yours.*"

"What is it?" Èvelyne calls from the door. "We have to move."

I can't respond. I can't look away from Gwen. At the blood in her feathers. The stillness of her body. She is always so full of light: now she lies still.

"*Viens! Maintenant!*" Èvelyne says. "Now, ladies! We must go!"

"High Priestess," Olivia says.

There is a shift in the room, as though all the air has gone out of it. Behind me, my mother moves to the bed. Seeing Olivia, noticing my expression at how still Gwen is, Èvelyne brushes past Olivia and me, pushing her aside. Sinking to her knees, an incantation tumbles from her lips. With her hands hovering above Gwen's chest, the words flow together in a dizzying rhythm. The longer it goes on, the more hopelessness seeps into my heart. Then, the smallest gasp, an almost inaudible sigh, escapes Gwen's mouth, glimmering in an undulating spiral of life-giving breath. Èvelyne stands.

"We have to get her back to La Maison," she says, gathering the blanket around Gwen and tucking it across her small body.

"Going back to La Maison is a mistake," Andres says. "Los Cazadores could be there already."

"If they were," Èvelyne says, "our sisters would have warned us by now. We need to get Gwendolyn back there. She must drink the Elixir if she is to see the night through."

Once Gwen is wrapped, Èvelyne takes her and moves for the door. Following her, Olivia passes; not bothering to move over, she nudges me aside. The arrow Olivia removed from Gwen's chest lays on the bed. I edge toward it, taking it in my hands. The hatred imbued within turns my hands cold. I pry away the metal talisman and pocket it before discarding the hateful weapon. Andres extinguishes the fire in the hearth, and when I turn, the smoky scent wafts toward me.

At the door, Èvelyne is on her phone.

She looks at me as she ends the call. "I've had a car waiting in town. They'll be here in five minutes to transport Gwen and Valeria and one guard. The rest of us will fly to warn the others."

"Is that wise, Èvelyne?" Andres says. "It's obvious some of us are weaker than others. With the Elixir fading within each of us—"

"We made it here," she says, holding up a hand as she cuts him off. "We shall make it to La Maison. It is better warded to protect us than it is here. There is no other choice."

With a nod, Èvelyne signals Will. He opens the door and steps aside, allowing Andres to exit. There's a quick snap of feathers outside as he transitions and takes to the sky.

My mother waits near the door. Olivia glares at me before she heads outside, taking off to fly back to the estate.

"I trust you will guard these two," my mother says to Will.

"With my life, High Priestess," he says.

Her eyes flash with anger before softening with worry. All these months, I'd been so content to keep her in the periphery of my mind. But now that we're face-to-face, I feel that same pull I did back at the ceremony. Our two planets are in orbit, an unending bond neither time nor distance can sever. I worry my actions have pushed her away. And from the anger, fear, and worry in her eyes, she feels the same.

"We'll be fine," I say, trying to take the burden of guilt from her. "I'll see you back—"

"At home," she says, finishing my sentence.

She pauses and then leans in, whispering something to Gwen before she hands her to me. I take Gwen, cradling her to me as Èvelyne turns, her cape billowing behind her. I watch her take a running start, her clothes disintegrating into nothingness with the shift. With a shrill shriek and clacking of her beak, she is off to join the others. Her wings outstretched, she soars above the pines like a ghost.

We wait. Will stands in front of us, his shoulders raised, his body a coiled spring ready to strike if need be.

From somewhere in the distance, a coyote bays, chilling my blood. My throat tightens. How many are coming? How many Hunters are they scouting for? Can Will and I hold them off? If they catch up to us, will I be able to protect us? Or am I putting us in danger again?

Distant barking disturbs the silence. Will backs up, his arms out to shelter us. Our preternatural senses allow us to hear sounds, even from miles away. They're so close, it makes the skin on the back of my neck crawl.

"We might have to barricade ourselves inside if the car doesn't get here in time," he says.

I glance over my shoulder. "The fire is smoldering. We can light it to fight them off."

Two more yelps in the darkness.

"It might not be enough."

As the coyote calls grow nearer and come closer together, a distant rumbling approaches.

"The car," I say.

I take a step, but there's a sound. Close. Closer than before. Branches snapping. I shield Gwen, clutching her to my chest.

Outside, a coyote howls, panting. Footsteps, at first plodding, now pick up pace and crash toward us.

Will crouches. Apparently, he's prepared to take off, transform, and leave us here alone. I pull out my charm bag. I can hold them off with incantations. But half a dozen coyotes? And who knows how many Hunters are following behind them? There's not enough time to cast a protection spell. I won't make it out of this cabin alive.

The car is almost to us.

Another cry from the coyotes is closer than I expected. Will lets out a growl. He's one of the more advanced witches, able to do so without his whistle or shifting into owl form. Èvelyne was right to leave him as our guard.

I can barely hear the response over the rumble of the engine.

The howling.

My heart races, flooding my bloodstream with adrenaline.

But there's a response from the car. They're almost here.

"Let's go!" Will shouts, bounding outside.

He's standing at the edge of the force field by the time I make it outside. There's an electricity in the air. The protection shield glimmers purple. As his chants increase in volume and speed, the charm grows, turning the energy field to glimmering gold.

Will leads us.

One step.

Paws squelching in mud.

Two.

They're coming.

Three more steps.

Branches snap.

They edge closer.

Rubber rumbles over rock and gravel. Headlights penetrate the inky blackness and cast lurking shadows skyward.

Breath. Heavy and hard. Saliva drips like poison. The coyotes are almost here.

We move forward together, and as we do, the energy field moves with us. But when we get to the dirt road, the animals come crashing from the shadows, careening for us, ravenous and rabid.

The first coyote flies head-first into the shield, bouncing off with a thud and sprawling on its back. The second and third attack from either side, lunging forward with dripping incisors, ready to snap and bite. Their spittle clouds the force field, and when they realize they can't get to us, they begin to dig.

Will and I chant in unison, but the animals claw and scrape at the dirt. One paces around the exterior. Will throws his arms to either side, and I spin until we're back-to-back. We turn as the coyotes circle us, monitoring them. The glimmer is fading. Our protection is wearing thin.

"Wait!" Will shouts.

Over the snarling and snapping, beneath the growls and guttural bays for blood, the car careens closer. We edge to the side of the road as fast as we can, our energy field following around us. The car speeds past us, skids and drifts a full revolution in the driveway, then comes back out to join us at the road, coming to a stop. The back door flies open.

"Ready to go?" Will says, eyeing the coyotes.

"Ready as I'll ever be," I say.

He takes my hand and we bolt for the back door of the car. Something hits the force field and pings to the ground—an arrow lands in the grass. Another hits the shield. And another.

"Go!" Will says.

We dart forward. Will calls out, ending the spell, and he shoves me as the force field drops. I run, but a coyote snatches my boot and I go flying. I have enough time to toss Gwen into the backseat before I fall to my knees. I swing my arm in a wide arc, thundering my fist into the side of the coyote's head. It snaps at me, its incisors grazing my skin. I spin on my knees, grabbing its leather collar to hold it back with both hands. Will shouts and punts the coyote to the side. I scramble to my feet and drag myself into the back seat of the car, lifting Gwen so I can slip across the seat and haul Will in after me.

Instead, he leans down and shouts, "Go!" before he slams the door between us.

"No!" I shout.

The car takes off down the road. I spin in time to watch Will transform. He spreads his wings and, in a flurry of down, takes off into the treetops with a shriek.

He departs just in time. Behind him on the road, I see the haunting glow of eyes. One set. Two. Then more.

"Go back!" I pound my hand on the back of the driver's seat.

But the driver, another of the Seekers, shifts gears and speeds away. Gripping the steering wheel, he glances over his shoulder.

"Your mother gave me explicit instructions. No stopping for anyone other than you."

"I don't care what she said. We can't leave Will out there to fend for himself!"

I turn again, but the coyotes are nowhere to be found. If they aren't tracking us, that can only mean one thing. Los Cazadores have a target in mind, and it isn't us.

When I turn back around and lean against the seat, I gather Gwen in my arms and check on her breathing. But all I can think of is the snarling. The snapping teeth. Their breath, rank and desperate, their bloodlust turning them into savage beasts.

Will is one of our most powerful flyers. But even the best of us cannot outrun an arrow.

For a moment, the coyotes gain on us, and our tail lights illuminate their harrowed faces in stark red. Behind them, a single headlight appears—some kind of motorized bike. We speed up the logging road, leaving them in our dust.

CHAPTER 4

Accusations

A half dozen of our defense flock stand stationed at the turn-off from the road to Maison des Arbres when we pull into the driveway. Specially trained Watchers line the exterior of the estate grounds and surround the main entrance. Prepared to protect the coven, they have replaced their cloaks with dark vests which, at first glance, resemble interwoven feathers. Instead, burnished steel plates fashioned into armor allow them free movement to avoid arrows, the weapon of choice of Los Cazadores.

Relief floods my body, warming me now that we're back in safe territory. Seeing my fellow sisters and brothers prepared to fight makes me realize this is no longer about the coven staying hidden. It's about survival.

I squeeze Gwen close to me as we pull up to the wrought iron security gate. Behind it, towering hedges block the estate from view. The gates fold inward in a slow reveal, and when the driver recites the spell that wards the grounds, the protective veil parts, allowing us to proceed into the courtyard.

Gwen has been quiet most of the way, but when the car stops and I open my door, she lets out a sharp cry.

Our healer, Victoria, races down the steps. Kneeling in front of me, she cradles Gwen's head. In her hand, she holds a vial of sacred Elixir the Assemblée des Chouettes use to maintain our Gift and protect us from harm and injury. She dips Gwen's beak into the Elixir dribbled in her palm, but it does nothing to pull my sister from her catatonic state.

"Drink, sister," Victoria says, dipping Gwen's beak again. When she doesn't react, Victoria lifts her from my grasp. "We need to get her inside. Now."

They take her from me and carry her into the foyer. I try to keep up with them, but I'm fading, barely able to stay upright without swaying. When they get Gwen to the wide set of stairs that lead to the upper floor of the main house, I lose momentum. I need to sit down somewhere. Every muscle in my body is screaming. Every ounce of regret weakens me. The farther I am from Gwen, the deeper the heartache I feel for getting her into this situation.

Animated conversation wafts from the parlor, where dark wooden beams open up to a triangular archway. Undulating patterns of candlelight shift and dance on the stark white stone walls, yet the soft light is anything but comforting. Instead, it has a dizzying effect that makes my stomach turn over.

"An extra portion of the Elixir is what she needs," Èvelyne tells the group. "With its benefits have run their course, getting the fresh supply is our most pressing matter. We must gather in the Yucatán so we can be there the moment it is restored."

Relief warms my face at hearing my mother's voice. She looks regal as ever, holding court over the other members of the coven.

Footsteps approach, stopping next to me. When I turn, Will is there, back in his sleek black and gray Seeker uniform. His eyes are wide and bright yellow, still in owl form from his journey home, but he is otherwise unscathed. When he sees me, they shift back to their usual blue. "Glad you made it back safe."

I bolt to hug him, and he holds me up when I start to stumble. "Jesus, Will. What the hell were you thinking, flying off like that?"

"Someone had to draw the Hunters away from you."

I pull away from him and glare, but it only lasts for a moment. If I could have taken off, I would have done the same thing if it meant giving them a head start. That he would risk himself like that for Gwen brings tears to my eyes.

"How is she?" he asks, keeping one hand on my arm and squeezing lightly.

"Well, she made it here. The Healers took her."

He glances to the parlor, where a group stands in discussion. "Must be serious if they brought the bigwigs in early."

Past him, my mother is deep in conversation with the High Priests from the east and west assemblies, with Olivia standing at her right hand. Each is dressed in their formal attire, dark suit coats that stretch to their knees. But there is an unmistakable bulk to them—body armor to protect them while they are in human form.

"I'm surprised they're here. Èvelyne said she would tell them not to come, that it was too much of a risk."

Will nudges me.

"What?"

"You don't call her Èvelyne to her face, do you?"

"No. I call her High Priestess like everyone else."

"Not Mom?"

I shrug. "It seems weird to call her that here."

"She's your mother, Val," he says, laughing.

But when I edge closer and study her—the way she moves, how her eyes flash in the light when she gets animated—a sense of pride washes over me at her power. Then doubt seizes my mind. I could have avoided all of this if I had stayed away.

There's a reason I've been practicing on my own for months. After Imbolc and the omen of the black witch moths, I couldn't come back here knowing the warning they showed me. Since I've been gone, I've been spared the reminder of their threat. But, on that fateful day when Los Cazadores took my father from me, the moths weren't a simple warning. They bonded to me, their warnings becoming a touchstone, my conscience, my guides. Staying away seemed like the right decision then. I tricked myself into believing that by keeping my distance, my fellow witches would be safe from the omen the black witch moths bring with them. That by not being here, the threat would dissipate. After tonight and the ugly reappearance of Los Cazadores, I realize that ignoring the moths and their message won't do any good. The threat lingers. Instead of running from them, it's time that I face them head-on so I can figure out what it is they're warning me about before anyone else gets hurt.

That stomach-tensing feeling that tempts me to leave for the last time comes back. All I want is to be as fearless as my mother is. To stand shoulders back, head held high, determined to face any and every obstacle I come across. The problem with wanting these things is knowing I wouldn't desire them so badly if I were already that strong.

As if sensing my thoughts, Èvelyne catches my eye. Her expression softens. She blinks and gives me a slight smile.

"See," Will says, nudging me. "She's glad you're here where you belong."

When he turns and pulls me away, I hesitate. I've always felt like I had one foot in this coven and one in my father's in the south. And I'm not sure where I feel like more of an outsider.

Before I can second guess being back here again, someone cries out from down the hall. Èvelyne spins and rushes away. It's Gwen.

I brush past Will to follow my mother; by the time I get to the small room at the back of the house, the scene is in chaos.

Victoria stands over Gwen, who has transitioned back to her human form. Thin black veins discolor her normally rosy complexion. They extend across her face and down her neck. A stark white blanket is pulled up to her chest and tucked under her arms, but her skin gleams with the feverish sweat of an infection. The other Healers work in unison with Victoria. Their chants encircle Gwen in a golden thread of curative power, pulling the sickness and injury from her body. But she lays there, unmoving, except for the rapid rise and fall of her chest.

At the foot of the bed, Èvelyne prepares the tinctures I have seen her mix a million times. Elderberry flower to reduce inflammation. Garlic as an antiseptic and to boost her immune system. Thyme to ease her labored breathing. As she moves aside, Olivia comes into focus, and even as she works, she glares at me.

The power emanating from her pushes me back a step, so I grab the doorframe and edge my way inside.

"Val, we shouldn't be here," Will says.

"I'm not leaving!"

"Let them do their work. Come on."

When Will tries to pull me away, I yank my arm from his grip and shove him inside the room.

"Either get out or do something productive!" Olivia says.

I spin, not sure of what to do or where to go.

"In the cabinet," Èvelyne says to me over her shoulder. "The Elixir. Take the vial and bring it here, please."

I go to the back wall where an antique armoire sits with drawers pulled half-open. In the center, there's a panel of two doors, locked when I pull on them. I face my mother. She glances over her shoulder and waves her hand. The door opens, revealing a brass stand in the center, the glass vial illuminated. Only a small portion of Elixir remains. I take it in both hands, gripping it tightly, holding it out in front of me to make sure I do not spill a drop.

"Now, please," Èvelyne's voice is steady, edged with alarm.

As I move to the bed, she glances down and then does a double-take. She meets my gaze and then returns hers back to the vial.

"Was this closed when you took it out?"

I nod.

Concern wrinkles her forehead.

"What is it?" I ask.

She shakes her head and takes it from me, removing the stopper and holding it out to Victoria. She takes it, but the calm alarm in her eyes gives her thoughts away.

"Is this necessary?" she asks.

"She won't survive without it," Èvelyne says.

"But High Priestess—"

"Our sister needs this help. We will all make do until we receive the next portion from Mexico."

That's when I realize what they aren't saying. There should be more of the Elixir than there is.

But Victoria continues working. The temperature in the room rises with all the energy they're channeling into Gwen. Olivia moves beside my mother and takes her hand. As the Healers open the stopper and take a drop from the vial, they hum.

The sounds create a magnetic effect when their two tones intertwine: one higher, one lower to conjure a harmonious note. When my mother reaches out, I take a step back. But she isn't pushing me out. Her hand slips into mine, and she nudges me closer to the bed. When I chant alongside her and Olivia, the power of our collective vibration amplifies our connection despite our differences: the only thing that matters at this moment is healing Gwen.

But she sputters and chokes, spitting up the Elixir the healers dribbled into her mouth. It trickles down her chin, staining the pristine white sheet. Victoria glances up at my mother, and with a nod, Èvelyne gives her approval. Taking another drop of the liquid, Victoria holds out the dropper, but Gwen's lips purse together in agony.

I am closest to Gwen. I can help. But I'm struck still, terrified of doing something wrong. Of failing her again.

Olivia steps past me and moves to Gwen's side. She uses both hands to part her lips so Victoria can deposit the Elixir on her tongue.

Olivia stands back, and we continue chanting. I offer my hand to her, willing her to take it so we can join our power. When she takes my invitation, she squeezes my fingers hard; it takes everything in me not to cry out.

As our voices rise, the air in the room swirls around us.

But Gwen convulses, her face bright red.

Victoria leans down to strip the blanket from Gwen. Dressed in stark white boyshorts and a white bra, the impact of the Hunter's arrow is clear. Blood oozes from a sore on her side where the arrow punctured her skin.

As Victoria places her hands on Gwen's side, she convulses. Olivia throws herself on top of her legs to hold her still. I do the same, flinging myself across her midsection, but her temperature is rising.

"Gwen! It's going to be alright," I say. "You're home now. You're safe."

But it does nothing. She convulses so violently that it flings both of us back a few steps. My mother grabs me before I fall and steadies me, but when we turn back to Gwen, the convulsions have stopped. She lies still, her head hanging limp. She isn't breathing.

I dart to the side of the bed, falling on my knees beside her.

"Gwen! No! Please don't leave me, Gwen! Please!"

Nothing. I brush her red hair from her cheeks, and a lock falls free into my trembling hand. Her skin is like tarnished porcelain. The black veins have ruined her face, spreading up her neck and expanding across her cheeks.

Someone places their hand on my shoulder. It sets me off. I spring up and stagger backward, spinning to face the others. But I can't see them. The moths have engulfed each of them, taking over their faces and smothering them until the only thing left is black nothingness.

I push through the group and make it out of the room, running into Will.

"Val, wait!"

"I... I can't be here," I say, holding out the lock of Gwen's hair. "Not now. I never should have come back here. This is all my fault."

But it isn't," he says, clasping my hand in his. "Los Cazadores would have come for us with or without you here. You belong here as much as anyone else."

"Like hell she does!"

I turn to find Olivia coming out of Gwen's room. She barrels for me. Will puts himself between us to stop her from getting to me.

"If it weren't for Valeria, Gwen would be alive!"

"Shut the hell up, Olivia!" Will says.

"No," I say. "She's right. If I didn't come here, if I didn't take off outside the walls, Los Cazadores would have only circled the estate."

"You can't know that, Val," Will says. "Even with the enchantment, they would come for us the moment we left the protection of the grounds."

"They would never have gotten Gwen if she hadn't come to find me."

"For once, we agree on something," Olivia says.

"Give it a rest, Olivia," Will says. "We all lost someone tonight. Not just you."

"The difference is I actually care about Gwen. If Val did like she says she does, she would have protected her better. Or not come back here at all. This is part of the problem with you, Val. You let others stand up for you, and that's how they get hurt."

I lunge for Olivia, shoving her back. "The nerve you have to taunt me when one of the people I care about the most has just died! You don't care about this coven! Or our sisterhood!"

"All right," Will says, moving between us. "This is the last thing we need."

"No, it isn't!" Olivia shouts, clutching the jet-black wire-wrapped pendant she wears at her throat for protection. "What we need to do is to kick her out of the coven. The only reason she's still here is because her mother is too soft to cut ties with her once and for all."

"That's the High Priestess to you," I say, lunging for Olivia again.

"Oh, look. The prodigal daughter is here to fight her own battles for once. It's about time," Olivia says, the taunt clear in her voice.

"Don't even test me right now, Olivia."

"Your little puppet Gwen isn't here to do your dirty work for you anymore," she says, forcing me back a few steps. Her aura burns bright red around her. "And whose fault is that?"

I back-step to avoid crashing into her, but she doesn't give in.

"How many more of us have to get injured for you to realize you don't belong here, Valeria?" With one hand, she swipes at the side of my head. I shove her arm away from me. "You just aren't that good. And you'll never be more than a pseudo-witch who's already peaked and will never learn to fly like the rest of us."

That last insult she hurls at me sets off a fire within me. I yell and throw my hands out, intense energy coursing from my fingers and knocking Olivia down and sending her skidding backward on her back. From all sides, a shroud of black moths, my eternal protectors, surge toward her, pin her to the floor, choking her. I gasp and lurch away, tripping over my feet, but Will catches me by the elbow.

I dart around him and take off up the corridor, tearing open the front door.

My breath comes out in gusts. I squeeze my hands together, feeling the pulse of energy beneath my skin. My heart thuds in my ears. The edges of the forest around La Maison shift and quiver. The moths are waiting. The voices, the judgment, all drowned out for once.

Will is beside me. His lips are moving. His face tilts in, his eyes back to his bright owl eyes. He searches my face, studying me, but I can't hear what he's saying. Instead, I focus on the cold wind that whistles through the bare birch branches. Fire crackles from large barrels arranged in a wide arc around the property where more of our most seasoned witches stand guard.

"Val? What the hell happened there? Are you all right?" His eyes flash, and the woodsy timbre of his hawk owl voice resonates so deeply, it makes me tear up.

"I...don't know. She...came at me. I had to stop her. Get her away from me."

"Did you push her? I didn't see—"

"No! I didn't touch her! I..."

My hands held out in front of me, I flip them over and back again. There are scrapes and cuts from the forest, but I'm otherwise unscathed.

"That was insane!"

Shivering, I wrap my arms around myself. Olivia is in the window, surrounded by half a dozen others, glaring out at me.

"I need to get out of here," I say, pushing past him. Back inside, I head to where I dropped my bag so many hours ago and grab it, slinging it over my shoulder..

When I glance up, Olivia has retreated to my mother's side. She makes a point of being seen at her right hand repeatedly to rub in her position as the High Priestess's Maiden.

My mother doesn't see me, but her voice carries down the hall.

"She should not have been out there at all. Her judgment has never been good. I only wonder if she'll ever become the witch she is meant to be."

Her words ring in my ears, drowning out everything else around me. The world goes topsy-turvy again. Everything is off-kilter, the same way it is whenever I come home. Maybe it's me. Everything else is right, and I'm the thing that's wrong here.

When she finally sees me, our gazes lock. For a moment, there's a glint of hope, of love, in her eyes. But in the next, their light tarnishes with disappointment. I leave before I have to witness it fill her eyes completely. I yank the door open, and I'm outside before anyone can stop me.

When I step through the door, I notice the soft light of dawn on the horizon. We made it through the night, though not without cost. The promise of Mabon seems so far away now. I'm halfway to my Jeep when Will calls out from behind me. After opening the car door, I toss my bag on the passenger seat, giving him the time he needs to catch up to me.

"You can't leave, Val."

"I can't stay."

"Your mother has called a lockdown. At least until the Seekers do one final sweep and we give the all clear."

I zip my jacket up and shove my hands in my pockets. "I don't belong here, Will. I never have."

"That's not true."

"But it is. You know it. Everyone knows it."

"If you're talking about Olivia—"

"I'm not. And that's okay. It's better this way. I've already done so much to screw things up here. Leaving is the best thing I can do right now."

"For whom?"

"Everyone. Trust me. It will be a relief to have me gone."

I move toward him, but he backs away. I see it in his eyes now. The hurt. The disappointment. I'm so tired of seeing that look—in the faces of others, in my own eyes. I'm exhausted.

"You need to stop thinking about what you need to be for everyone else. Be who you want to be. For yourself."

"I tried. I don't think I did it very well."

"Maybe you didn't go far enough. Or look deep enough. Maybe you looked outside yourself when what you need to do is look within. Leaving won't solve anything, Val. Not when what you need is right here."

"You don't know that."

"Neither do you," he says.

"Maybe not...but for once, I can't stop myself from looking. I can't hold myself back because it's too hard. Or too unknown."

The weight of my words sits between us like an invisible barricade and already, I feel far away from him.

"But...where will you go?" he finally asks.

"Somewhere where I'm not judged by every move I make."

I pull him in for a hug, but he is stiff and barely relents, so I get into the driver's seat.

"It's not safe out there, Val. Not alone. Let me come with you."

I close the door and start the engine, and the sound of it makes him jump back. As I buckle up and put the car into drive, the hint of movement is like an insult to him, and his eyes go darker than I've ever seen them. I can't bear to open the window to say goodbye. To hear his voice break. Or maybe he wouldn't even respond. Instead, I lift my hand in a final wave, but he doesn't move. Doesn't blink. He only looks back at me, his jaw set, no emotion in his gaze.

So I drive. I edge toward the front gate, waiting for the guards to open it so I can pass. In my rearview mirror, Will gets smaller the farther I drive. La Maison lingers like a phantom in the fog, like my past, already forgotten. The amber glimmer of the lights from within the manor isn't enough to warm me. Too much has happened here—too much loss, too much disappointment. The only way to put it behind me for the last time is to avoid looking back, no matter how much it aches.

CHAPTER 5

Decisions

Back in Montréal, I cruise past the park that runs along the blood-red maple-lined boulevard where I live. Fallen leaves scrape across the sidewalks and land in the slushy sleet where early morning joggers and dog walkers stride by. The air is different here. Even though I'm in the heart of the city, I feel free. Like I can breathe.

I pull into the spot outside my townhouse, half-expecting a car to be waiting for me, sent by my mother to force me back to La Maison to answer for what I did to put the coven in danger. But there's no one there. I'm not sure if I'm relieved or disappointed. Maybe both.

La Maison des Arbres was once my refuge. The surrounding forest, my solace. Not knowing when I'll return fills me with a yearning for a past I can't live up to and a future unknown.

Beneath the uneasiness, my nerves percolate with a secret longing. A hunger I didn't realize was there. Am I a traitor for leaving my coven when they need me the most? A betrayer? To break trust with a fellow witch is second only to harming another. But the pull of nettle and thistle, of fragrant juniper and smoky mesquite, stirs my wanderlust.

I want to go south. Let sand buff away my turmoil. Let the sun awaken what's stirring inside me. I want to crawl from the earth and let the heat and flame burn away everything I no longer need, shaping me into my true self. Maybe if I explore, I'll find my path. Learn what I need to so I can become the witch I am destined to be. Maybe by leaving our northern assembly for our southern sister coven, it will draw away any lingering threat from Los Cazadores. Maybe the black witch moths will stop tormenting me.

I park and turn off the ignition, leaning my head against the seatback and closing my eyes for a moment. I can't help but think about the past twenty-four hours. Maybe if I had stayed away and ignored Gwen's plea to appear at the ceremony, she would still be here. The coven would be safe. Los Cazadores wouldn't have come for my brother and sister witches. If last night's events didn't show them that my being there is a danger to everyone around me, then I don't know what will.

I slam my hands against the steering wheel, gripping it until my knuckles turn white. What the hell do I do?

To go where my father was High Priest has been a dream of mine since I started studying the Craft. And even though Èvelyne and I have always butted heads, it feels wrong to leave her when she's suffered another loss after so many others over the years.

My mother. Her last words back at La Maison, when she was talking to the others about the attack, haunt my thoughts like those flitting moths.

I only wonder if she'll ever become the witch she is meant to be.

Her voice echoes in my head, the ultimate insult coming from the person whose opinion I value the most. Hearing shit like that from Olivia is par for the course. But from my mother? Maybe I'm fooling myself. Maybe I won't ever fly to the heights I imagined I would.

"You know what? Watch me."

I yank the keys from the ignition and shove my door wide. Crossing the sidewalk, I head to the black wrought iron staircase that leads to my apartment on the second floor, clamping my jacket closed at the neck to protect myself from the biting wind whipping down the boulevard. I bound up the stairs, but when I reach the top, I stop suddenly in front of my door, where a crude symbol is spray painted in dripping black paint.

Sorcière métisse.

Half-breed witch.

I only notice my hands are clenched when my fingernails press into the fleshy part of my palm hard enough to leave a mark. I stride to the door and try to wipe away the hateful words, but the paint has long since dried.

I check to make sure there's no one on the boulevard watching and hoping for a reaction, but there's no one suspicious. Only a faint aura of black at the edge of my vision lingers to show their ill intent.

Sweeping my hand in front of me to reveal the crystalline veil of protection draped across the threshold, I exhale, blowing a clear spot in the middle that allows me enough time to slip through the boundary to the other side before it closes, crystallizing before it goes invisible again. How did they get past it?

Livid, I unlock the front door, flicking on the lights and tossing my bag on the tiled floor near the door.

I've never been so relieved to be home, but the tension in my back doesn't unknot, and my shoulders don't loosen like usual. Who would do something so vile? The insult is personal. Someone who knows not only my past but also how I live my life.

My phone chimes in my pocket. I ignore it and peel off my coat, throwing it across the arm of my slate-hued sofa before I sink into the cushions. The morning light, gray and diffused, filters in through the prism hanging in the massive arched window overlooking the back of the property. Soft orbs of light dot the room like fireflies. Even with the dull light from outside, being here allows me to breathe. To settle. To feel like I am wholly myself and not just putting on a face for whoever might be watching me. I was once filled with a sense of community at La Maison, but there's something delicious about being alone. How it feels like you can breathe deeply. To feel your emotions and honor them without having to please anyone other than yourself. I used to love being at the coven house for gatherings and dinners—that sense of family when I stepped inside to music and laughter filtering down the long hallway. Somehow, that feeling has gotten more hollow as the years have gone on. I'm not sure why. And that makes my heart ache the most.

I take in a breath, hold it, and then let it out again. But something tickles my mouth. I brush my fingertips across my lip and pull away a hair —coarse, dark gray. A tuft of fur.

I pluck it off and fling it away. Knowing Los Cazadores's coyotes were close enough to leave such a reminder makes my pulse race. My phone chimes again. Anticipation of checking the message tightens my throat. I pull it from my pocket. There are five missed messages. I jab at the screen. They're all from Will.

I pause before I read them.

Val. Please. Don't do this. I get it. Tonight was insane. But you belong here, now, more than ever.

Los Cazadores are out there, Val. This is what the Elders warned us about all our lives.

This isn't only about you. They would have attacked with or without you here.

Val???

Answer me. Please. Tell me you're okay. I'm coming over there if you don't text me back.

A pang of longing hits me, and for a moment, I'm tempted to text him. To tell him to come to me. My fingers go to my bone whistle and I think about putting it to my lips. To will him here with my call.

But in the next moment, the thought of seeing him, of seeing the anguish in his eyes all over again, is too much. La Maison feels too close. I need to get away from here, away from the pressure of expectation, the reminder of everything I am and all those things I'm not.

Closing my eyes, I see myself soaring over La Fontaine, away from the city and high into the Laurentian Mountains, where the air is cool and bursts of autumn color glimmer with the first hints of frost. But the thought fades when reality creeps into my daydream.

Even if I could transform and fly, is this what I need right now? Is this really the time to leave with Los Cazadores on the prowl? When my mother is preparing to go to Mexico for the Elixir? Is leaving the comfort of home the right thing to do? Will it solve anything? Will I—

Rattling. Outside. The back gate. Someone's trying to get in.

I jump up and cross the room in half a dozen steps, crouching low to stay below the sight line of the window. When I make it to the back door, I pause. Back pressed against the wall, I keep my lips together, slow my breath, and stay quiet so I can listen.

With my preternatural hearing, I pick up the sound of the hinges on the back gate squealing as the door groans open and then closes again.

I strain to look out the window. A figure is hunched over, standing still for a moment before it moves a few steps toward the patio.

I dart for the tall mahogany bookcase near the door. On the bottom shelf, there's a box. Not filled with herbs and crystals, but a taser, one I haven't needed for a long time. I almost got rid of it in a purge last week. But something told me to keep it.

I unlock the door and crack it open slightly. The figure has moved closer to the steps leading up to the landing.

I slip into the oversized snow boots I keep for when I'm working in the garden and edge open the outer door. How the hell can I stay hidden and sneak down there without tripping, keeping the taser in front of me?

He's closer now. I have no choice.

"Protect this home from all that is dark."

I go down one step.

"Protect all who dwell here too."

Another step.

"Protect this place where I reside."

He hasn't noticed me yet.

Three. Four.

His back is to me. He's still hunched over. Maybe readying his weapon.

"Protect with light that is true."

Five. Six. Seven. Eight.

"Hey!"

He jumps and faces me. His hood falls back against his shoulders before he sinks to one knee. It's my landlord. His wrinkled old face and nose are bright red.

"Jean?"

"Mademoiselle Val," he says. "You scared the crap outta me!"

"I could say the same about you."

With one hand, I help him up and ease him to the small wooden bench beside the planter where the last of the black-eyed Susans are wilting; the edges of the delicate bursts of Queen Anne's lace have turned the color of spilled tea.

"I thought you were breaking in or something!"

He nods to the taser in my hand. "I can see that."

I hold it down and away from him. "I heard the gate open. Guess you startled me."

"Just out for my morning stroll."

"Good for you," I say. "Best to get out before the first snow."

"Went up to the market," he says.

I smile and nod.

"And then to the pharmacy for my vitamins."

"I'll go for you anytime, Jean," I say, touching him on the arm. "Just say the word."

He chuckles and shrugs me off, but when he chats about his weekend, his voice fades from my consciousness, and my senses take over. There's a residual musk in the air; I recognize the scent from the woods. And as I nod and smile, acting like I'm listening, I scour the yard. Something seems off. Like an enduring heat lingers around me. Then I notice the fresh paw print in the mud next to the walkway. Up the path are more prints—a heavier pair—that stop at the bottom of the stairs in a dusting of frost. They're pronounced like the animal sat for a while. A long while. Waiting.

"Val? You hear me?"

I try to keep the concern from my expression. "Sorry, what?"

"You hear anything last night?" he asks.

I shake my head. "I wasn't here. Only got home a few minutes ago. You?"

"Nah. Fell asleep watching the tube. Wouldn't have heard a lion even if it jumped in my lap and growled."

I glance down to get a closer look. The print is big. Bigger than your average coyote. Los Cazadores—it had to be them. First, they come to La Maison, and now my house. They would never be so careless as to allow their coyotes to leave a print if they didn't want me to know they were here.

As owls, our covens think we've got one up on Los Cazadores. We're able to shift. To hide in plain sight. It is how we've been able to survive for so long. It's what lets us preserve the legacy given to us by Lorenza, the First Witch. With Hunters unable to differentiate us from earthly owls, we have been able to exploit this divine Gift of our Craft. But Los Cazadores have the advantage of their coyote packs. For centuries, each Hunter has undergone a binding ceremony to supernaturally connect him to his coyote. It allows the pair to act as one mind. Scouting. Hunting. Killing. They are predators in the truest sense of the word—and we're their prey.

For years, this went on. Before I was born, Los Cazadores and our covens came to a truce. For whatever reason, they seem to have tossed that peace aside. Their coming here is no coincidence. This is a warning.

"You hear that story on the news? About some kinda cat?" Jean says, interrupting my thoughts.

"What cat?"

"Tourists near La Fontaine said they spotted some big cat. Or dog. Or something. Probably just a fox, huh?"

La Fontaine is up the block.

"It's ridiculous." He hauls himself up and starts for the back door. "Probably a dog got off its leash, eh?"

I try to smile when he waves goodbye, but my ears are ringing. They attack La Maison on the same night someone reports some sort of large animal in the city? And this paw print outside my apartment? That's no coincidence.

When Jean is safely inside, I run upstairs, taking the stairs two at a time, and bolt up the hall. I'm outside the door to my bedroom when my phone pings in the living room. When I grab it to pick it up, it isn't Gwen or Will. Panic floods my system.

I tap the screen and hold it out in front of me, answering the video call.

"Desi?"

"Hey, cuz."

"What's wrong?" I say, searching my cousin's face for some sign of what's going on. "Everything alright with you?"

He nods and scrubs at his thick curls, as haphazard and messy as always, with two tufts poking up at either side of his temple. "Yeah, I'm good. I'm more worried about you."

I roll my eyes and move to the front window. Morning traffic is busy, with cars heading to office jobs and the postal vans out on their daily routes.

"Let me guess. My mother called and told you what happened last night."

"She didn't have to," Desi says, yawning. "The entire coven's buzzing about it. You freaking Canadians and your drama. *Loco de la cabeza*, man."

I laugh for what feels like the first time in years. When we were kids, Desi taught me the best of Spanish slang, even though I was the older cousin.

"What do you expect after being snowbound for months?" I say. "We all go a little crazy sometimes."

"Yeah, well, you sure know how to stir things up. You okay after everything that went down?"

"I guess."

"Oh, that was real convincing, *prima*."

"What can I say? It wasn't how I expected to spend Mabon, that's for sure."

"You can say that again. You had another one of your visions, huh?"

That's the last thing I need. It's bad enough the coven saw me freak out, but now Desi knows too? I love my cousin, but he's got the monopoly on the gossip gene in our family.

"Look, I get it," he says. "You been through some stuff. If anyone gets it, it's me. But girl...you gotta be your own person and stop trying to be who you think your mamá wants you to be."

Desi wasn't born yet when my dad died, but he grew up hearing the stories. It gives us a shorthand, one I'm glad for. That time in my life isn't anything I want to explain to anyone right now. But he's experienced my mother firsthand. He knows how she's expected me to take her place in the coven.

"What you need," he says, "is a vacation."

Great. Another person telling me what I need.

"I know you don't like it when people give you advice," he says, laughing like he could hear my thoughts. "But maybe a few weeks down south will help you clear your head."

I prop one hand on my hip. "Why do I get the idea you knew I was thinking about leaving? That my mom asked you to check in on me?"

He tries to hide it, but the way his mouth curls up at both sides says it all. Then he lets out that hideous cackle he does when he knows he's caught.

"Okay, so maybe I got a call, but it wasn't from your mom. Your boy Will called me."

"Seriously?"

"Yeah. He said you might bail outta town for a few weeks. And since you ain't been back here for what, like five years? Now's the perfect time for you to get your pale ass down here and get some sun. You can crash at my place. Or at El Rancho. There are these sweet little guest houses on the property. Real private. Close to the woods. Perfect place to lose yourself for a while. What do ya say, huh?"

I have to admit it sounds a lot better than heading to the airport and picking up the first ticket available for standby. Being in San Diego wouldn't be so bad right now. It would give me time to catch up with family and would let me get away from the tension here. Let things settle.

It's where my dad practiced his Craft. The place that made him who he was. There are worse things to do than go to The Strand and stare at hot surfers while grabbing tacos and beer on the beach.

"So...you coming? Or am I gonna have to come up there and haul you back with me?"

"Alright, alright. I'll think about it."

"Good. Last thing I wanna do is buy snowshoes or some heavy-assed parka or...what do you call it? A torque?"

I laugh, shaking my head at him. "It's a toque. A knit cap."

"Well, whatever you call it, I don't want it," he says. So, how soon you gonna leave?"

"Hey, I didn't agree to anything yet."

He shrugs at me and kicks back on the couch. "What's there to think about? On one hand, you got snow. On the other hand, you got sun, sand, and surf. Oh, and your favorite cousin to hang out with."

I move through the living room and stop at the large bookshelf against the far wall. The sunlight has moved across the apartment and one beam highlights the last family photo we took. My mother, looking ethereal as always, stands with both arms wrapped around me. I've got that teenage look about me. All attitude with pursed lips, head tilted to one side. It seems like a lifetime ago. It makes my stomach sour at how good things were back then, and I was too much of a surly teen to notice. Those halcyon days of my youth are behind me, and now I'm the one dealing with the reality of life in the coven.

"I'll be out of here as soon as possible. I can pack and head to the airport now. Grab the first standby flight I can find."

"Damn, girl. You're serious about getting the hell outta Dodge."

"I mean, I can get a hotel if you—"

"Bite your tongue. Just lemme know your flight number when you get it. I got some stuff to do for Los Muertos. So it'll either be me or my girl, Dree, to pick yo' ass up. Got it?"

"Okay."

"Good. I'll see ya soon."

"Yeah. Hey, Desi?"

"You're welcome," he says. "Later, *loca*."

After he hangs up, I linger at the photo a little longer. I always wanted to be like my mother. But maybe I've been using it as a crutch. Maybe trying to live up to her reputation is the very thing keeping me grounded. Is Desi right? Should I just let it all go? Move on and be who I'm supposed to be instead of who I think she has always wanted me to be?

The second thing missing? My dad. The only thing I ever wished for was for him to come back to me. Maybe going to the place where he spent most of his time will help me learn about the pieces of him I never knew. To bring him back in a way.

Desi's vibe is exactly what I need: seeing him and getting away from life up here for a while may help me put things in perspective. Putting as many miles between myself and Los Cazadores to protect myself and the coven. Maybe it will help keep the black witch moths at bay. The thought of their relentless fluttering, their tiny clawed toes scratching…

I pad down the hallway to my bedroom. I kneel and yank out the suitcase stashed beneath the box spring, unzipping it and tossing it on the unmade bed. Everything I own comes in various shades of black, with some burgundy and olive green thrown in. Something tells me a little retail therapy is in my future, along with the San Diego sojourn. There's no way Desi will tolerate me being dressed in dark colors in the California sunshine.

I toss my clothes, and a few other necessities into my bag and zip it closed before moving to the living room. I grab my purse and dump the contents onto the sofa. My owl mask sits at the top of the pile. Sections of the feathers are gone. Others are stained and dirty, the ends stuck together with dried blood. I toss it aside, trying to ignore it. But it doesn't matter. The mask has a pull on me I can't shake, even from ten feet away. When I glance at it, I feel it on my face. When I take a step closer and reach for it, there's a soft tickle of feathers in my hand before I even touch it. I have worn it for so many rites, some of the most important nights in my life. Seeing it in this state crushes me. The blood sullies it and all it stands for, and the thought of putting it back on brings back the chill of the forest. The thrumming of my pulse at knowing Los Cazadores were so close. My skin crawls, knowing they saw me before I even knew they were there. I can't bear to touch it.

I go to the bookshelf and take my passport from a small locked metal box before I take another smaller wooden trinket box. The top is carved with owl wings, the same as the ones I got tattooed on my back the minute I turned eighteen. I dust off the top and open it. My nose tickles with the lingering scent of incense. Inside, a small square of velvet protects my cherished set of tarot cards. In another bundle, a worn deck of Loteria cards with a simple pattern on the back. The fronts were decorated in still vibrant hues, though a little faded after all these years. Tia Lena gave the deck to me when I turned five. I've always loved the pensive expression of La Luna, the scythe of La Muerte, the sinister grin of El Diablo. Instead of fearing them, the designs entranced me. They still do. I secure them in the box before reaching for a compact bundle of crushed purple velvet.

Inside sits an amethyst pendant and a moonstone ring, given to me by Gwen at last year's Yule celebrations. I slip the pendant around my neck.

Gwen. The thought of her makes my stomach queasy. Images of her flash in my thoughts: her excitement at seeing me there for the ceremony, our chat in the woods, and her unending support. Then, the attack. The memories come faster now: breathing beyond the trees, Gwen shifting, her feathers snapping, the slicing of metal through feather and flesh, her high-pitched screech. And then...the thump of her body hitting the forest floor. Her injuries. Her final moments, riddled with poison from the arrow. Los Cazadores may have been the ones to hurt her, but it's my fault she was in harm's way in the first place. The best thing I can do now to protect everyone else in L'Assemblée de la Terre is to get as far away as possible. In my pocket, I still have the lock of her hair that fell into my hand back at La Maison. I place it alongside my other treasures before closing the box and slipping it into my bag.

In two swift moves, I've got my phone in my hand, and I'm calling a cab. I'll worry about eating when I get there. And sleep? Who needs it? I shove my feet into my Docs, classic black and creased at the toes. People wear Docs in the desert, right?

I sling my bag over my shoulder, but the mask... It sits there, empty. Staring up at me. So hollow without my eyes to bring it to life. It's a shell, a façade. I can't even stand to look at it anymore. I take it and toss it onto the couch, then head to the door, ignoring the pull of the mask's importance on my heart.

Then I remember the coyote fur. It draws my gaze back to the table where I'd set it. I'm repelled from it and drawn to it all the same. I gather it up and go to the bookshelf, rifling around until I find an empty medicine bottle. I palm the lid, dropping the fur inside the bottle, screwing the cap back on, and shoving it into my bag before I grab my jacket and head for the door. When I step outside, I close and lock the door, trying to ignore the disgusting slur on the front.

Slipping my hand into my pocket, I find the talisman that I took from the arrow that ended Gwen's life. Instead of spitting on it and stomping on it with my boot like I want to do, I pocket it again. They took something important to me. Now I have something that belongs to them—something I can use when the time is right. Whether or not Los Cazadores are the ones behind the vulgar spray painting job on my door, they were here.

I breathe in the crisp air and the faint ashen scent of fireplaces wafting from the older townhouses on the block. The air is a blanket of earthen spice. It almost reminds me of the forest where I once belonged. But that time is gone, too.

I'm at the curb when the driver pulls up. He exits the driver's side to open the door for me.

"Val?" he asks.

I nod and hand him my bag, which he deposits into the trunk. I start to slide into the backseat, but a sharp whistle stops me.

It's from miles away, but it's there. Under the din of the car horns and sirens, it comes again. It nags at my nerves, pulling them taut. I get into the car and close the door, but it's still there. The driver gets in, and we head off. I wait for the traffic light to change, drumming my fingers on the window ledge to the beat of the song on the radio, trying not to hear the persistent whistle.

The sound comes anew. My mother. She's calling me, willing me back to La Maison. It isn't her whistle, though. It's her voice. I would know it anywhere. I knew it before I was born.

For a moment, I almost tell the driver to take me there. Out of the city, back into the forest. Back to La Maison, where Èvelyne is calling for me. I daydream about pulling up to the front of the house. Getting out of the car. Running up to the door where she wraps her arms around me, and everything feels like it will be okay.

But the days when my mother's hugs solved all my problems are long gone now. Sentiment will solve nothing.

"Where to?" the driver asks.

"The airport, please."

He shifts the car into drive and heads out into traffic. The further we get from downtown, the more doubt sits heavy in my stomach.

Yet thoughts of visiting Desi, memories of my childhood when we were all together, and a time before I knew nothing of Hunters and being chased and people dying pull me forward. The initial wave of uncertainty I felt was slowly being replaced by a sense of adventure.

But Èvelyne's voice doesn't stop, only fades like the mourning song of a spirit. I pull out my headphones and jam them on, loading up my favorite satellite station and blasting it. I only hope California is far enough away that it drowns everything out.

CHAPTER 6

California

By the time I land and grab a cab to Barrio Logan, sunset illuminates the buildings in Old Town San Diego, painting them with candy-colored hues. The buzzing energy and dry heat make it feel like I'm on another planet, not just the other coast. But it's a welcome change from the cloud hanging over me from Mabon and the attack on La Maison.

Not that there's anything that can truly erase the horrors of the past few days. At some point, I have to process everything that happened—the moths and their omen, the assault from Los Cazadores, losing Gwen—but for now, I'm keeping those thoughts pushed to the back of my brain. It's the only way I'll be able to survive without letting that darkness swallow me whole.

I get the cabbie to drop me off in the Chicano part of town where Desi lives. When I step out and grab my luggage, I take in a breath, letting the heat energize my soul and draw me from the hibernation I've been in, not only this winter but for years. The rhythm of the city combines with the distant swish of the ocean against the sand. This is where I'm supposed to be right now.

Before Èvelyne was High Priestess, we spent our winters here. La Asamblea de la Lumbre, the fire assembly of the Assemblée des Chouettes, or the Aquelarre Búho as they call it, is based here. *Papá* was studying with a local *Curandero*, Don Vega, to enhance his craft and learn the ancient ways of healing and plant wisdom. Being back here, snapshots of moments past aren't the only memories floating to the surface. Phantom images of my father linger in the air like he's still here. The nearer I get to the desert, to the ocean, the more I sense his energy around me.

A multicolored mural beneath the overpass draws my attention and lures me in. With her arms outstretched, the towering figure—a woman painted in red and purple with a skirt of snakes—holds the sun in one hand and the earth in the other. Moving closer, I trace my fingers over her eyes, her lips, her face. This was one of my father's favorite places when we came to visit. He would hold me up on his shoulders and whisper to me about the ancient gods and goddesses. Their names rolled off his tongue so smoothly; even without knowing the language, I still remember this one. Coatlicue, the Aztec Goddess of the Earth. It makes sense she would draw my attention. I'm an Earth witch, after all. The way the lights dance across her face, illuminating her eyes, it's like she is calling me to her. Pointing me home.

Around her, the vibrant colors swirl into one another until I can't see straight. Peacock feathers and desert scenes, yucca trees and crosses, snakes and cacti. La Catrina holding a sacred heart, the thorns leaving a trail of blood dripping from her palms. In the middle of it all, something pulses. Hidden within the elaborate painting, a white symbol throbs as though embedded beneath it. But as I touch it, willing the dark magic instilled within, low breaths draw my attention.

Behind me, tourists snap photos of the colorful paintings and gather around objects tied to the middle of the palm trees that line the street. Some are compact bundles, in hot pink and white. Others are small wooden shelves nailed to the trunk. Tall glass votive candles with La Catrina and Our Lady of Guadalupe flicker in the darkness. And there, again, lurking under the din, breathing.

Tinny salsa music thrums from speakers set up in Chicano Park. But beneath the pulsing beat, a thread of hostility snakes its way through the crowd. Something is hungry, but not for the chorizo empanadas or *elote*—buttered grilled corn covered in queso fresco and lime—from the local food trucks. Something craves me, craves my blood, and that determined hunger washes toward me in waves.

I stand still, slowing my breathing and clearing my thoughts, allowing my tracking skills to hone in on the source of this dark energy, but it's too

THE BONE KEY

elusive for me to see clearly. It warps the music around me, the rhythm becoming choppy and the melody souring into discordance. The park, with its revelers all spinning to the tempo, goes fuzzy and off-kilter like I'm looking in a funhouse mirror. My face flushes as my throat goes dry, my hands trembling like I am cornered prey. Overhead, the paper lanterns and wavering *papel picado*—the colorful garland banners—make my stomach somersault.

I reach behind me, pressing my palm to the hidden symbol on the wall, which turns warm under my hand. The world comes starkly into focus, the music and laughter drops away. The air cools, and the sky darkens. In the distance, a lone figure stands unmoving, watching me.

A surge of panic pangs at my temple. I need to get out of here. It doesn't matter how many witnesses there are around me. I'm completely exposed with no backup. And I'm being hunted.

My phone chimes in my pocket. I almost don't accept the call, but there's a tingling in the back of my mind, and the distinct scent of fire tickles my nose like an omen. I keep my gaze locked on my pursuer, who still has not moved and take out my phone.

"What the hell, cuz? Where are you?" It's Desi.

"I'm downtown. Chicano Park."

"I told you my girl, Dree, was gonna pick you up at the airport."

"I know. Something didn't feel right."

"It's dangerous, Val, with what happened to you back home."

"You can say that again."

"Why? What's going on?"

"I've got a tail," I say, watching the figure advance. "I'm not sure how long he's been on me, but he's here. And he's headed right for me."

I sling my bag over one shoulder and head in the opposite direction. When I glance back, he's still following me.

"Who? What the hell you talking about, Val?"

"A Hunter."

"Damn, you sure?"

"He might be blocks away, but his stench is unmistakable."

I dodge around two families, nearly slamming into a toddler in the middle of the sidewalk. She screams, jolting me from my dream state and bringing everything back into loud, sharp focus. The shrill pomp and circumstance of the mariachi trumpets set my nerves on edge as I try to put as much distance between myself and the Hunter as possible, but he's gaining on me.

"You serious? Yo, where you at exactly? I'm coming to get you."

"No!" I say. "I'm not letting Los Cazadores hurt another person I care about."

"Val..."

"I'll be fine."

I end the call before he can protest and pocket my phone. Up ahead, countless cafes, galleries, and taquerias create the perfect place to get lost in the crowd. I spot a group filing in through barricades—looks like a street festival. Must be an early start to Día de Los Muertos.

I bolt to a tree in a large planter on the sidewalk and move behind it, trying to make myself as small as possible. When I peek around, the Hunter is gone. For the moment, at least, I can breathe.

The radio in one of the shops across the street blasts Reggaeton, the perfect backdrop to the party atmosphere. A thumping bass line plays under a blistering Latin rhythm. Music has always been an escape for me, and that's what I need right now. Even with the brief nap on the flight, every muscle in my body feels like a stretched piece of taffy, aching and overworked. The melody helps loosen my shoulders, helps me unclench my jaw so I can breathe.

But when the song changes, the overwhelming sense of aggression hits me again, snaking around the tree and dotting my skin with goosebumps. I try to make myself smaller, to stay in the shadow of the tree, but the longer I remain hidden, the more my body tingles. Around me, the shade from the tree grows, and a *flicker-flicker-flickering* starts high in the branches before descending around me.

The black witch moths. Somehow, they're here with me again, this time seeping down around me like a veil, shrouding me the same way they did at Hacienda en Las Lomas when I sat beside my dying father, and the mysterious dark woman in the trees was there, then gone, swallowed by the swarm.

They don't swallow me, though. Instead, they hover around me in a protective circle, shielding me from the party-goers walking past, who don't seem to notice me. As the surge of aggression comes closer, I hold my breath, praying for it to pass. As he draws close to me, my knees go weak, but the moths gather to brace me. The Hunter paces past, pausing to glance around in confusion; I clench my teeth together to keep from reacting to his nearness.

On his face, he has a long scratch. A wound healed years ago, stretching from just above his left eye to his cheekbone. For a few moments, his face shifts into a younger one. A face I recognize.

#

Cries pierce the silence. The tang of blood hangs thickly in the air, choking me. All I want is for someone to save me.

A low-pitched screech from a dark owl in the trees above makes me jump. Its black wings swoop overhead, circling a spot near the firethorns that acts as a barrier between the charmed land of our coven and the canyon beyond. The bushes rustle and shift with movement from within.

A figure, not much larger than me, kneels in the bushes with one arm pulled back, holding the bow at full draw and pointing it at me.

We lock gazes, and he hesitates long enough for the owl to attack. It dive bombs toward the boy, peeling a long, shrill cry. With its wings extended and legs outstretched, the owl slashes at the boy's forehead with its talons. He screams and flings himself backward into the thorns.

Hovering there, the owl beats the bushes with his wings, kicking out its feet to get to the boy. But somehow, he scurries through to the other side and gets away. As a flurry of arrows whizz past the owl's head and land in the grass, it turns and flies toward me. Swooping overhead, it releases a long call and lands, using its wings to shield me as everything goes black.

∽

The memory dissipates, and I stare into the face of Nico López, whose father took mine from me, the man who wants to do the same to me. I've heard my mother speak the López name with such ire that my blood surges hot through my body at the sight of him. He inches closer, looking right through me. He scans the crowds gathered for the festivities. His brow wrinkles, sensing something he cannot place.

With my lips pursed together, I whisper an enchantment to keep myself hidden.

He takes another step toward me, edging deeper into the shadows.

I hold my breath.

He lifts one hand, reaching forward into the darkness. I press my back hard against the tree, fighting to control my breath, my heartbeat. The back of my neck prickles with a desperate desire to flee, and it takes every ounce of magical energy the moths possess to keep me from moving.

His hand reaches closer. The moths surge for him, the fine hairs on their wings growing into tiny barbs. Their little clawed feet elongate and slice at him.

He cries out and draws back his hand, shaking it and inspecting his fingertips, bloodied from the moths' attack. But he doesn't see me and races away.

Only when Nico is halfway down the block do I pitch forward, clutching my ribs: they ache from holding my breath. A jolt to the middle of my forehead forces me to my knees. A sharp whistle tickles my ears, the same way it did when I left Montréal. My mother. She senses my panic. She knows I'm being hunted, and she's calling to me. I inhale and breathe back out, trying to quell the pain long enough to cast my thoughts to her.

I'm safe. I'm alive and can fend for myself.

The whistle comes again, this time an undulating call to return. To go back home. But I've come too far: I can only move forward now, not back. Right now, that means getting as far away from the Hunter as I can.

My entire body is flooded with adrenaline, enough to push me through the veil of moths in the opposite direction from the Hunter. I need to get away from here. Now.

I make it back to Chicano Park when my phone pings. I reach for it as a blast of dark energy hits me from behind, sending me staggering, falling to my knees. When I get my bearings, I spot Nico running toward me from the street.

My phone rings again, but I can't stop. I have no time. He's coming for me.

Some passerby reaches down to help me up, and I let him, but only long enough to get to my feet and race away.

Curious onlookers gawk at me like I've lost my mind, but I ignore them—he's gaining on me.

I clutch the amethyst pendant dangling at my throat and speak low. "Send back the harm that is put upon me. Send it back where it came."

Up ahead, there's a trolley with tourists hopping on to take a guided tour. As it drives away, I try to catch up, but my muscles are spent. I can barely keep up. I spin back around in time to see Nico run straight into a drunk girl who careens in front of him, nearly falling into the street. He catches her, and she distracts him enough for me to lunge for the back end of the trolley. When it slows, I slide into one of the open-air seats and shove my bag beside me. Just as it takes off, Nico catches up. He lunges for the tail of the trolley, hopping up onto the back and reaching for me. I dart to the side, narrowly missing his grasp. He's hanging on as it speeds up, still swiping at me to grab onto me. I lurch away from him again; this time, he catches me by the hand.

I cry out, yanking away from him, but he holds tight, somehow hanging over the back of the seat. With a closed fist, I pound on the side of his head, trying to free myself from his grasp. When he doesn't let go, I yank the cord around my neck and clasp my bone whistle between my knuckles, slashing at him.

The needle-sharp bone, filed into a talon, catches him in the face, reopening his old wound. When he brings his arm up to fight off my next attack, he slips from the back of the trolley and falls to the pavement.

Collapsing to the side, gasping for air, I spin in my seat, making sure he isn't following. In the middle of the street, he stands with a cacophony of car horns blaring at him as vehicles swerve around him.

Then he starts running.

I take my bag and fling it around me, then push myself up and barrel to the front of the trolley.

"Go!" I shout, fighting to keep myself upright as I battle the bumpy ride.

"Miss, please sit down," the driver calls over her shoulder.

"Please, I need you to keep going!" I shout, making it to the front of the trolley as it slows.

"Sit down, please. We're almost at the next stop."

Nico is limping, but he's moving fast. Getting closer.

"I'm being chased! You can't stop. Please!"

The driver doesn't listen, slowing the trolley as we approach another tourist signpost. When she stops, I push through the oncoming passengers, ignoring their annoyed glares, and take off.

But he's relentless in his pursuit. His poisonous energy weighs me down, and there are no moths here to protect me.

I spin in circles. The sun is down. I'm trapped. There is nowhere to go—only the park on one side and the overpass leading to the Coronado Bridge on the other. But it's not like I can stop. I have to keep pushing forward, even if I feel like I'm about to collapse.

I make it to the center of the park before I hear him behind me.

"You might have some tricks up your sleeve, but I'm still faster than you."

I face him so he won't have the satisfaction of coming up behind me unseen. He's a hulking shadow in the darkness, the streetlights behind him hiding his face.

"You might be faster," I say, "but you're as alone out here as I am."

He stops running, and before I can wonder why, a distinct rumbling growl sounds from behind me. I freeze, my stomach dropping. A pair of bright yellow eyes shimmer in the darkness a few yards away.

His tracker coyote.

They have me on both sides.

I clench my hands into fists, only then remembering my bone whistle clenched between my fingers.

I prop it to my lips and play a short tune. A distress signal.

There's no response.

"Nice try," Nico says, taunting me. "That's what happens when you leave everything and everyone you know behind."

He strides forward a few steps.

I play the tune again. Nothing.

The coyote paces toward me, salivating, its eyes blazing bright. It opens its mouth, ready to devour me.

From beyond the wan circle of the streetlights comes a whistled response. The other half of my song. Only another member of the Aquelarre Búho would know this melody—I'm not alone.

Nico speeds toward me. He might think he has the upper hand, but only members of our owl coven can hear the song. He doesn't know I've got backup.

I move to the side, glancing quickly to find his coyote. It has paced closer to me. They are closing the gap, trying to box me in. I'm about to play another tune when the Hunter lets out a quick whistle.

The coyote snaps its teeth together with a sickening snap and sets off at a bloodthirsty gallop.

I steel my nerves for the impact, but as the animal nears, I dive into a thicket of bushes alongside the road with my heart in my throat. The coyote goes skidding past me, flipping onto its side from the momentum. It scrambles up and comes at me again, and I hold my bag up in front of me for protection when it throws its weight into the bushes. Its weight lands on top of me, but I push back with every ounce of energy I have left. It goes flying onto its back as a car horn blasts from the road. A pair of headlights illuminates the bushes, blinding me.

Nico shouts something as a dark shadow races past in the other direction. A car door opens and slams beyond the park. Footsteps race toward me, getting louder.

My body tenses, anticipating hands reaching in to drag me away, probably belonging to another Hunter. Or two. I can't see anything. There could be half a dozen.

"Val?"

Oh God, no.

"I know you're in there, Val."

He knows my—

A trill, a song from my childhood. It's Desi.

I lift the whistle and play the second half, the answer to his question. When he finishes, all the pent up anger, the fear, the guilt all boil over at once. By the time he gets to me, I'm curled on my side, sobbing.

Desi hauls me up out of the bushes. He cups my face and pushes my hair out of my face, brushing the dirt and dried leaves from me.

"Damn, girl. I know you're an Earth witch, but this is taking it one step too far."

I throw my arms around him. Squeeze him until we're both laughing, and I fall into him.

"Come on," he says, steadying me. "Let's go home."

I climb into the back seat of the car. Doors closed, we head off. I lean into him, let him cradle me like I'm the younger cousin for once. For now, I'm safe. But that doesn't stop me from peering into the mirror, making sure Nico López and his coyote aren't following us. But the only thing illuminated by our taillights is a shadowy veil of blackness escorting us home.

CHAPTER 7

Darkness Begins

The air here is scented with incense and sea salt. Jasmine and smoke. When I roll out of bed, I am drawn to the window. Sunlight burns everything hot white, but when my eyes adjust, I'm greeted by an oasis in the desert. Lush palms surround the vast grounds, and on either side, set amongst brush and flowers, are several pale brown stucco guesthouses. Across the grounds, a low stone wall separates the greenery from the main house, where a criss-crossing string of fairy lights hovers above the tiled patio.

In the distance, the heartbeat of a drum coaxes me to slip on my shoes and head toward the door. When I open it and wander outside, I shade my eyes. The heat and sun of the morning make me realize I am way overdressed. I'm still on Montréal time and sure as hell still in urban fashion mode.

I'm sweating. Instantly sweating. I strip off my long-sleeved shirt and pull my hair up into a messy bun. This will take some getting used to. Then again, I have no plans about when—or if—I'll go back.

As I start for the house, my phone chimes from my back pocket. Checking the screen, my mother's number flashes with each ring. I'm tempted to silence it, but that will only encourage her to keep calling.

"Hi, Mom," I say, bracing myself.

"Valeria...you're all right?"

"Of course I am."

"You aren't hurt then?"

I sigh, tilting my head to one side as I glance skyward, willing strength and trying to keep the bite in my tone at bay. "I'm fine."

"After last night, I had to be sure. Esmeralda told me what happened when you arrived."

I bite my bottom lip. I would have thought Desi would be the one to rat me out, but it was Esme.

"She's High Priestess, Valeria. She thought it was important for me to know that Los Cazadores followed you there."

"They did, but I managed to hold him off. I made it safely to El Rancho. You don't have to worry."

"But I do worry. And that isn't a bad thing, you know. I'm concerned—not only for you but all of us. The way things happened at Mabon... That was unfair. Not to mention Gwendolyn. The attack..."

"Which is why it's better I'm here. To keep Los Cazadores away from La Maison. I feel protected here. Like I can breathe for the first time in a long time."

Her silence on the other end of the line hurts my heart. I don't want her to think I don't appreciate everything she's given me.

"You need to move forward," she says. "I understand. I only want you to be happy, *mon amour*."

"That might take some time. But I'm trying."

"Good," she says, softer now. "*Ma petite plume.*"

"I gotta go," I say, hanging up before her words, her earnest tone, can soften my resolve.

I stride for the house, but the unmistakable scent of aromatic evergreen and mesquite lingers like a whisper. Trying to pinpoint where it's coming from, I follow the scent across the expansive grounds toward a small cabin set amongst the palm trees. The front platform has two well-worn wicker chairs. Bone wind chimes hang from the awning that spans the length of the house.

I tip-toe, trying not to snoop, but from somewhere inside, a low, chanting voice entices me to sneak a look through the half-opened window.

The interior is smoky, the lighting subdued. It looks like the inside of a campfire when the coals have burned down, and all the embers simmer. Amber-hued light filters everything with an ethereal glow.

I edge closer, trying to see who's inside, and fail to notice the stack of clay pots to my right. Like a clumsy oaf, I knock them over, giving away my presence in a clattering cacophony of shattered earthenware.

I freeze. The front door flies open, and a woman around my age, dressed in a black top and leggings, strides toward me. Her gauzy flame-colored wrap flits in the air.

She stops just short of colliding with me and stares, studying me. Dark hair frames her delicate face. A half-moon tattoo adorns the middle of her forehead between thin, pointed eyebrows. Kohl cat's eyeliner flicks from her eyelids.

"*Hola. Me llamo,* Valeria. *Soy*...I, uh...I'm so sorry," I say. "I didn't mean to—"

She holds up a finger to her mouth. Her upper lip is painted black. The bottom one has a single black line painted down the center.

"Don't," she says. "There's no need for it. Come." She takes my hand and pulls me inside, where the perfumed cloud of opium incense hangs like a spoken daydream. "I'm Lidia."

"Nice to meet you," I say, glancing around.

Stacks of books fill the well-loved interior, with bunches of dried flowers and an army of cacti lining the windowsill. Lush red pillows encircle a canary and orange-colored tapestry of a sun draped across the floor. She directs me to sit and then plants herself opposite me. I plunk myself down, feeling like a gangly deer with coltish limbs and knobby joints.

"I'm so sorry for intruding," I say. "I was only—"

"Looking for guidance."

"Uh, yeah. To the main house? Can I just walk in there or... I mean, I'm visiting. So, I didn't want to intrude. Like I've done here. To you."

She doesn't speak. Her lips don't move. But I swear I hear an incantation under her breath.

"I'm looking for—"

"An escape," she says. Her lips barely move, making it seem as though her voice comes from everywhere and nowhere all at once. "From someone or something holding you back."

"Uh...I guess."

The way she stares feels too personal. Like she can see into my head. Like it's all written on my face, ingrained in my soul, and she has a way of tapping into it. It feels so intrusive, but I can't pull myself away. There's something about her, the way she looks at me so intently. Maybe it's the swirling smoke, the candles, the dark coolness of this room. There's something familiar about her, even though we've never met.

Her eyebrows knit together as she studies me like she's trying to pull something out of me. "You have something with you. Something you wanted to leave behind but could not."

Is she talking about my regret? Because I've got a hell of a lot of it.

"Something you've kept hidden," she continues. "Something that makes you recoil, but you cannot resist it."

My hand goes to my satchel. My comfort. The thing I never leave home without. I know what's inside. It feels like a secret, burning to expose itself.

"What is it?" she asks. "Something from a lover? A friend or foe? Something you want? That you revile?"

"I don't even know why I kept it," I lie.

I knew exactly what I was doing back at my apartment when I plucked it from my coat, even if I didn't want to admit it to myself. I squirreled that bit of fur away for a time when all the chaos and craziness subsided long enough that I could gather my crystals and herbs, call a circle, and do some damage to the animals who hunt us.

"But you did. Keep it, I mean."

Of course, I did. And when Desi called and invited me down, I brought it with me. I knew as soon as I could tell him what I had, he would be the first one lining up to conjure a response for Los Cazadores—even if Èvelyne would go on about how they are the ones who set out to harm when we only want to thrive.

She holds her hand out like a schoolmarm, waiting for me to spit out my gum. Her eyes shimmer with anticipation, waiting for the big reveal.

There's something about the determination in her eyes that I can't resist. It's so different from my mother's stoicism. From Will's bravado. From Gwen's earth-child chill. There is a fire in her, one that taps into something lying dormant in me. Something I've caught glimpses of over the years, alight with passion and power. Before I can resist, I reach into my bag, pull out the medicine bottle, and hand it to her.

She takes it like a magpie snatching a shiny bauble, and for a moment, the fire in her eyes flashes with lust before quelling. She opens the bottle and holds it under her nose, looking down into it and sniffing the contents.

With eyes closed, her expression shifts. When they open again, something darker disintegrates her enthusiasm. She upends the bottle. The fur falls into her palm, and she holds it out in front of her.

"This is from the one who harmed your friend."

I nod.

"And you want to hurt him in return. For what he stole. For what he put you through."

"Yes."

"You are done with hiding. Done with being stuck in the shadows. You want your other self to take over. To be your *true* self."

Something about the way she speaks entrances me. I nod, even though I don't want to admit it. Los Cazadores put my coven at risk. They trespassed on our sacred land. And they killed Gwen, one of the most loving witches I know. My incantations aren't enough any longer. Not if Los Cazadores continue to persecute us for what we are.

"They hunted us for hours," I say, clenching my hands into fists. "Chased us through the dark. The cold. Stalked us through the backwoods."

Cold sweat percolates on the back of my neck. The scent of burnt wood from the fires at La Maison floods my senses.

"I had to use every charm I possessed. Recite every spell of protection, of strength, to keep going." My breath hitches in my throat. "Branches lashed at my cheeks. I had cuts and scrapes over my arms and legs. My face. But I kept going, no matter how cold or how my body weakened at the toil. It took everything in me to protect myself. To protect Gwen."

The mere mention of her name makes my chest tighten. I reach into my bag where I secreted away the lock of her hair, which I tied into a braid on the flight over here. I don't see her as a vibrant, smiling young woman so excited by the prospect of her Gift. I picture her seized with pain, pale and tormented. The black veins from the poisoned arrows scarring her face, her body wracked in agony, and then unmoving forever. My blood boils at the indelible image Los Cazadores have left me with.

"They hunted you, Valeria," Lidia says, sitting up and clasping her hand over mine. "Stalked you. Waited until you were at your most vulnerable. Murdered one of our sisters."

Her eyes flash bright yellow, and then they darken like the full moon blocked by passing clouds. "They killed your friend and tried to kill you too. Are you going to let them get away with it?"

She knows. She knows everything, even my name. Desi wasn't kidding when he said word had spread.

"We are all family," she says, taking the hair from me and setting it aside. "When one of us hurts, the rest hurt, too. When one of us cannot find their strength, the rest of us lift them up."

She reaches toward a low table to her left and takes a scarf, unfolding it and spreading it on the floor. She places the tuft of coyote fur on top. Next, she pulls a length of black silk cord from the bottom shelf.

"What are you doing?" I ask.

"Do you want to protect yourself? Protect our sisters and brothers?"

"With everything in me," I say.

"This will help." She lays the length of cord in front of me and hands me the bundle of coyote hair. "Take a single hair. Lay it across the string."

I do as she says. While I do so, she pulls a worn, hand-bound journal from the table. She unlatches the copper closure and flips through several pages. Some are sparse, with only a few scribblings. Others have elaborate illustrations. She stops, turning the book to me and tapping the page.

"Tie a knot around the hair. As you bind it, recite this."

I take the book from her and place it in front of me. A spell in thin, scraggly black script spills across the page. I lift both ends of the string and follow Lidia's instructions.

"I call upon the spirit of Lorenza de Salazar," I say, "who gave us our Gift. I ask you to guide and protect us. That you give us the strength we need to overcome our enemies. May their cruelty forever disappear."

I lift the long end, laying the hair across it before I secure it in place.

"You will do this once every night for a week," she says, jumping up and moving to a wooden cupboard. She rifles around in a drawer before she returns with a black candle and a small cigar box. She sits cross-legged across from me. "Do you know the name of the person who harmed you and your friend?"

I almost don't want to tell her. But I feel the talisman burning a hole in my pocket. I slip my hand into my bag and feel around. The pendant is cool to the touch, but I swear it is burning a sigil in my palm as I pull it out.

"I know this belonged to him."

I hold it out to her. She leans forward, studies it, nods.

"Do you have your athamé? If not, I can—"

I pull it from my bag before she can finish.

Her mouth curls up at either side. "Good. If you know nothing other than his initials, take this and carve them into the candle."

I reach for it, hesitating. This is it. There's no turning back from here. I can hear Desi's voice.

"Girl, you're getting into some crazy shit."

But I'm tired of it. Tired of hesitating, of constantly talking myself out of doing things because I'm afraid of what everyone else thinks. I have power. Power darker than what I've shown so far. Is this why the black witch moths come to me?

I take the candle. As I carve, a snippet of conversation floats in like a wisp on the wind. My mother's voice, hushed. Huddled together with Andres at the cabin. She spoke a name. The name that would haunt my dreams, tainting the happiest memories I had of my father for the rest of my days. The same one whose initials are on the talisman in front of me.

Nico López. It has to be.

I carve his name, first and last, on either side of the candle. Done, I look up and catch Lidia's gaze.

"What you do to one, you do to the other," she says.

I nod.

"Now, think about what happened to you. Every evening, you tie another hair to the string the same way you did just now."

She takes the candle from me and lays it in the box.

"On the seventh night after tying the knot, burn this."

She lifts the string, so delicate that just looking at it might break it.

"Light the candle, take the string and the hairs, and burn it all until you leave nothing."

She lays it beside the candle and then folds each side of the scarf into the middle, then folds the top and bottom points down.

"When you gather the ashes, you will take it all to the stream at the San Dieguito Trail. Throw the ashes into the current and say the spell once more to seal it."

She tucks the bundle tight and places it in the cigar box. When she hands it to me, I feel the impossible weight of it, even though I know it is nothing more than a small candle and a bundle of fabric. But it has stirred something in me. Something I thought I'd left behind.

That night comes back to me.

My breath grows shallow at the memory of being chased. Gwen, so fragile in owl form, in my arms. Tripping over downed branches, trying to see my way through the dark woods, keeping my gaze focused on the path ahead while listening for Los Cazadores. Their coyotes. Blood on my lip from biting it in frustration. Sweat beading on my forehead. The grit of dirt under my fingernails. Wind lashing my cheeks as I race through the shadows. All of it swirls around me. I blink, but I'm gone from this place. I'm back there: in the forest, with the stately pines, the willows, tangles of vines and brush, and soggy moss under my feet.

But instead of bothering me, it stokes a darkness in me that has lingered below the surface for so long. Thinking about Los Cazadores, how they were so close, close enough I had the coyote's fur on my clothing, makes my blood burn in my veins. They thought they could get away with their attack. But I'm going to use this fire within me, the fire I got from my father, Alejandro Salcedo, fire witch, High Priest of La Asamblea de la Lumbre, and I'm going to make them pay.

A hand on my arm makes me jump. When the memory drifts away like black sand, Lidia is standing in front of me, studying my face the way she did when I first showed up, snooping at her window. Instead of her fiery aura, something colder surrounds her.

"You all right?"

"Of course," I say, tucking the box into my satchel and gathering up the pendant and Gwen's braid.

She laughs and stands, stretching, her golden robe shimmering around her. The way the candlelight catches her angular face throws me off. Her face changes, filling out, the light reflecting like gold thread in her hair until she stops, her appearance returning to normal.

"I know. Not how you imagined your homecoming, huh? Might as well hit the ground running, *sí*?" She takes me by the arm and moves to the door. "You hungry? I'll bet you ate nothing on your flight."

"How'd you know?"

"You went through a significant trauma. Probably haven't slept much either since it happened."

"Not really," I say.

"Well, you're in the perfect place then. Let's go up to the main house. There's always a good spread there, and I need my *café*."

I follow her outside just as others emerge from the guesthouses on the grounds. They look in our direction, studying me and whispering to one another.

"Oh, don't worry about them," Lidia says, waving her hand. "They want to know all about the daughter of the High Priestess of the north."

"So, what is it you've heard about me? And my mother?"

"Oh, nothing bad," she says, putting a hand on my arm and coaxing me forward. "I mean, we all know she's the High Priestess. Esme always talks about the time she spent here."

She's being nice. But there's a veil between what she's saying and what she's trying to hold back.

"And your father too, of course."

Just hearing him mentioned makes my stomach lurch. I want to know everything about him, to learn all the things I never knew because I was too young to know anything other than his face. The things my mother never said because just the thought of him pained her so. But I can't ask. I'm too hopped up on adrenaline from the spell and the newness of this place.

We go to the back of the main house, wandering through a towering archway that leads from the spacious grounds to the back. At the top of the pillars, a set of weathered bones hang down like giant talons, razor-sharp, that come to a point at the end. The perfect weapon to impale any nosy coyote that gets too close.

"Rancho de las Garras," I say, breathing out the last word.

"House of Claws," she says, reaching up and touching the tip of the talon with her finger. "How long since you've been back home?"

"We came a few times after my dad passed, but…"

"It's too difficult. But it's good you are here, especially now with Los Cazadores lurking in the shadows." When she says their name, her eyes go black for a split second. "*Cabrones*. I look forward to the day I can use *mis garras* to pay them back for what they do to us."

Your talons, I think. I wonder if she knows enough about me to know I'm, as of now, flightless unless you count flying the coop from Montréal to spend who-knows-how-long down here.

As we head inside, I feel apprehension creeping in. I was never the one to jump into things headfirst and now, seeing the others inside, moving around one another and indulging in early morning chatter—clearly in their routine—I instantly stop myself from going inside.

When I feel a hand on my back, I expect it to be Lidia. Instead, Esmeralda Vasquez, my mother's counterpart from La Asamblea de la Lumbre, stands behind me, smiling. Her hair is dark like the sky at night, and her eyes glitter with welcome.

"Valeria. I am glad you're safe," she says, her voice is smoky and dazzling. "We were all very anxious after hearing about the attack."

"Thank you, High Priestess," I say. The past few days have been the strangest dream—the beauty of rekindling my connection with my coven colliding with the nightmare of the attack by Los Cazadores.

But there's something else in her warm tone. An undercurrent of love, of acceptance. There is no judgment there—no hint of the dark glint of disappointment I'm used to seeing in my mother's eyes and the eyes of my fellow witches because I'm not what they want me to be for them. Not even a hint of it.

She cups one hand on my cheek. "You grew up to be a lovely young woman. *Tu papá* would be so proud of you, his *pequeña pluma*."

A cry catches in my throat. Little feather. My father's nickname for me.

"What is it, *mija?*" she says, leading me to a long wooden bench against one wall. "What troubles you?"

"There have been so many changes in such a short time. Coming back here after so long…everything seems different. But still the same. And I'm not sure where I fit in. Or if I do at all."

She leans in and places her hand over mine.

"Sometimes we get so caught up in thinking about what we need to be for others that we become lost. Even in those places where we were comfortable for so long. You need to explore to find your true path."

"I tried that. It didn't go very well."

"Maybe you didn't go far enough. Or look deep enough. Maybe you looked outside yourself when what you really need to do is look within."

The thought thrills and terrifies me all at once. To look deep within? To examine everything I am, everything I am not? What if I can't do that? What if everything I believe I need is wrong?

"Listen," she says, "you come from a powerful mother. A fearless father. I know they are both in you. There is always space for you here where *tu papá* called home. This is *your* home, Valeria. Where you belong. You are always welcome here."

She links her arm in mine, and we walk to the back door, moving inside. The warmth of the morning sun dulls. Everything is cool and fragrant, and natural light floods in from outside and illuminates stone and wood in the interior. Glass orbs hang at various heights, pastel glass filled with water so they give off the look of a natural disco ball.

The way the witches move around one another is entrancing. Some are singing. A few dancing. It's a huge change from the polite coolness of my Assemblée de la Terre brothers and sisters to the north.

But as they move, as their laughter lilts in the air, I can hear my parents talking to one another, a memory of the happiness we shared here when I was young. The memory sends a pang of nostalgia to my chest, a fleeting vision of the three of us together so long ago when I was still too young to know those moments can't last forever.

As Esme leads me to a chair at the long table and I settle in, I don't feel as out of place as I'd expected. In the sitting room, there's a wall of portraits. I find my father straight away. My breath catches in my throat, tears stinging my eyes. He is valiant in his portrait: the jaguar skull propped high on his head, a spray of feathers for the mane. One incisor extends down either side of his temple, and a necklace of feathers and animal incisors juts out from his chest. Seeing him there, in a place of honor on the wall, swells pride within me.

"He was the last," Esme says beside me, nodding to the gallery. "We've never had another who could live up to his example as our High Priest. No one else to honor her the way he did."

In the center of the gallery, a massive oil painting hangs, connected to the others by thin black vines tracing generations of witches from Lorenza De Salazar, the First Witch of the Owl Covens. She is dressed in a cloak of mottled brown and black feathers that extend up her neck, wrapping around her shoulders to splay down her chest. Perched on her head, a crown of bones supports an owl skull, with river stones and acorns interwoven between them. Dried flowers and clay beads cascade in a veil of thorny vines around her face.

Esme leans in and slides her hand on the small of my back, and whispers, "You see. I told you. You are home."

Her voice is soothing, her touch comforting me. But the *flick-flick-flicker* outside the window catches my attention. A shadowy assembly of black witch moths pings against the window. I stare into my father's eyes, willing his strength into myself and wondering if the moths are coaxing me to come to them. If I do not heed their call, will they come for me instead?

CHAPTER 8

Road Trip

In the hills east of El Cajon, I'm riding shotgun in Desi's car with its shocking pink and orange interior. Yellow cotton fringe tacked to the dashboard wavers in the breeze blowing through the open windows. Dree, sprawled out in the backseat, bops her head to the salsa on the radio as she snaps her gum, and we head away from the city in a convoy. Our destination? The house of Silas Vega, *Curandero*. He's the Healer of La Asamblea de la Lumbre, a guru to our coven, with the gift of folk magic, medicine, and ritual healing for all aspects of the human condition. He was also my father's best friend and mentor and a surrogate uncle to me. Family.

It's a slow drive, but that's just as well. Normally, the coven would transform and fly here, but they need to save their energy for what's ahead, especially with the Elixir fading and, with it, their ability to shift forms and stay hidden from Los Cazadores.

We turn off the main road onto a winding one-lane trail through a dry valley. I feel like everything I've been through has been leading up to this reunion, so my anticipation grows with every mile, excited and anxious to be back in the place that played host to such a defining moment in my life.

The narrow two-lane road bisects the arid desert landscape. Every few miles, we blaze past a bright yellow sign for horse and rider crossings along the side of the road. Gone is the dewiness of the coast, replaced with a dry heat that takes my breath away.

I lean my head back with my arm hanging out the window, feeling the warm breeze on my bare skin. "How often do you guys come out here to see Don Vega?"

"All the time," Desi says from behind a pair of ridiculous rhinestone-encrusted sunglasses twice the size of his face that makes him look much younger than me. "Every witch in La Lumbre goes to Don Vega at some point."

"I remember," I say. "When I was little, and we'd visit, there was always a steady stream of people coming to him for advice."

"He's big on passing down the ancient traditions. Cool thing is, he spends time getting to know everyone individually. To know their strengths. Their talents. Then he gives you a masterclass in honing them. He's a freaking genius, cuz. I mean, you know that. *Tu papá* studied under him long enough, huh?"

I nod and look out the window. I can picture Don Vega, but only in dappled memories of the past. The sleek, tanned skin. His long, dark hair pulled into a ponytail or flowing freely down his back. I was a small child when we spent time here. The last time we visited was a few years after *Papá* died. I wished I'd kept in touch with him—if not for the wisdom he could share, then for the connection he had to my dad. Tío Silas was always loving and welcoming to me, but things between him and my mother were strained. I always thought it was the pain of being back here, but now I wonder if it might have been something more.

We leave the trail for hard-packed dirt and gravel. That's when it hits me—I've been here before. I didn't expect him to live on the same property, given what the Hunters did here. How they came onto Don Vega's sacred land and took so much from the coven. So much from him. From me. My muscles tense, and my pulse quickens with my memories of that day: panic, fear, devastation. Only a few snapshots of that day remain in my memory, but being back here has each one flickering through my brain, vying for attention I'm not sure I want to give them.

With my thumbs interlocked and my palms flat to my chest, I squeeze my eyes closed and try to center myself. With each slow, deep breath, I lift and then lower my hands intermittently, tapping my fingers against my chest, visualizing these dark memories as a storm cloud passing over me, drifting away.

Desi's voice pierces the silence. "Oh, damn. Sorry, cuz."

"For what?"

"I didn't think how hard this might be, coming back here again."

When we pull through an elaborate wooden archway, darkened by time, I remember looking up from the backseat of my dad's black El Camino with music playing on the radio. I was so excited to be visiting Tío Silas, knowing he would welcome us with enthusiasm. I can't help but wonder if he'll feel the same way about me now.

It's an oasis in the middle of the arid landscape as we pass through the gates from the desert into a garden of lush greenery. Alongside the road, a ditch with an irrigation channel carries snowmelt from the mountains down into the valley. We continue toward the house, and it strikes me how things come back to me so easily. I know where things are before we get there. The old barbed fence separating the garden from the grass, the line of sunflowers up the drive, the old hacienda, and its colorfully painted tiles that set it apart from the hillside. But it's also the feeling of the place—magical, yet comfortable. Wide open and lush but secure. At least, that's how it used to feel. Because no matter how far removed I am from that day and how much I try not to remember, there's a darkness creeping in from the periphery. And instead of cowering from it like I did back home, I feel a pull toward it that I'm wary to admit I can sense.

Desi slows the car and parks behind the truck carrying Esme and her Maiden, Lidia. She exits the passenger side, her gold shimmering skirt billowing out behind her. When Lidia exits, she smoothes out her skirt and fluffs her hair before she glances back at us. Her eyes are blank with an iciness that surprises me. She's different from how she's been in the few days I've been with the coven, her fire changed to something deeper and darker but colder, too. I get out of the car and wave, but she only stares at me for a moment before she follows Esme.

Hacienda en Las Lomas sits in the center of a tract of land bordered by a circular entanglement of shrubbery. I remember the shrubs dotted with bright orange berries and studded with thorns. In the distance, rolling ridges in variegated shades of green and brown fade off into the horizon. The House in the Hills. No other name could be more fitting.

A pathway made from wide slabs of stone leads through an archway toward the hacienda. Climbing roses intertwine around two thick posts capped with a weathered beam.

As we proceed, following behind Esme, I get *déjà vu*. When you're a kid, you don't pay much attention to time or places. I had no sense of the importance of this space when I was young, but we spent a lot of time here before my *papá* died. When he was off with Tío Silas, I played with the other kids. Other times, I spent with Don Vega, my tío not by blood but by connection to my father, watching him tend to his fields, learning.

Esme stops at the entrance long enough to whisper an incantation and then she passes through the archway. Dree and Lidia do the same. Only the core members of La Lumbre are here—less than there were at the Mabon festival back home—but given the current threat, it doesn't surprise me that only those living at Rancho de las Garras would be here today.

Desi walks through the gate before me. When I pass under the archway, I have a brief flash of my father carrying me under the cypress beam. When he taught me the name—*ahuehuete*—I giggled at the sound of it. He lifted me higher so I could feel the baubles and feathers adorning it, careful to avoid the thorns.

He told me it was good luck to touch it, that any person who did so would lose any weariness they felt. Back in Montréal, I would have hesitated, fearful of feeling some lingering remnant of his soul here. Back home, so many of my memories feel frozen in time; just thinking about them, I worry about disturbing what once was. But here, the urge to revisit those fragments of time, to bring them back out into the sun again, inspires me to stand on my tiptoes in the hopes of feeling my father's enduring energy. A flashing memory comes to me, the sound of his voice reverberating in my head, but in an instant, it's gone. The moment gives me a flush of happiness instead of the bittersweet nostalgia I expected.

When I rejoin Desi, he squeezes my elbow and nods to the house where Esme stands, hugging Don Vega. Dressed in a white linen shirt, he wears worn jeans around his thin waist with a leather belt adorned with silver and turquoise cabochons. His hair is glossy black, like raven feathers, with a hint of blue and gray at the temples. But his face is impossibly young. I feel myself being pulled closer like he is a planet unto himself, and we are all gravitating toward him.

"Silas," Esme says, hugging him. "*Gracias por tus bendiciones.*"

They kiss one another on the cheek before he greets the others. Some with hugs, others with a slap on the back and a gravelly laugh as they briefly catch up.

Desi moves to him, and they share a bro-hug, one hand on the other's back and a chest bump while exchanging a few words. When Desi moves aside, I stand there awkwardly, feeling everyone's eyes on me.

There is something else in Don Vega, something deeply ancient and wise. I see it when he looks me up and down, his gaze a combination of playfulness and authority. I expect he's trying to place me. Trying to figure out how he knows me or if he knows me at all. There's something otherworldly in his aura, as if he has been here longer than I can imagine and will be here long after I am gone.

I step forward, prepared to explain who I am. Who my mother is, my father. Why I'm here uninvited, crashing the party.

Instead, he grins, chuckling, and comes toward me to wrap his arms around me. I stand there, not sure whether to reciprocate. Desi is laughing his face off at my awkward expression. Esme stands off to one side, smiling.

"*Pequeña pluma*. You've come home, huh?" He pulls back, holding me at arm's length. "You may have been born in the north, but your blood—your bones—they call to you of this place, no?"

"Well, I definitely don't miss the cold," I say.

"That's because you are made of fire and sun, not just mountains and fields. You will feel more like yourself now that you're here. We're blessed to have you."

With a wide sweep of his arms, he coaxes everyone to follow him.

As we do, Desi wraps an arm around me and pulls me to him. "See? He remembers you!"

I can't help but smile. Maybe this is what I've been missing all these years: this connection to my roots, to the past I've been trying to suppress. I've spent so much time in the north that everything within me was unbalanced. I can already feel myself becoming more grounded. My body tingles as long-dormant parts of my soul awaken.

We trail behind the group, moving toward La Hacienda, where it sits in the middle of the circle of cypress trees. Rounded stones—some amber-colored, others slate and brown—offset the clay roof. Two tall cacti flank either side of the front door, painted bright turquoise. Orange-tiled steps with various planters on each filled with flowers, aloe, and yucca lead up to the door, each step offset by vibrant Spanish tiles with elaborate floral patterns in lemon, cherry, and eggplant hues.

Don Vega bypasses the door and takes us around the side of the house to a patio beneath a pergola made from tall, dark wood pillars. Wicker chairs sit around an outdoor oven overlooking the vast downward slope of the hillside.

On a cliff overlooking the valley below, a phantom lurks in the smoky distance. My parents stand together. My mother tilts her head to one side, and *Papá* has his arm draped around her shoulders. They talk softly to one another. I'm running up to join them in pigtails and my favorite baby blue ruffled dress.

By the time I shake off the vision, everyone else has taken a seat around a massive clay *chiminea*. Desi pats the spot next to him, and we squeeze into it together as Esme takes the last seat.

"Thank you for taking the time to see us, Don Vega," she says.

"*De nada*," he says, moving to the fire pit in the center. "Anything I can do to help my fellow brothers and sisters at this important time. What news do we have from the south?"

"Our scouts have been doing their best to monitor the regeneration," Esme says, "and our most skilled witches are performing their protections daily to know when the power of *el árbol sagrado* has bloomed."

Don Vega prods the fire with a long poker. "This time is most important for La Lumbre. Our sister, the First Witch, sacrificed to bring us our Gifts from the Sacred Tree—the Gifts of transformation and flight. But she paid a great price. Each time we take that power into us, we must honor what she gave so we can carry forth this Gift to future generations."

"So shall it be," Esme says. "Your wisdom is always welcomed. Any blessings you may offer can only help us as we prepare to travel to *la cenote* where our Gift was first born."

He nods, but caution thins his smile. He looks at each of us in turn. "The past is never gone, *mis amigos y amigas*. When we honor those who came before us, they share their wisdom. This is how we keep them with us."

Don Vega's voice takes me back in time. Even if I don't fully remember most of what happened to me here, it doesn't matter. His voice stirs something in me, dredging up all the nostalgia hidden deep within. I didn't expect to feel so emotional coming here. I thought it would be a trip down memory lane that would help me tap into those lost memories of my father and help me feel closer to him. Even as the happy memories return, I can't help but feel the bitter sense of mourning I thought I'd put behind me a long time ago.

Moving to the house with Esme, Don Vega gestures to the group. "Now please, everyone relax. I will take some time to prepare. You should ground yourselves before we begin."

As the others break apart, Dree and Desi stroll the grounds. While Lidia sits in quiet meditation, I head toward a sizable garden beyond the hacienda. A rough path winds through a maze of plants and blooms of all kinds. I trail my fingers through wildflowers bursting with color and perfume, bees buzzing lazily in sunbeams.

I kneel and lift the bright red flowers of lilting pineapple sage, inhaling the fruity scent, one that reminds me of those sunny days when the three of us—my mother and *Papá* and me—were happy together.

"Why am I not surprised you would go straight for those?" a voice says behind me.

When I turn, Don Vega is standing, watching.

"So many people look at them as weeds, but I've always loved them."

He nods. "I remember. *Tu papá* used to gather them. Two bunches. One for *tu mamá* and one for you, his *pequeño pluma*."

I close my eyes. Hearing Don Vega call me by the nickname my father gave me makes me feel more at home than anything else.

"It isn't what you thought, coming back here, is it? It's too raw, even now."

"I don't want to seem ungrateful. Everyone has been so welcoming. I couldn't ask for more."

He moves toward me, putting his hand on my shoulder. "Maybe that's why you feel this way. You are no guest here. You're family. You belong here. And *tu papá* is so proud you've come back home. Don't you feel it?"

He smiles and lifts both hands to the sky, tilting his head back, his eyes squeezed closed.

"He is here. He always has been and always will be. Maybe that's why it makes you so emotional to be here."

I wrap my arms across myself, hugging them to my chest. "I can't shake what happened to him here. Even though I only remember bits and pieces, it left something in me. An angry scar that feels like it will never heal."

He lifts both hands and holds them, palms out, in front of me. "Mmm-hmm. I sense that. A darkness from the past you cannot shake. But you're here for a reason, Valeria. There is meaning in coming south. It is the first place we go to become self-aware. To heal and grow through understanding and discovery. Because you came here, I can help you get back the parts of you that are lost."

I reach out for his hand, warm and strong like my *papá's*, and clasp it in mine. He offers me a slight smile.

"Losing *tu papá* isn't only about him. It's about you, too. About the part of you connected to him, the part that *came* from him. That connection will always *be*, even though he's gone. He is still *tu papá*. And you will always be his *pequeña pluma*. Not even his death can separate you. He's with you, always."

I didn't expect him to get so deep so quickly. Then again, I would be disappointed if he didn't. This is exactly why I was looking forward to seeing him again. Back when I was little, he was just my cool Tío Silas, telling stories. Now I can fully understand the lessons he gave me back then. His wisdom. His passion. I can learn from the master, the same man my father looked to for his own spiritual guidance. This isn't only about me connecting to my Craft. This is my heritage: the very thing I've been craving, the connection I hope will make me feel more complete.

"The death of Alejandro was a trauma for you," he says, tucking his hair behind his ear. "When we suffer those traumas, we lose a part of ourselves. And all this time, you have been feeling something is missing, but you are not sure what it is or why. That is why those of us who have lost parts of our souls struggle with the same issues over and over again. It is us trying to retrieve those parts of us that have been lost. Until we address them, until we resolve them and get closure, we go on mourning that final piece that makes us whole."

Everything he says is a revelation. It gives words and structure to everything I've been feeling and sensing more deeply the older I get. Maybe because all my struggles felt so insurmountable until I could get closure. Staying away from this place that was so important to my dad, living my life amongst my northern coven, the life of Assemblée de la Terre, meant I'd been allowing that other part of myself to remain not only hidden but broken.

"How do you do it?" I ask. "How do you stay here after what happened that day? How do you live with those ghosts?"

He lifts both hands and raises his arms out over his head.

"There are *fantasmas* everywhere, Valeria. No matter where you go, there will be spirits that linger. Remembrances big and small. But should that stop you from going somewhere? You cannot be afraid. To live there again, in those memories. What are we if we don't remember the things that have happened to us in our lives? The good and bad. The sweet and the bitter. Who are we if we do not live? Would I give up any of my time here simply because I have loved and lost some of those I loved?" He spins and looks out over the grounds, watching the others in conversation for a moment. "Never. Not for a million years. You see this?"

He points to the fine lines radiating out from the corners of his eyes. "These are a badge of honor. The worry and the love. Time gone by. I can only hope it's a life well-lived. The only regret I could ever have when I leave this place is to do it without having lived. I suspect that is why you've come back home. *Tu papá* was the same. He was never one to stay in one place except here."

He cups his hand to his ear and listens. "Do you hear that?"

I shake my head, confused.

"He loved *tu mamá* and would follow her anywhere. But there is something here he could never escape. Something he never wanted to escape. There is wisdom in the wind. The whispers of those who came before us. Our ancestors. They called you here. They called you home."

I look to the hills in the east, at the valley to the west, and the hint of the ocean beyond, and I feel my connection growing. Instead of getting emotional about my father, at all the things I'd lost, or the chances I had been too hesitant to take, I was taking them in now. Connecting to the past and to the future all at once. Everything is in its right place, and so am I.

He smiles and takes my hand in his. "You seem happier than when you first arrived."

"I am."

"But?"

I shrug and smile. "It's a lot of emotions all at once. Emotions I've put off dealing with, I guess."

"Valeria. *Mija*. Don't explain how you feel. And don't apologize. *Feeling* is good. It's how we know we're on the right track. It's how we know we're still alive, huh?" He drops my hand and kneels, trailing his hand over the flowers blooming at his feet. He hovers his fingertips over bright orange Mexican honeysuckle flower bursts and stops to caress the Yucca plants, their deep green leaves broad and fat. He comes to another and pulls a two-tone blossom free from the dahlia plants. Then he stands and lifts it to me, gesturing for me to take it.

I do, and I lift it to my nose, closing my eyes and breathing in the slightly bitter perfume, allowing its musk to diffuse my sadness.

"Keep them closed," he says when he takes it from me and places another stem in my hand.

This time, it is flat, cool. Prickly on the edges.

"Aloe," I say, feeling my anxiety starting to wane.

He laughs and squeezes my shoulder. "Even as a child, you knew the plants."

"I had two excellent teachers."

The smell of this place is a time capsule, unveiling a memory in my mind. My father standing barefoot in dirt-stained jeans, no shirt. His black hair combed back in a thick ponytail, two tendrils stuck to his sweaty forehead. He lifted me on his shoulders, trailing the flowers under my nose, teaching me how to pick out the scents. He tied a red ribbon on the aloe plants to ward off destructive energy and bring only good things and protection to those he loved. Like the faded ribbons on the plants at my feet.

"We had a wonderful student, huh?" he says. "One can only learn so much, Valeria. Sometimes, you just know. It's deep inside you, inherited from *tu papá* and *tu abuelo* before him."

I brighten at the thought. Maybe my dad was whispering to me after all these years. Teaching me. Instilling in me the same talents he had. Maybe those traits extended further and deeper than the Craft. Maybe I only needed to be in the right place to receive them.

The thought itself fills me with caution but also excitement. It's easy to wax nostalgic. It's a lot harder to do the actual work and face the tough choices. To really look deeper than the surface, than wishes, than what sounds good. Somehow, being here in this place, the iciness and my cold resolve melt away.

When I pull myself from my thoughts, Don Vega is studying me. Not quizzical, but like he is half amused, half cautious.

"I see something in you," he says finally.

"Oh? Should I be worried?"

I chuckle at my joke, but he doesn't reciprocate. A flutter of nervousness washes over the back of my neck at the look on his face.

"Something is holding you back. Some...one."

My eyelashes flutter at the comment. "Are you trying to nicely say that I'm standing in my own way? Because you wouldn't be the first to tell me that."

He stands still, his hair billowing, rolling down the hillside. The longer he remains silent, the more nervous I feel. When he steps toward me, he places a hand on mine. "There is a darkness. It calls to you. The way it called to you when you were a child."

When I catch his eye, I remember. After the attack when I was five, after those we lost were put to rest, I sat on Don Vega's knee, my surrogate father, to mourn. I told him about the black witch moths, how they came to me in a dream. How I knew they would come for real. And they did.

"It calls to you now. Still."

I nod.

"The question is," he says, starting for the house, "is it the sorrow moth? One that comes to you in a time of your life when you are mourning the loss of one thing to prepare for another? Because sorrow not dealt with can turn dark with a vengeance."

As he speaks, the memory of that day when I was just a child plays out in front of me. The slender woman standing near the trees waiting, watching. The moths and their swirling dance as they swarmed her before she dissolved into nothing. I realize now the moths came to me in mourning. But why do they keep coming for me when I'm not here when I am up north?

For so long, I thought I imagined them. But when they swarm around me with an almost deafening flickering of wing-beats, when they prickle with their tiny clawed feet and leave dust from their wings on my hands, my face, wherever they've touched me, I know they're real. Even though no one else can see them, I've always felt their magic and their warning. Sharing this secret knowledge with Tío Silas means more than I thought possible. They are, in fact, real...and that energizes and frightens me at the same time.

"But if they are instead *la mariposa de la muerte*, cautioning you, warning of something more devastating," he says, "then it is good you are here where we can protect you."

"How can I know why they come to me?" I ask.

When he turns to me, it is with a look of warning. "You cannot truly know until you let go of the thing keeping you from seeing your truth."

"If I knew how to do that…"

"There's nothing wrong with not knowing how. That's why you have come to see me, no? For guidance?"

I squeeze my hands together. "You were always so encouraging to me. I need that."

"Good. Then the next step is up to me."

He turns toward the house, and as I follow, I know this is only the beginning of our conversation. When he passes Desi, he stops for a moment to say something low in his ear before going inside.

Desi is standing next to Dree, who is chatting to Lidia in staccato-rhythm Spanish so fast I can barely pick out the handful of words I recognize, and he waves me over.

"Did you and Don Vega have a nice *platica*?" he asks.

"Huh?" The shame I feel at neither of my parents teaching me much of my second and third native tongues bubbles to the surface.

He nods, smiling. "You guys talked, right?"

"Yeah."

"And he gave you some guidance?"

"He did."

Desi slips an arm around my shoulder and squeezes me to him. "That's how he does it, man. He's giving you counsel. *Platica*. Sorta like therapy."

"That was one of his spiritual talks?"

Desi laughs. "Hell no. That was just him seeing if you're ready."

"For what?"

He lifts both hands skyward. "The ritual. *Él es un curandero*. He won't only be talking things out. He's gonna tap into all parts of you to see what's missing and what you need to retrieve to be whole. Changed my life, man. I'll bet he does the same for you."

I can't help but hope he is right. I already feel so much better from our five-minute chat. How will I feel after taking part in one of Don Vega's infamous ritual cleansings?

"Come on," Desi says, taking my hand.

"What...you mean now?"

"No better time, cuz. This is exactly what you need."

I smile and follow alongside him. But something is haunting about the look in his eyes, no matter how hard he tries to hide it. I know there's something he isn't telling me. The darkness—could it be the omen of the black witch moth? Could Don Vega have seen them? If anyone can tell me what the omen means, it is him. I'm just afraid I won't like what I learn. Or maybe I'll like it a little too much.

As we continue forward, locked arm-in-arm, darkness encroaches from the hillside, sweeping down upon us like a black veil. Instead of rushing to where the fire would warm me and offer refuge in its light, my skin tingles at the prospect of this darkness meant only for me.

CHAPTER 9

A Spiritual Awakening

A stone path leads from the lush garden to the back of the property at Hacienda en Las Lomas. At first, it is unassuming, but the further I get from the house and the others, the more my skin buzzes with anticipation from the intensity of the surroundings.

A large firethorn bush over six feet tall glows with ambient light in the darkness. As I draw nearer and reach out, the dark, woodsy smoke of a fire intoxicates me. The thorny branches unlock their grasp from one another and part, revealing a fiery hut. Its door stands open, lit from within.

I duck as I pass through the archway into a large room. On one wall, a dazzling mural shimmers in the firelight—a massive tree stretches up to the sky, its roots cascading down into a cool, blue pool of water below. It draws me in with a desire that stirs deep. When I smooth my palm over the surface, shards of tiny glass shimmer, catching the light and projecting it onto the surrounding walls.

In the center of the room, a large fire pit blazes. Red and purple flames lick the sides of the burning logs. When the sparks jump and rise with a disturbance in the air, Don Vega enters through the open door carrying a worn book with him. Desi, dressed in a simple outfit, follows to assist him.

Don Vega is dressed in white linen pants and has tied a length of bright red woven headband around his forehead. His hair is wild and free, and frames his face, which is painted with a series of triangles that accentuate his features. An elaborate collar of owl feathers drapes his shoulders and falls down his chest. He opens the book, smoothing down the pages to reveal strange symbols scrawled across the interior.

When he turns away to warm his hands over the fire, I notice the pattern radiating across his back and down both arms—a jagged pattern of branched veins branded into his skin.

I remember a time when we were visiting: Don Vega carried me across the room, swinging me from side to side. My curious fingers found the ridge of wounds, and he told me they were his battle scars. I didn't realize what that meant at the time.

Then he turns back to face me.

"Tonight, this undertaking will help us cleanse the mind, body, and soul of our sister, Valeria Salcedo."

He nods to Desi. Stepping forward, he offers me a small cup. "Take this offering. It will aid in your healing."

Taking the cup, I inhale the fragrant, lemony liquid, enjoying its underlying hint of peppermint before I drink it down and return the cup.

Holding out a clay tray decorated with turquoise cabochons, Desi waits for Don Vega to take salt and liquid, splashing them into the flames before sprinkling in a handful of dried herbs.

Next, he lights a charcoal tab on a round plate and adds resins to it. Their pungent earthiness smolders, filling the room with a heady fragrance that makes my head swim.

"Why are you here, Valeria? Why do you undertake this cleansing?" Don Vega asks.

I swallow hard before answering. "To find out why I feel so out of place."

"Why does this matter to you?"

"I feel...like something is holding me back."

His eyes bore into me, and the harder he stares, the darker the room turns. The fire licks the air, throwing light in strange shapes across his face. My body is feverish; sweat beads across my skin.

"How does that make you feel, Valeria?"

I blink away the tears forming in the corners of my eyes. I lift my dress away from my skin to allow cool air in, but it does me no good.

"Like a failure. Like I don't belong here. Like I've failed my coven again."

"Again," he says, crossing his arms over his chest. "When did you fail them before?"

I shake my head, not wanting to give my darkest thoughts a voice, but they bubble to the surface. "With Gwen. I failed her. With my mother. I failed her, too. Over and over, I face obstacles and can do nothing better than stumble. Just like that day…"

"Which day, Valeria?" Don Vega asks. "Which day did you falter?"

I close my eyes, hoping it will keep the memory from coming back to me, but I see him again.

"My father," I say. "The arrow hits him. He falls. The light leaves his eyes as I try to help, but I don't know how. I don't know how to help him. I'm just a child, but I can't save him. I fail him in the worst possible way."

Underneath the crackling of the fire and my tormented voice, a soft thumping begins.

"Lie down, Valeria," he says.

I obey and lie back on the woven blanket beside the stone pit with my hands clasped together, my eyes closed.

Using a small drum, Desi taps out a decisive beat as Don Vega moves over me. With both hands out—one holding a bowl of water, the other a hand-sized wooden rattle—Don Vega says a spiraling loop of words I don't understand. His voice rises and falls, and as his tone grows more commanding, the heat in the room follows suit.

I get lost in the intensity of the pulsing rhythm, the tang of the sweaty air, and the nose-prickling burn of charred wood. As Desi's drumming intensifies Don Vega's voice, it carries around me in a tumultuous loop, inspiring an undulating flicker of shadows under my eyelids.

"Relax, Valeria. This will help rid you of unwanted energies so you can tap into your true potential," he says. "Your strength comes from within. Only when you free your inner darkness can you access those abilities."

I try to calm my breathing, and when a cool rush of air breezes across my body, I feel like I can breathe again. Don Vega dips the rattle into the water, spraying droplets across my body. Over me, he shakes the rattle in a quick staccato rhythm and then recites something in Spanish. I feel the air of a feather fan waft across me.

I squeeze my hands together, trying to let go of my apprehension, but when the intense vibrations and the shifting shapes become too overwhelming, I open my eyes.

The patterns take on a life of their own, forming into a dark cloud that spins and dances around me, splitting into two shadows that race across the walls, dispersing and then gathering into shapes I struggle to identify.

When Don Vega's voice rises, one cloud comes together in an animal shape. A long, lean body with thick, powerful legs and a long, sturdy tail—a jaguar. As it takes off, running across the wall, another cloud forms. Pointed large ears sit atop a thin face, and as the jaguar circles the room toward it, the second shape lets out a high-pitched howl.

The two shadow animals face off, the jaguar hunching as it stalks the coyote. When the jaguar opens its powerful jaws, the coyote lunges at it, and the two shadows explode into one another, sending the room into darkness.

I cry out, grasping for something secure to cling to, but the room turns bright white. I shade my eyes with my hand, and when they adjust to the light, I find myself somewhere else.

∼

Forest, thick and dark, surrounds a clearing on all sides. Carvings of pumas and jaguars, of suns and moons, decorate thick stone slabs set into the earth. My father's voice tells me of the old city, cherished by the ancient ones and cursed by those who came after them.

A dozen rough huts with thatched palm leaf roofs sit scattered within the natural walls of the remote village. The walls are made up of thin, upright branches, the gaps packed with mud and grass. Inside, simple woven hammocks hang from wood beams, and a substantial stone fire pit is set off to one side for cooking.

This is not a welcoming place. An air of foreboding lingers like a shroud, and as I move toward the houses along a well-worn path lined with enormous stones on either side, someone cries out ahead of me.

I follow the sound to a small clearing. Barefoot villagers race in all directions. Women carry children at their hips. A few men usher them along while others gather at one side of the village.

"No!" someone shouts. When I turn, the woman from Hacienda en Las Lomas, the one I saw the day of the attack on my father, stands behind me, a mirage of beauty against a backdrop of horror.

Lorenza de Salazar. The First Witch.

She rushes from the darkness of the forest like a shadow, but as she approaches, she becomes clearer. The same dark eyes. That same flowing hair. The angular face that looks so familiar. As she rushes past me toward the gathering men, I put both hands up even though I have no idea how to explain what I am doing there, wherever this place is.

A loud noise comes from beyond the village. The long groan of a conch shell trumpet joins the deep bass of beaten drums. Without warning, a flurry of stones descends from the sky in an arc. The women and children duck, running for cover as a second wave of arrows and darts rain down on the village from above. With a blood-curdling shout, an army descends on the villagers, ransacking everything in sight, upturning pots of maize, breaking looms, and using torches to light the palapas on fire.

Lorenza doesn't leave. She stands behind the men who form a line, bracing themselves. As the drumming gets louder, harsh voices cry out from the forest, and, all at once, the men are beaten back. Before Lorenza can reach them, three women rush from a nearby hut and pull her inside to safety, even as she struggles to remain in the fray.

I crouch down and move toward the hut. Inside, the women cower in one corner, but Lorenza remains in the doorway, defiant. Cradled in her arms, a tiny bundle squirms. The baby cries out, her tiny hands balled into fists.

At the front of the attackers, a group of half a dozen men with shaved heads mock the villagers, lunging at them. With only a braid of hair on their otherwise bald heads, blue, yellow, and red paint decorates their skin. They force their way into the village, knocking back any man who dares to defy them. One of the men, dressed in an elaborate woven cloak, shouts in a language I don't recognize. The villagers respond, their words rushed and pleading, trying to reason with him, but he paces and turns away, refusing to listen.

When the attackers advance on the men, most back off. The one villager who fights gets a swift hit from a raider wearing a reed headdress, the spray of bright teal feathers set into a handwoven intricate design swishing as he moves.

Lorenza starts through the doorway, but the other women cry out to her. They take the child from her and beg her to stay. The attackers, drawn to the commotion, bully their way past the men, striking any who try to prevent them from moving further into the village.

As shouts and cries distort the tumultuous air, Lorenza stands rigid, chanting under her breath. The raiders stream into the village, using their round shields to push the men back, jabbing short spears at those who stand up to them.

Behind them, men dressed in dark cloaks scream from under masks covered in the animal's fur they personify with ire and hatred—the coyote. Using leather slings, they hurl stones at anyone standing between them and Lorenza. I crouch there, watching as she paces toward them, her chant rising as the wave of shouts and screams assaults her. Every muscle in her body is taut as they move in, but she doesn't back down.

One man carrying a brightly colored shield decorated with feathers stalks toward her. He stops before her, glaring down at her, his chest heaving. When she doesn't relent or cower, he strikes her across the face. She falls to the ground.

I gasp, covering my mouth with my hand hoping he doesn't hear me, but like Lorenza, he doesn't register I'm there.

Before she can counterattack, the warrior reaches for her, grabbing her by the hair and dragging her away. She kicks, screeching, but no one comes to help her. Taking her down a slight slope, he yanks her through the dirt, past a tall tree whose thick, gnarled roots trail off toward a fast-flowing river at the base of the hill.

I follow them, feeling compelled to be with her. By the time I make it there, he turns her over onto her back and is leaning over her, shouting at her in a language I don't recognize. She glares back up at him, refusing to comply. He continues his attack, lunging at her as he shouts, spinning around, and coming back at her again, but she remains firm and doesn't respond to his attacks.

With his eyes rabid and his body coiled like a snake ready to strike, he turns and roars. A group of warriors runs toward him. As they approach, Lorenza lets out a shattering scream, and a poisonous loop of words falls from her lips. The warriors stagger back a few steps, her tirade so oppressive they can barely remain upright. Nevertheless, their rage overcomes her verbal onslaught, and they press on, striding toward her. Arming themselves with long tubes they hold to their mouths, they shoot tiny darts at Lorenza, striking her arms, her legs, and some hitting her in the face and neck.

She winces with every barbed projectile but doesn't cry out. Not when another round of darts assail her. Not when her body seizes with pain and shadow crosses over her face.

The warrior king towers over her, reaching for her hand. He yanks her arm up, bending it back at a grueling angle. When she doesn't relent, he breaks her fingers.

I race for her, my hands out, wanting to help her because I know this agony. I've seen it before. Gwen's face swims in the forefront of my mind—the agony she suffered in the forest after she was hit by an arrow from one of Los Cazadores, the torment she endured at La Maison as the poisons wracked her body with such invasive venom she couldn't stave it off. It stole her from me. And now I am watching it take Lorenza.

But even as I move toward her, I sense the fruitlessness of my actions. There's nothing I can do for her. I am here, but not here, a silent witness to this horrific day.

When she finally cries out, it's so earth-shattering it drives the warriors back, and they clutch at their heads as though she has transferred her pain to them. It's enough of a reprieve to give her fellow villagers the chance to make their move.

Working together, the men beat back the warriors, who retreat after a final assault of machete slashes and spear punctures, but not before they trounce any woman who tends to the wounded or strikes down any unfortunate child who has lost his guardian. As they slither back into the forest from where they came, they set the remaining trees surrounding the village alight.

The women from the hut race past the encroaching fire, falling to the ground beside Lorenza. But she pushes them away, turning over onto her hands and knees. Clawing at the dirt, she drags herself to the river, plunging herself into the water. It washes over her, sizzling her skin and sending ribbons of smoke into the surrounding air.

Panting, she thrusts herself up, but the magnificent tree beside her sends fire-singed pods of its fruit raining down around her. The others gather small clay pots discarded on the river bank and desperately try to use them to douse the tree. But the bark is already blackened. The trunk, knobby and cracked, angrily glows bright red from within.

Lorenza crawls forward, grasping for a pod that has fallen into the water and threatens to escape downstream. Catching it up, she cups it in her palms and uses her thumbs to break it open. Inside, milky juice bubbles

THE BONE KEY

up, and she wrings it into one of the pots. She adds fresh water to the pot, then holds her battle-scarred arms over the brim and presses one of her wounds, crying out as she squeezes blood into the concoction.

She studies her maimed hand, her pinky finger bent to one side. Seizing one of the obsidian darts left behind by the attackers, she holds it against her hand.

"Please! Don't do this!" I say.

But I've seen this same action play out so many times over the years it finally makes sense. This is why we sacrifice a part of ourselves for the coven—to show our devotion to the First Witch. This is her act of allegiance to those she loves, paid in pain, blood, and sacrifice as she slices away her finger at the first joint.

As it lands on the ground, she lets out a tormented scream before she slumps forward. She reaches for the severed fingertip and strips off a portion of the bone with the point of the dart. Once she adds the sliver of bone to the pot, she falls on her side in exhaustion.

Seeing her collapse, the other women come to her. One cradles her as the other takes the bowl from her and places it in the sand. As she stands and looks down inside, she, too, reaches for the dart, creating a gash across her arm. She holds the wound over the bowl, adding her blood to the mixture.

The other two women do the same, and when they have each added their contribution, they kneel beside Lorenza, gathering her into their laps to comfort her.

One of the women holds the child out. Only then does Lorenza stir, clutching the bundle to her chest. When the infant cries out, Lorenza prods her to nurse, but as she suckles, insidious black veins spread across the baby's perfectly unblemished skin.

Without hesitation, Lorenza whispers. Her voice is hoarse, but her devotion never wavers. As she continues, the three women join her. The mantra grows, drowning out the tortured cries of injured villagers up the hill, but their voices become more desperate the longer they speak.

Somehow, Lorenza regains enough strength to stand and, still nestling the infant, she paces toward the charred tree with the others following behind. There at the base, a villager dressed in a feathered collar joins them. As they hold the clay pot out to him, he raises both hands over his head and shouts an incantation to the skies. His spell complete, he nods to the women, who scoop their hands into the pot, taking out handfuls of the glimmering Elixir and smearing it across the tree. Seeping into the wounds, the concoction cools and heals the damage. But a chunk of the bark falls away in Lorenza's hand. Pockmarked where the fire burned through, she holds it up to her face. Using it as a makeshift mask, she peers through the small holes at the others.

When their work is done, the women huddle together, following the healer up the incline toward the village. As they do, the river rises, filling in the scorched earth scarred by the attack. Cracks in the limestone fill in with groundwater that soothes and comforts. I watch the water overcome the damage and protect the ancient womb in the earth that gave birth to our Gift.

Before I can contemplate the meaning, Lorenza turns her head. For the first time, she sees me. I cannot breathe. My heart races and stops at the same time. My blood runs cold, then burns hot under her gaze. Fluttering, the moths come flickering down from the treetops like singed leaves. As they dance around her, their wings are whisper-soft against her wounds, comforting and protecting her. But then they surge and come together in a gust of wind. The blackness seeps around me on all sides. The village is gone. The people, my people, disappear. Only Lorenza remains, her eyes dark with determination. Then everything goes black.

CHAPTER 10

Imaginings

When I come to, I'm on my back beside the fire. The light from the flames blinds me, so I shield my eyes and jolt away from the heat. When the scene comes into focus, I find myself in the hut. Kneeling in front of me, Don Vega remains still with his eyes closed. Sweat beads on his face, smudging the painted shapes.

When he opens them again, they are stark black, like the vast emptiness of an underground cavern, but they shift to bright orange when he blinks —his owl eyes—before returning to their usual brown.

Something soft drapes over my shoulders, and I jump, spinning to find Desi beside me. He places a light linen cloth soaked in cold water around my neck and I lean back against him, letting out the breath I'd been holding in.

"You've come back to us," Don Vega says.

"Was I out long?" I take the tall glass of water Desi hands me and drink it down in two long swigs.

"You were gone, cuz. I mean..." Desi makes a flapping motion with his hand over his head. "Gone. Your body was here, but your soul was someplace else."

I nod. There is no other way to describe what I just experienced. "I imagined something...incredible. There's no other way to describe it."

"These are not imaginings," Don Vega says. "They are your abilities, showing you the truth you seek, if only you will allow yourself to see."

I let Desi tend to me as Don Vega leads me toward the door, where the cool night air beckons me. I'm relieved to be here. But seeing what I did, experiencing what Lorenza endured to become who she was, to create what we are... I am so blessed to have received such a vision.

Don Vega takes bundles of carnations and sweeps them down my body, starting at the back of my head and moving to my feet. Turning me, he does the same from my feet to the top of my head. With each motion, the flowers exude their perfume. Once done, he shakes them, casting off the negative energies I experienced.

Placing the bundles down, he brings out a bowl filled with water. Flowers and herbs float languidly inside, and he dabs the fragrant concoction on my chest.

"I bless you with the power of the winds of the north and the east and with the winds of the south and the west. May they carry you and help you rise anew."

I want to hug him, but it doesn't seem like enough. I want to collapse and absorb everything I've seen, but I know if I do, my spent body, every muscle pulled taut from exhaustion, won't get up again.

Luckily, Desi is there. He takes me by the arm and leads me through the door, down the path between the firethorn branches toward Hacienda en Las Lomas, where it glimmers like a jewel set against the San Joaquin.

"Why didn't you tell me you were training under Don Vega?"

He let out a sly smile. "I wasn't sure how you would take it."

"Why?"

"You know..." he said, looking away from me. "*Tu papá* was the last one Don Vega believed should be the next *Curandero* for our coven. I was worried you'd be...I dunno, pissed or something. Feeling like I was taking something that shoulda been his."

"Well, I think it's amazing."

"Really?" He says, the trepidation fading from his eyes. "Because I've been dying to tell you. I just didn't wanna stir shit up, especially with everything else you got going on."

I realize that he's been holding onto something he was really excited about to avoid upsetting me. My own hang-ups are affecting everyone around me. Putting Gwen in danger. Making my mother go out on a limb for me when I wasn't contributing to our coven. And now, Desi. To be chosen by Don Vega as his protégé is an honor of the highest degree in the Asamblea de la Lumbre. Everyone knows it. I can tell by the way they look at Desi. They have faith in him.

The further away I get from the hut, the more deeply I feel like fragments of myself are no longer with me. Like they're in the past, in that *other* place, as if singed away by the torment I witnessed. I feel raw, exposed, but I am glad to be with family, to feel the embrace of their love and devotion after the ordeal I experienced. But my agony, my loss, is nothing compared to what Lorenza endured.

"You'll make an amazing *Curandero*, Desi. I know it," I say, easing down onto a log opposite a massive outdoor stone fire pit.

Across from us, Dree and Lidia share a low wooden bench.

"Hell yeah, he will," Dree says. Desi beams with pride, then turns back to me.

"You gotta rest now," Desi says, "You'll be sore. Probably for a few days. It might not seem like it, but the *platica* takes a toll on your body. Now it's time to relax and have some fun. You need it, especially after what you just went through."

"What makes you think I went through something?"

"I was there, cuz. I saw what happened to you. I'm telling you, if I didn't know you were in a trance, I woulda thought you were dead. Your body went still. Your face was expressionless. But in the middle of it all, your eyes flew open, black like onyx. Chilled me to the bone."

"That must have been when...when I slipped under the dark waves."

As I say it, I can't help but think of what Don Vega said about the darkness inside me. It reminds me of the aftermath of the Los Cazadores attack. Back at La Maison, during my argument with Olivia—the look on her face when I sent her flying across the room without even touching her. When the moths surged, smothering her, choking her. It was the same with Lorenza when she let out a blood-curdling scream to stave off the village attackers.

My mind goes back to that moment. My face was flushed, and everyone's fear and anger were directed at me. I was utterly exhausted, but my abilities emerged without even trying. I didn't even think about what I wanted to do. I reacted and sent Olivia flying across the room without a single touch. Just like Lorenza did.

My gaze flicks to Lidia. A dark smile curls the corners of her mouth like she can see the same memory I do.

"What are you thinking, cuz?" Desi asks.

I shake my head, trying to cast off the chill of the cool night air. "It reminded me of something that happened back home. Something…unexpected. Power I didn't know I had that came out when I needed it."

Desi narrows his eyes. "Oh? What's the tea, cuz? Tell me!"

I lower my voice and lean into him. "You know how Olivia is."

He sucks his teeth and wrinkles his nose. "That *cabrona* is always up to something. What'd she do now?"

"She got in my face. So…I defended myself."

"Val…"

"Honestly, I didn't even touch her. But that didn't stop me from sending her flying across the room."

His eyes go wide. When he moves in closer to me and links his arm in mine, I'm not exactly sure what will come out of his mouth.

"Oh, snap!" he whispers.

"What?"

"You've got it."

"What? A bad attitude?"

"No, *loca*. The gift of La Primera. The First Witch, Val. La Lechuza. You're a natural *bruja*."

Just the mention of her makes my skin go hot like I am back in Lorenza's village with the forest blazing around me and her fiery gaze trained on me. My temperature is rising. Before I lose control, Don Vega exits the house and approaches the group with Esme at his side.

"So, those scars?" I whisper to Desi, nodding to the lightning-strike patterns peeking out from Don Vega's unbuttoned shirt. "How did he get them?"

"That's from when he was chosen," Desi whispers. "He was young when it happened. Mid-twenties, I think. Got sick. Like real sick. The spirits called to him long before that, but when they saw he was ready, they chose him. Struck him down and waited for him to heal himself. To prove himself."

As Desi speaks, images flash in my mind of playing with Tío Silas, of closing my hands behind his neck, my fingers trailing across the marks, soft yet tough: jagged, raised scar tissue.

"You think *Esme's* strong? He had to fight tooth and nail to survive what he went through. He went down to the depths, man. Had to get up in the face of *los espíritus y los muertos* and show them he was worthy of their messages."

Dree, who up until now had been in intense conversation with Lidia, turns to us, propping her forearms on her knees and leaning in. She tucks her long purple hair behind her ears. "From what I hear, there was a storm in the desert. Lightning bolt came down and hit him square on. The charge went right through him. Any *gringo* woulda died right then and there. But not Don Vega. He's a beast." She thumps her fist on her breastbone. "*Uno guerrero*. A freaking warrior, man."

This is the first time I'm getting the complete story about a man who meant so much to my *papá*. To me. It's not like my mother hadn't spoken to Don Vega over the years. But after my dad was gone, Èvelyne put him in her rear-view mirror as she did with the rest of our family down south.

It strikes me that I haven't spoken to my mother in a few days. Not that I'd never gone weeks without speaking to her. But without contact with my family up north, not even Will, my head is clearer. I feel a twinge of guilt for not reaching out to let them know I'm okay.

"Hey," Desi says, nudging me. "Looks like we're getting started."

Esme moves to the front of the gathering, taking her place next to the altar as Don Vega moves to address us. He is still wearing the bright red woven headband around his forehead.

"We gather here, we spirits of fire," he says, "those of us made from the fire of volcanoes, to prepare for the Opening of the Flower. The most important time for Aquelarre Bújo, our owl coven. As we feel the seasons shift and the power of the Elixir fades within us, we must draw upon our inner reserves to endure all we face."

One by one, everyone stands. I follow Desi's lead and move into an informal circle with the others. As Don Vega makes his way around the group, he pauses at each one of us, starting with Esme, who upturns her hands and lifts them skyward.

"Our fire may dim, but the only way to keep it from going out is to keep fighting. As we await the blooming, we gather our collective sparks and unite as a coven to channel our energy and use it to propel ourselves forward."

Next, he stops at Lidia. Her body language is completely different from the witch I hung out with yesterday. Her fire is subdued, and in its place, a frostiness emanates from her in waves, making my scalp tingle. At the edge of my perspective, darkness flickers; I blink it away. I don't need that, not now.

"When one of our coven ails," Don Vega says, "we ail with them. When one of us aches, we take that pain within us and rise anew."

He lifts both hands to the sky, and a breeze lifts and rolls down the hillside, sending dahlia blooms floating in the air like butterflies. They float down, singeing and turning to ash around me.

I reach for Desi's hand. The blackness seeps around me with a heaviness that leaves me breathless. It is a swirling torrent spinning around Lidia's face.

"You okay?" Desi says, leaning into me.

I nod. No one else sees it. But instead of cowering from it, I feel a surge of energy like I felt with Lidia when we did the beginnings of the spell yesterday. I don't want to look away from it or fear what the vision has to say. I want to understand it.

When I look back at her, Don Vega has broken the connection with Lidia and is staring at me. His gaze slips upward and around. Does he sense what I do?

As he starts toward me, goosebumps rise on my skin from the thrill of being under his gaze. I get what Desi told me earlier now. When I first arrived, it was light, the two of us getting reacquainted. But the entire vibe is different after what we went through in the *platica*. It's more serious. More focused. Like he can sense my every thought. Like every emotion I feel touches him, too.

When he stops, I want to turn to avoid having the focus all on me. But I can't. There's a pull within him, like Desi said. We're connected even more than before. We share the same tragedy. The same loss. What happened here, on this ground…it affected us both. The repercussions of that day traumatized me. They traumatized him, too.

"When we lose someone," he says, "it's like a scar on our soul. But one that is only skin deep. What they meant to us, the strength and wisdom they once gave, is never gone. Because they are with us. Always and forever."

He places one hand on either of my shoulders.

THE BONE KEY

"I give you this blessing that you shall find your strength. That which you seek is not outside of you but within."

This time, when he speaks, the darkness blacks out everything in front of me. The faces of the others dissipate into nothingness. The night sounds of the crickets and the wind through the trees fade, and instead, there's a lone voice whispering. The voice comes closer, grows louder. I can't understand it, but there are words I can pick out here and there. Spanish.

Valeria. Mija. Nosotros somos tu familia. We are all family, Valeria.

In the blackness, a pair of eyes appears—stark white, the pupils and irises missing. Then a face. No color, only a blank expression. It slides forward, long dark tendrils of hair hanging down either side. At first, nothing is there at all, then it turns to me.

I step forward unbidden. The pull, at first, slack like a thread, carries me toward her. Lorenza.

Don Vega's hand on my arm wrenches me back to the present. Everyone stares, but no one says a word. Instead, Esme moves to the fire pit, where the flames dance behind her, making her appear golden and fluid. When she speaks, the fire responds, lashing the air.

"Brothers and sisters. Now is the most important time for our coven. For our eastern brothers and sisters of Air," she says, gesturing to the east before motioning to the other directions saying, "to our Water brothers and sisters of the west, and our Earth sisters and brothers of the north."

She steps aside, allowing Don Vega to move to the center. Behind him, Desi presents a collection of owl feathers. Don Vega takes them and holds them in both hands, blowing on them. A lofty brightness perfumes the air, like the ocean salt drying in the sun. He dips the tips of the feathers into a clay bowl of water Desi holds out to him.

"We thank our sisters and brothers," Don Vega says, "for sharing with us their guidance and knowledge."

Starting with Esme, Don Vega sweeps the feather down from her head and around both her front and back. He dips his fingers into the cup and anoints her forehead, her throat, and the center of her spine before moving to Lidia. As he makes his way around the circle toward me with Desi accompanying him, the sky darkens, and with it, the horizon turns from gold to red. He sweeps the feathers across my body before anointing me.

"I summon, stir, and call our ancient ancestors to guard our circle and witness this rite. As we await the Opening of the Flower, the life-giving power of the Elixir it sustains grows weaker in each of us. For those who have had the Elixir, we feel our abilities waning."

Taking the feathers from Desi, he cups them in his hands. "We thank our sisters, our brothers, that we may use their energy to help us connect to our earthly abilities. And yet we long for the wisdom of our ancestors, of the Elixir made by their ancient methods, to instill in us once again the power to see even when the shadows threaten to engulf us. To hear that which, to others, is only a whisper. To soar to heights once only imagined by those of us who dared to dream."

Desi places the cup down and takes up a bundle of smoldering palo santo sticks and moves around the circle again, wafting the incense smoke around each of us.

"This Elixir gives all *hermano y hermana búho* the ability to fly. But for us in this Fire Coven, it is most important. It is our ancestors who brought forth this gift to us. It is our sister, La Primera, Lorenza de Salazar…"

The face from earlier flashes in the shadows again.

"…La Lechuza, the owl witch…"

Her face is clearer now, her eyes a bright white. Her nose, not long and slender like in my vision, is now a dark, pointed beak. Her skin is pale, gray, and haggard.

"…Who practiced with a *curandero* to gain the wisdom she needed to take her Craft to new heights."

It's Lorenza, I see. La Lechuza. But why is she coming to me? Why now, after having just seen her in the past? Why does no one else see her? We all come from her—why does she only appear to me?

"As we bless our sisters and brothers, we give to them the last of La Néctar Sagrado, that it may grant them the Gift of flight…"

Esme has moved beside Don Vega. She takes the glass vial set in a tarnished copper capsule from around her neck. It is almost empty, but the liquid remaining within glows bright purple. She pulls the stopper from the top and reaches out for Lidia; as Esme cups her chin, she tilts her head to deposit a droplet of the Elixir on her tongue.

" …The ability to see things that are hidden," Don Vega continues. "To hear not only that which they wish but that which shall help them."

What does it taste like? Is it sweet? Does it tingle when it touches her tongue? I've wondered about these things for so long, and I have never wanted to taste it more than I do now.

Esme moves down the line to Dree, who takes a droplet and bows before her. Esme moves on to Desi, who drinks next. When she comes to me, she stops and winks before moving on. I know this is meant as a sign of encouragement that I, too, will join my fellow Assemblée des Chouettes and share in the Elixir soon to gain my owl abilities, but that doesn't mean seeing each of them drink doesn't sting from humiliation and desire.

Having moved away from the group, Desi returns carrying a tray laden with cake and glimmering glass goblets. He pours wine into each of the glasses and offers one to each of us.

When he comes to me, he smiles, handing me a glass, and then holds up the tray.

"May you never thirst," he says.

I take the glass and hold it up. "And may you never hunger."

Having finished the blessings, Don Vega pulls on a linen shirt and takes a seat next to the fire. He strums a guitar, breaking into an intense session that sets everyone off laughing and dancing. Joy fills the valley, reverberating up the hillside and creating a cocoon of soothing music.

Before Desi returns, he speaks to Don Vega for a few moments. When they're finished, Desi comes toward me, a satisfied smile on his face.

Suddenly, I feel like I can breathe a little easier, too. The black witch moth didn't touch Desi in my vision. Maybe this was a true omen. Maybe him studying under Don Vega and learning the skills it takes to heal our kind is exactly what he needs to protect us all. I can't fault him for that. We're each reaching for things that can give us peace of mind, especially when so much is caught in a cycle of turmoil.

Suddenly, Don Vega lets out a long, drawn-out cry to the skies. One of love and lust, of pain and sorrow. One of life and death, all intertwined. A *grito*. A flash of memory comes to me of him and my dad, standing in the light of the full moon and doing the same call, just like their fathers and grandfathers did before them. So moved by the time and place, it's an expression of so many swirling emotions, the same you hear when the mariachis play. Don Vega doing it now makes me feel truly at home.

Desi starts for the others, most of whom stand looking up at the now violet sky like he's been called to action. He pauses and looks at me. "I don't have to go, you know. It's no biggie."

"I'm good. Go on. You deserve it."

He winks at me and then spins and bounds over. By the time Desi makes it to him, Don Vega has transformed. Even though it's dark, his feathers almost black, his bright orange eyes give him away.

As I watch the coven lift up and take off, flying in circles overhead, swooping and diving, I feel a pull in the pit of my gut. I want that. But I don't feel as angry as I did before. Somehow, being here makes me feel like I'll be flying before I know it.

"You will," Lidia says beside me.

I turn to her, only just realizing she remains with me as she nods to the sky. "I'll bet you'll be up there sooner than you think."

"I hope so."

"I can almost guarantee it."

There's an angry flash in her eyes, reminding me of that day in her room and the darkness that seemed to take over her. It's like she is two distinct people. I wonder which one I'll meet next.

CHAPTER 11

Los Muertos

A few nights later, over in Old Town, the crowds gather near the Presidio Mission, the ghostly landmark where the souls of the first Spanish and Mexican residents of San Diego linger. The mariachis tune their guitars on stage in *el mercado*, waiting to coax forth the old spirits with songs of love and loss. The taco and tamale stands fire up, the sizzle and smell of mesquite and char intermingling with incense and melting candle wax. The Catrinas, in their long frocks and fancy, feathered hats, prepare for a night of remembrances of the dead on the steps of the Church of the Immaculate Conception, lit softly from within.

At Asamblea de la Lumbre, though, we do things a little differently for La Día de Los Muertos. No tourists. No cameras. Only the invited few.

When we pull up to the Mission, the weight of souls in the air is palpable, like an invisible curtain we have stepped closer to. The surrounding energy vibrates with an intensity I've never felt before. Maybe it's the freedom of being here. Maybe it's Don Vega's influence encouraging me, allowing me to accept the changes I've gone through, and opening me to the possibilities of what the future holds. Or maybe it's because the veil between our world and the one beyond is thinning, allowing in the remnants of those souls we've lost but not forgotten to return to us.

Boxes brimming with marigolds in various shades of yellow and orange overflow into the backseat of Dree's truck, where I sit behind Desi. The air is intoxicating, heady with their perfume. We exit our cars, a convoy of witches dressed in white and black ceremonial robes, each embroidered with the interlocked vines of the strangler fig, bright gladiolas, and pomegranates spilling open with jeweled fruit. Everyone moves quickly into their assigned roles, with some removing the flower bundles and others taking boxes filled with platters piled high with treats: oranges, grapes, sweets, and *pan de muertos*. Candles of various sizes and colors fill trays we pass from hand to hand. Some are thin tapers. Others stand short and stubby. A collection of prayer candles with Christ the Redeemer, La Virgen de Guadalupe, and even Santa Muerte sit on trays, waiting to be lit.

Esme is off to the side. Wearing a black veil draped over her dark curls, she looks like a goddess, a widow, and a queen all at once. In her hand is a mask, its face obscured from view, but the crown of feathers is brushed smooth.

Beside her, Don Vega stands with his hands crossed in front of him. His hair is pulled back in a ponytail. His feathered collar billows in the breeze. Charcoal lines his intense eyes.

Grouped behind him, two dozen witches from other houses within La Lumbre wait. Their masks are familiar, all owls, but authentically southern. Feathers encircle each mask, but the face itself is decorated with intricately carved designs—swirls and flowers etched into the clay, all painted with vibrant hues. It's as if they are living *calaveras* reminiscent of the molded, vibrantly decorated sugar skulls sold at the markets in *el mercado* for the Day of the Dead celebrations.

I've been to La Presidio once before—the November before that terrible day at Don Vega's *hacienda* when Los Cazadores took so much from me. We stood in a procession, the way we do now, and when the bell in the tower struck midnight, my father took one of my hands, my mother the other, and we started along the path. The scent of the tuberose blooms that lined the path, intermingling with the smell of incense and damp soil, drew us back into the past. They do the same for me now. The reality of being back here, where those we love are waiting for us, where we wait for them to return, brings tears to my eyes. It isn't only about losing my father or the time spent with him here, the stories and love, or that connection to my Mexican family. All the things I lost that I didn't realize had been taken away from me: the connection to my history, a sense of feeling whole, the confidence that comes from having those who love you unconditionally.

Maybe that's why I've been pushing people away from me over the past few months. Maybe I'm not afraid of what the black witch moths will do to me. It's what they can bring to me that scares me: not what I'm afraid of becoming, but that I might fail at becoming all the things I want to be. Being here is like being at the source of my power and the power passed on to me by ancestors who are accomplished in their Craft. I'm terrified to fail, to not live up to my potential. But not trying would be even worse.

We stand in solemn silence, only moving when the bronze bells in the mission's *campanario* toll to honor the dead. In front of the group, Don Vega throws both hands skyward and recites an incantation so quickly it creates a dizzying effect. I take Desi's hand to steady myself.

When he finishes, Don Vega holds still for a moment. No one breathes. Then, the clinking of iron sounds as the gates unlock and open. As a band of musicians standing to one side starts a slow dirge, their trumpet, drums, and guitars at the ready. The rattling maracas keep the beat and signify the beginning of the celebration.

Don Vega and Esme lead the group, and together, we make our way past the red and black willow trees through the gate where the market and the city beyond fall away. At first, there's nothing, but as Don Vega proceeds through the resting place of our ancestors, the shadows vibrate. As they shift and move, the darkness transforms into a fluttering blanket, revealing itself not as mere shadow but mourning moths resting on the graves. Awakening, they bask in the moonlight, fluttering their wings until they transform from black to the bright orange of marigolds, spread in unending blankets across each gravesite. When they take flight, they rise into the air, flittering in the sky like flower petals.

Headstones, some small and stout, others tall and slender, spread out across the space, each vibrating with the energy of their departed. Crosses, some made from plain wood and painted vibrant turquoise, others made of iron and tarnished from the elements, jut from the earth. Dried flowers from past remembrances reinvigorate and blossom with fresh sweetness. Desi holds a box in one hand and leads me to the back of the plot, where a canopy of walnut trees hangs low. The others in our group split off to where their lost beloved lie.

As Desi and I approach, the nuts on the tree burst and spill open, showering the ground with their fruit-like confetti. A fleeting memory of coming here in a procession with my mother makes my skin prickle with sorrow, but as we near my father's altar, an intense wave of love blossoms across my chest. Taking candles from the box, Desi kneels. I follow suit, and as I take one, I cup it in both hands and softly blow. The wick lights shimmer as I place the candle in the dirt. We continue until gleaming light surrounds the entire grave, and when I sit back, the photograph of my father blazes from black and white to vibrant color.

I cup my hand around the feather Don Vega gave me. Its feathery sleekness is soft beneath my touch. My father's headstone is old and weathered. Dried leaves litter the top. Scattered around the base, withered flower petals look like tarnished gemstones in the dirt. As the light from the flickering candles warms the space, the leaves fill out with new life. The dried flower petals plumpen and become fragrant with renewed perfume. I hold out my hand, placing my palm flat on the front of the stone. It feels more hopeful than I expected but bittersweet, with all those lost moments lingering like whispers in the breeze.

Etched into the stone, the epitaph.

Alejandro Salcedo. Father. Protector. Defender.

Intertwined with the music, the monotone sounds of a voice filter toward me. Don Vega stands in the center of the plot of land. Hands out to either side, he chants in a continual loop, his voice lilting in a thread that filters up and around him like tendrils of smoldering incense, so intense his words take shape around him like smoke.

I take out the narrow garland of tissue paper *papel picado*—intricately cut banners with skulls, flowers, and candle designs—and lay it across the top of the headstone. I find small woven bowls in the box and place one on either end, placing fruit and nuts in one. Tamales, *Papá's* favorite, go in the other. Along the base, I lay out a garland of marigolds sewn together with orange string. The smaller candles I bunch together, placing them alongside the larger ones, whose energy ignites the others at the foot of the cross.

From my bag, I produce the wooden box I brought from home that my dad carved for me for my fifth birthday. I open it and inside, among the incense and talismans I brought with me, is a photo. I'm sitting on his shoulders, facing the sun overlooking the ocean at Silver Strand Beach, the two of us in silhouette. I don't remember what we did that day. I only know we were together. We were happy.

"Now we're together again, *Papá*."

I take the photo and place it with the *ofrenda*. When I stand and look down, I notice Desi out of the corner of my eye, watching me. He steps forward, a bottle of tequila in one hand and three glasses in the other.

He hands me one and pours me a shot, which I place on the altar. When I turn back, he pours two more, holding a glass out to me, which he clinks to his when I take it.

"*Que sus almas descansen en paz.*"

I smile and turn to my dad's photo. "To those who are gone. May they be with us always. May they rest in peace."

My glass raised, I'm about to drink the tequila, when Dree joins us. Holding out a shot glass, she waits for Desi to fill it, then holds it up to me.

"I know this isn't easy," she says. "But it's good you being here tonight."

I lift my glass and clink it against hers. "To *familia*."

She nods, drinking her shot in one swig. When I take my turn, the tequila burns going down my throat. Desi laughs when I cringe at the taste, taking the glass from me as another group joins the celebration. Cousins, sisters, and brothers of those buried here all gathered in remembrance and celebration. Someone strums a guitar. Another sings a lament, deep and emotional, creating an atmosphere of family and home.

As the music rises, the wind surges all around us, and the moths descend from the trees where they've been watching, waiting. As they spin and flit, they come together, forming the shape of a man. I clasp Desi's hand, unable to look away as the moths remain gathered in my father's likeness. Reaching out with one hand, I sweep my fingers through the swarm. Their wings graze my fingertips as they disperse, only to come back again. As they do, they whirl around me, and for a moment, it's like my father is there, embracing me. Even though it's touching, there's a feeling of unrest in the swarm, the way they hover there with vibrant intensity. Can my father's spirit sense the turmoil? Does he know what I'm facing?

Around us, the excited chatter of my fellow witches drops away to subdued celebration, revealing each of the other altars and restless swarms of mourning moths lingering like a black cloud over all of us.

As the music swells from the mariachis, the spirits shift, and the multitudes of moths break apart in a dark wave. I reach up, skimming the swarm over my father's altar until the last one floats away.

When I turn to the rest of the group, now gathering and chatting quietly, Esme catches my eye and motions for me to go to her. I leave Desi with Dree and join Esme, allowing her to take my hand.

She pulls me in for a hug. "It must have been hard for you to return here after so long."

"I thought it would be," I say, "but it's also comforting, being closer to him instead of mourning him from afar."

She smiles and nods. "That's good. It's sad, yes, but it doesn't have to be. Not thinking about those we love and have lost is more painful than remembering them when they were here."

Lively chatter replaces the quiet solitude, filled with anticipation of joining the procession with the others. When I find Desi, his sly smile makes me chuckle.

"What?" I ask, afraid of what he's up to now.

"Now?" he asks Esme.

When she gives him a nod, he laughs and darts past the others to where we left our things when we first arrived.

He goes to a large box, removing something before sprinting back.

"We got you a little somethin' somethin'," he says with a self-satisfied look on his face.

I'm really hoping it isn't a pair of those gaudy sunglasses he was sporting the other day.

"We thought you would only feel truly at home once you received a new mask fitting of your heritage," Esme says, taking me by the elbow.

When she gestures to Desi, I turn to see his offering.

With both hands extended, he holds a mask out to me. The face is clay with various designs etched into the face—a sun on the forehead, white curlicues on either temple, red poppy petals around the eyes, and a spray of stars across the cheeks. White eyebrows jut from the center of the head into a point over either eye. Fine orange feathers outline the eyes like fringed eyelashes. Deep chocolate brown feathers frame the mask on the crown of the head and the sides of the face. White dots speckle the rest of the feathers.

I take the mask from Desi, holding it out before me.

"You deserve one that shows your other side," Esme says. "Your passion, your fire. *Tu sangre Salcedo.*"

Pride warms my skin as I look out at La Asamblea de La Lumbre. Knowing they accept me enough not only to welcome me but also to give me a mask of my own, one that shows my heritage, makes me feel I truly belong here.

"This means more than you know," I say. "Thank you."

"Well, put it on, *idiota!*" Desi says, cackling.

Standing among them, a twinge of guilt needles at me for so coldly leaving my snowy owl mask behind in Montréal, the one my mother gave me. I've been so desperate to connect to my father's heritage that I completely tossed aside my mother's. At the time, I didn't think of it that way. I was distraught by what happened to Gwen. It was more about casting off the memory of what I'd lost, of the danger I'd brought to the coven. Now, I can't help but feel a longing to have it back. But as I raise the mask, and each of my brothers and sisters do the same, I'm soothed. They're my family, too. Maybe I'm where I need to be right now. Being here doesn't mean I can never go back. But will it still be the same? Will all those I've left behind? Will I?

Around me, there are masks representing grayish-brown burrowing owls. Don Vega wears his almost black feathers, a white tuft in the middle of his forehead. Esme has her red screech owl mask. All the other variations of our cultures are represented here, all so beautiful. And when I slip into my mask facing Desi, he, too, is in his Mexican wood owl mask, slightly darker than mine but so much my kin.

I take his hand and we burst out laughing. When he hugs me, every lingering doubt about being here, about trying to fit in, is gone. I already fit in. I'm part of La Lumbre. And they're part of me.

Everyone gathers in an informal procession and as the music picks up, we take to singing and dancing, twirling around one another in a celebration of life.

Laughter percolates over the music, and suddenly, someone thrusts a bottle of tequila into my hand. I don't even think about it—I take a swig and then pass it to Desi, who's swaying his hips to the music.

We stay that way for a while. Laughing. Some howling. Others letting out a long, forlorn cry into the sky, then ending off with a deep, joyful belly laugh.

Somehow, we make our way out of the *cementerio*, skirting toward La Presidio, where the festivities are in full swing. Like two waves coming together, we slip into the flow of song and dance, getting carried up the cobblestones with tourists and families alike.

The tequila is already going to my head, but I embrace the buzz. I let loose, dancing with anyone who crosses my path, spinning and shaking my hips to the beat.

As we continue, I stagger, getting caught in the wave of people, and suddenly, I'm in another current, being pulled away from the main road to a wide field of grass. When I break free from the group, spinning and almost tripping over my feet, the current ebbs the other way, and I am on my own with only a few others around me. I search the group for Desi and Dree but they're gone, carried away in the opposite direction.

I laugh, peeling off my mask and propping it on my head, taking in the cool air. In the shadows, crickets sing their forlorn tune; I can hear not just their song but also their legs scratching together. High in the trees, it isn't only the breeze playing through the leaves but the rustling of animals burrowing in for the night. Somewhere high in the hills, a turkey vulture whines overhead.

I can't help but laugh and twirl at the wonder of my owl abilities sharpening. My hearing and sight have advanced in leaps and bounds since I've been here. It gives me hope it won't be long before my wings and feathers come.

I stop spinning, realizing it only makes the effect of the booze even worse, and look for a place to rest before I meet back up with the others. Ahead of me, there's a low wall surrounded by cacti, its pads flat and wide.

I propel myself toward the wall, staggering, but catch myself before I fall. I sit, and when my head stops spinning, I laugh at the mess I must be: a drunk woman sitting in the middle of a cemetery with an owl mask propped on the top of my head.

I fish around in my bag for my bottle of water and remove the lid, closing my eyes and swishing down as much of it as I can stomach. Around me, a few people mill around, but the next time I open my eyes, I'm the only one left.

From where I'm sitting, I watch as the multicolored procession glimmers in the distance, the revelers making their way down the hill overlooking Old Town. Muted waves of music waft up the hillside, and I swear I can hear Desi's laughter and Esme's rolling trill she likes to do when she gets excited, Don Vega's cry that unleashes his other side, the one that thrives in shadow.

Then there's something else. The soft pitter-patter of wings in the shadows around me. I can't see the moths but they are there, enshrouded, watching. When I stand to leave, their wings sting as they flit against my bare arms in warning.

Another noise comes, deeper and more robust than the moths. Not from the old market square. Somewhere closer.

The treeline.

Between me and my escape route.

Breathing.

An animal. Tracking me.

I take a step backward. The breathing moves closer.

I glance up. A pair of glowing eyes advances.

In the folds of my poncho, hidden pockets bulge with crystals. Sage. Black powder. Matches. A candle. My athamé.

I slip my hand into the pocket, feeling around until I find the small sachet Lidia had given me that day in her house. Sewn safely inside are elderberry, fennel, juniper, and mugwort.

I turn, undaunted. I'm sick of cowering or feeling threatened by things or people who seek to harm me and my coven.

Grasping the sachet in my hand, I set out, taking a precarious step toward the road.

"By the light of the lady moon," I say, moving with cautious determination. "I will reach my destination undaunted."

The scent of pine floods my nostrils. The char of burned logs scratches the back of my throat, and a shrill whistle sounds in my head: a warning from someone no longer on this plane but somewhere else—my gaze darts to the side. I speed up, putting as much distance between myself and the treeline as possible. But branches crack. Footsteps pace after me. The eyes and the creature behind them still follow.

One hand goes to my whistle as I continue my incantations. "My trip shall be safe."

I can't hear Desi. Nor Esme or Don Vega. They're gone; they've left me behind. I'm on my own.

Breathing.

Coming faster.

Moving closer.

A low growl pierces the quiet.

My pulse makes me dizzy.

"For all those concerned as well as me. So shall it be."

I take off running, making it to the main road, but a field of energy forces me back. No matter how I fight, there's a weight to the air, an unseen wall preventing me from returning to my coven.

Footsteps advance, galloping toward me. I lose my footing, but a swift gust, like an unseen hand, keeps me upright. When I stagger forward, my vision shimmers and then changes. Instead of the forest before me, I see myself as though I am someone else, watching myself from behind. I spin until the scene returns to normal, even though it is anything but. I fish around for my bone whistle and pull it from under my collar. I put it to my lips and let out a quick warning call, but keep moving. There's no response from the others. I curse myself for straying from the group.

Behind me, the determined exhalation of my pursuer follows. I try to catch a glimpse, but it only makes me lose footing.

The path narrows, taking me into a grove of trees. I don't have time to find another route. So I take it. I make it through quickly while memories of that night in the forest with Gwen flash.

It's behind me. I keep running, trying to ignore the sound of its breath, its feet hitting the ground. Its heart is thundering in anticipation of catching me. I scan the sounds rushing at me from all sides, hoping to catch a wave from the coven, wanting more than anything for them to realize I'm missing.

But I'm getting tired. It's gaining on me. I feel a snap at my heels, and I spin, screaming out and conjuring enough energy to force the animal backward. Still running, I grasp for the whistle at my neck. It takes a few tries to grab it. I prop it between my lips as something hits me from behind. I go flying forward and fall flat on my face. I let out a breath of air, but the whistle pops free from my lips and falls limply around my neck.

I flip over onto my back. The coyote lunges for me, but I lift both feet and kick it away. It goes flying back a few feet into the dirt with a yelp, scrambling onto its feet for another attack. When it comes for me again, I rise onto my elbows and throw out both hands to stop it. Letting out a shout, I channel all my energy to my fingertips as the coyote bounds toward me. In a flash of bright red, the animal catapults away from me, and it lands on its back ten feet away. Somehow, it gets up again. This time, I am not ready for it.

I fall onto my back and use both hands to keep it from attacking my face. But it snarls, growls, snapping at me. Its hot breath is on my face, and its saliva is dripping onto me. Somehow, I can hold it off, but as I struggle to keep it away from me, I get a better look at its face. There's something very wrong with the animal's eyes. They don't glow like I expect them to. They don't fit this face. They look almost human.

The thought chills me, and in a surge of energy, I scream out, using all my strength to throw the animal off me. I let out a sharp, shrill call, my owl voice coming to me without using my whistle.

A shadow emerges from the trees—a man. His sharp whistle evokes a Pavlovian response in the coyote. It backs away and circles him before sitting at his flank.

Towering over me, Nico López drops his hood and steps into the moonlight to reveal his face. He's dressed in dark gray from head to foot. There's a large circle in the middle of his chest with a gold and turquoise stepped fret design in the shape of a spiral in the center. A blood-red coyote is embroidered above his heart. Flashes of my cleansing ritual with Don Vega come back to me. The face of the ancient warrior with his head shorn and his face painted in vibrant colors slips over Nico's face like a ritual mask. They have the same slender nose and high cheekbones. That same dark determination pushes me back a few steps. Somehow, I knew what they were without realizing it. His ancestors are the same warriors who pursued mine from the beginning, starting with Lorenza and culminating with their obsessive pursuit of me from Montréal to California.

I scramble to get up, but he steps on my ankle, pinning me to the ground. His coyote dips its head and snarls. I kick at him with my free foot and scramble up.

"It's going to take more than that to keep me down. I got away from you before, remember?"

His laugh is laced with disgust. "You really think you got away? If I wanted to take you, I would have."

"Really? I saw you hesitate. The same way you did before, that day at Las Lomas, when you were a scared little kid hiding in a bush. What the hell do you want with me anyway? I've done nothing to you. Los Cazadores are the ones who've stolen things from me."

"Doesn't matter. Not all enemies are made because of what they've done to one another."

"So, you hate us just because we exist? How small-minded of you."

"And you think your Gift is the only magic in this world. How self-righteous of you."

The coyote snaps to attention, and when Nico raises his hand, his eyes turn bright yellow. Coyote eyes. Somehow, they're interchangeable. They are one.

"Why did you let me get away only to chase me here?"

Before he can answer, a large dark owl dive-bombs the coyote and lands on top of it, talons out. It lets out a yelp, snapping at the owl as it lifts again. All at once, Desi and Dree are beside me with extended hands, conjuring a forcefield of protection around us. I join them, adding my power. Our energy surges in a blaze of bright yellow, sending Nico staggering back with his coyote limping after him.

He reaches around his shoulder, sliding the crossbow out and pointing it toward me. He raises it and aims, but Esme appears and rushes past me. In a burst of bright white, she sends him flying away from us long enough for me to get behind her. Nico cries out, fighting the wall of energy. I move beside Esme and hold my hands out before me, joining my power with hers. Nico's body convulses, forcing him back, his boots dragging in the dirt until he wills enough of his power to break free from our attack.

When he's far enough away, we lower our hands, and the protective energy subsides. From the trees, Don Vega appears, having slipped back into his ceremonial robe. He stands and looks out over the field, making sure Nico is gone. Dree and the others have split off, circling us and inspecting the treeline.

Beside me, Esme places a hand on my arm. "*Mija*. Are you all right? Let me see."

She turns me around to face her and inspects me, touching her fingertips to a tender spot on my cheek. "Just a scratch. It will heal quickly."

When she pauses, her hand poised on my cheek, she grins. "You are strong, Valeria. Like *tu papá*."

"The coyote wasn't that big," I say.

"I meant your power. You knocked that animal back."

"With your help," I say, smiling.

"Don't do that, Valeria. Never downplay your abilities."

I nod, glancing over her shoulder at Desi and Dree as they return from patrol.

"Everything all right?" I ask.

"Looks like he's the only one."

"For tonight," Don Vega says, coming toward the group. "Los Cazadores never hunt alone. We should prepare for more."

There's a palpable tension amongst the group as we return to Old Town, where music thumps inside the square, and the smell of food and incense and the sound of laughter and singing come at me in waves.

This should be a celebration. The night of all nights to honor our ancestors, and Los Cazadores can't even let us have that.

I'm livid. As Desi pulls me in and talks a mile a minute to see if I'm hurt, I want nothing more than to make the Hunters pay. Not only for what they have taken from me but also for how they continue to persecute us.

As we merge into the partygoers and meet with the other Lumbres who were at the cemetery earlier, the music drops away. The revelers remain in the throes of celebration, but no one else seems to notice. Desi and I share a knowing glance, and then he leans over to murmur something to Dree.

On his other side, Don Vega stands stoic in the middle of the street as dancers twirl around him, but the music is gone now, the animated voices and revelry muted. There, in the endless silence, I hear a high-pitched whirring.

From the edges of the buildings, Los Cazadores appear. One stands in the alcove of a storefront and another on a balcony above the street. Two more crouch low to the ground next to a large water fountain. They have us surrounded. There's no way out except to go through them.

Don Vega throws his hands out, sending our group staggering to the side just before a flurry of arrows whizzes through the air, narrowly missing us. But there is the wet *thwack* of a projectile making contact and one of the other witches—someone I don't know—goes flying backward. He falls in the middle of the cobblestone road, unmoving.

Everything erupts into chaos as we duck and dive, reaching out to keep one another safe. Ahead of the group, Don Vega retreats behind a massive wall of fire conjured from his fingertips. As his voice rises, a painting on the sidewalk of the Old Adobe Chapel comes to life. The streets take on a three-dimensional look, stretching below ground, and the stark white façade of the church shimmers, beckoning.

With her palms pressed together, Esme chants as she pulls her hands apart. Between them, golden light glistens. As she continues to whisper, she holds her hands out over the ground and then pushes the energy toward the cobblestones.

"Come on, *prima!*" Desi says, grabbing my hand.

As we approach the mural, I gasp at the teetering effect as Dree walks toward it and into the painting, moving below ground level into the other world. I follow Desi, tentatively stepping toward the drawing. But when my foot touches the ground, I'm pulled through to the other side. When I continue forward, I'm transported to the steps in front of the church on the other side of Old Town, where we first began our evening.

Once we've all come through the portal, Esme and Don Vega follow as he recites a verse. The light on the ground disappears, and the sidewalk is once again solid, the doorway closed.

"Come. We must get back to the safety of Las Garras." He waves the group on, coaxing the others to follow.

"Let's go, Val. *Now*," Desi says.

I follow him and Dree, who huddle together as they walk, but when I glance over my shoulder, I notice Don Vega stooped over the body of our fallen witch. I can sense the pulse of his heartbeat: rage radiates from him in waves. His dark thoughts crash into my own, the anger of being attacked this way. The creeping sensation of being watched, followed, hunted. And the skin-crawling feeling of looking into those coyote eyes and seeing Nico López again, the man whose father killed mine, now intent on doing the same to me.

I hate him with every dark fluttering in my soul. But he let me get away. I need to know why.

CHAPTER 12

Regrouping

It's well past 4 am when we return to Rancho de Las Garras. Desi and Dree follow Esme and Don Vega inside, but my emotions are a swirling intensity of smoke and dank soil that keep me buzzing too much for me to go into the meeting house. My spirit is a restless animal, incensed and infuriated. Los Cazadores should never have provoked me. Nico López can save his platitudes. They'll do no good here.

On the flat stone threshold, looking out over the grounds, I stand with my hands balled into fists at my side and hold my breath so I can hear better, so I can sense if someone is lurking in the shadows, waiting for when we least expect them to mount another attack.

My first instinct in Montréal was to pick up and leave to keep myself and my coven safe from Los Cazadores. But to have them attack us on the most sacred of nights when we gather to pay respect to our ancestors who instilled in us their wisdom and their abilities? It imbues every cell in my body with ire.

Across the grounds, the pale orange glow emanating from Lidia's cabin proves she can't sleep either. I'm tempted to go over there and take her up on her offer to go deeper and darker with our Craft, but after the attack and my confrontation with Nico, after fighting off his coyote, it's clear that darkness is already within me. The black witch moths have been coming to me to draw it from within me, not to torment me. They've been the shining light I needed all along, and I won't turn my nose up at this power. I'm not afraid of tapping into something darker. I welcome it now more than ever before.

I snatch up my cigar box from the deck and bound down the steps, striding to the edge of the land where the shadows seep into the grounds of Rancho de las Garras. Surrounding the property, a field of protection invisible to the mortal eyes shimmers in iridescent red-gold. Arm outstretched, I wave my hand through the forcefield. Faint electricity percolates on my fingertips like the flare from the sparklers we used to get to celebrate Canada Day.

I approach the shoulder-high hedges planted as a natural barricade. I stop, my mother's voice ringing in my head, telling me it's too dangerous to go outside the barrier. That things lurk in the places beyond our walls, things that can hurt me. Things that threaten my safety. But I'm tired of being afraid. The phantom call of her whistle, which I heard when I left home, lingers like a warning.

The further I move into the field, the energy travels up my arm, across my shoulders, and up my neck until I'm standing in the center. Sounds far down in the forest are closer than my heartbeat. The sweet fragrance of dew on the leaves tickles my nose before turning sour and spoiled. The musty brine of the ocean miles away stings my lips with its saltiness. My entire body tingles with the thrill of magic. Of taking my power back and being fully myself. I part the tangle of firethorn branches and push through. They pull at my clothing like claws, trying to keep me inside the circle of protection, scraping my hands and cheeks, but I make it through to the other side.

I feel an electric buzz as I push through the energy field and move beyond the invisible barrier of safety, and my senses perk up. The wind calls to me in whispers. I hear the far-off screech of a condor high in the hills. And beneath it all, there's the almost imperceptible rhythm of water rushing downstream.

The *acequias* between El Rancho and the neighboring lands are abundant with life-giving water. Without these water channels, nothing could thrive here. It makes me wonder where La Lumbre would be if they did not have this fount so close to their property. Would we be in the desert, living in stone houses like Don Vega? Would we be somewhere else entirely? Would we be any less protected? Any more vulnerable?

After the attack at home in the forest surrounding La Maison, after being separated from the coven in Old Town, I know I should remain on the secure grounds. But that is what Los Cazadores want—for us to live in fear, to go into hiding again, as we have for years. I won't allow them to scare me into living my life in the shadows any longer. Not when I have the power to teach them a lesson.

I step toward the channel and crouch over it, the cigar box tucked under my arm. My hand unfurled, I skim my fingertips in the icy flow. I don't know why I expected it to be warm. Maybe it's the fire here, the sun, the way the land absorbs and protects that heat for when it's needed most.

As the water percolates and bubbles around my fingertips, I can hear my father teaching me about the channels and how they were a source of power and protection to us. As much as Los Cazadores want to attack us, they can't get past the defenses. The water repels them and protects us from their attacks.

This source is not only for the horses, plants, and animals here. It's an important element to our work. I don't take lightly having water so close to the desert, especially since I need it to complete my spell. I am about to begin when a sharp, shrill call sounds from afar, its fierce energy hitting me in the center of the forehead with an intensity that causes me to stagger sideways.

My mother. An alarm call from her bone whistle. She's here somehow. And she's in trouble.

I try to pinpoint her location, and when it screeches again, I jump across the *acequia* and take off. My feet can't carry me fast enough, but that doesn't matter. The moths are all around me now, carrying me faster, further. They become the wings I so long to sprout. I bolt down the well-beaten path to the south, where the hill drops away, leading further down into the canyon.

When I come to a ridge, I stop. The call comes again, closer now. Sharper. I scan the ridge below me and spot a copse of trees. It's the perfect place to hide, exactly where Èvelyne would seek refuge if she were in danger. I take off, staggering in my desperation to get to her.

Nearing the woods, I slowly crouch low and edge toward the trees. Why wouldn't she come to Las Garras, where her brother and sister witches would protect her? Did she sense Los Cazadores lurking and want to avoid leading them directly to our doors?

My heart thrums with bittersweet pain. She probably tried to make it here in time for La Día de Los Muertos to visit *Papá's* grave, to be with him on the night when she could feel close to him, if only for a few moments. She must have sensed the Hunters around. Maybe she saw the attack at Old Town and remained hidden, and now she's in danger trying to get back to us and our protected grounds.

The pause between her calls is too long. I need to hear her, to know she's safe. I pull out my whistle and let out a low call, one only another of our kind can detect. A few moments later, she responds with three sharp blasts, her warning signal. She's injured.

I step over brush and thorns, heading into the forest where the crickets trill their nighttime symphony. But as I approach, they fall silent: the only sound is my heartbeat, so loud it's maddening.

Moonlight filters through the trees in shards, piercing the veil of black moths that filter up to the treetops where they settle, wavering like leaves. Ahead of me, someone faces me. It's too dark to make out anything other than the ghostly white face of a snowy owl mask.

I continue, but the closer I get, the darker their aura burns—dark red, deep and foreboding. It comes to me at first like a hint of perfume lingering in the air, with a deep smokiness to warn me of its sinister source. A hint of something else. With each step, the shadows seep toward them, and an almost imperceptible haze of cunning encircles them, swallowing them in a silhouette as deep and endless as a moonless night.

One step.

Darkness like black ink floods into my field of vision.

Another step.

It spills across my sightline.

Two more steps and my arms prickle with little claw-tipped feet and the flutter of inky black wings. I look down to find both arms covered with moths. Some sit still while others open and close their wings in an enchanting dance that makes their spots look like owl eyes blinking at me, signaling me.

I lift my whistle to my lips. With careful breaths, I play a tune, one that only Èvelyne and I know. One we created when I was a child that we have protected from everyone else—from the coven, even from my father. One, we can play to signal our true identity to the other.

I wait. As the masked person lifts her whistle, there's nothing. No sound. No song. No answer to my call.

It's not Èvelyne.

Grasping at my father's feather, I hold one hand out before me, about to cast a spell, when the figure collapses, and the mask falls to the dirt. I bolt toward it and when I stand over it, there is nobody. No person. No one. There was never anyone there. It was all an illusion, a trap to get me out here, alone and vulnerable.

A beam of moonlight illuminates the face. Staring up at me, the vacant eyes. White feathers. Speckles on the forehead. It's my mother's. Panic surges through my limbs with an electric shock. When I lift it, the feathers are rigid in my hand, matted with dried blood.

Every muscle in my body seizes with panic. When I glance upward, the figure has moved to the middle of the path a few yards away. They lift their hand, press an object to their lips, and blow. Not a trill. Not a high-pitched bark. The tortured cry of my mother comes from the whistle. A memory of the torment inflicted upon her shrieks from the bone—the torture she endured before the whistle was taken from her. I clamp my hands to my ears, stunned. There's no way she would willingly part with her bone whistle. For an owl to do so would put them at the mercy of those who have harmed them. If they're too injured to call out, the bone whistle is a backup plan. A last resort for help from other witches. She can call without it, but it's a piece of her, made from her finger bone the same way mine was. To give up a part of herself is giving another being the ability to harm her and use her bone against her the way it's being used now.

Terror keeps me planted in place. Where is Èvelyne? Why does this person have something she would rather die than give up?

The figure shifts. I tense, waiting for an attack. Instead, they take off through the woods in the other direction. I snatch the mask and follow, barreling at my tormentor, trying to keep up with them. When I make it to the clearing, there's a Jeep waiting beside the dirt road that disappears into the valley. The figure stops. When they tilt their head to one side, studying me, the moonlight illuminates their face, and for a moment, their visage flickers the way a glint of light gets thrown from a mirror, the face taking on a more angular shape.

"Goddess. Ancestors," I say. "Help me see this dark force persecuting me!"

All at once, the moths dive-bomb from above, pushing the figure into the light, and the face inspires a moment of clarity. A hint of smoke tickles my nose, and the forest fades beyond the veil of moths. The crisp coolness of the thicket around La Maison, not Rancho des Las Garras, prickles my skin.

I gasp, sending the figure spinning, running away from me. Like coming out of a tunnel, the starkness of home gives way to the darkness of this place. The figure is gone. I need to warn the others. I need to find Èvelyne.

I race up the path toward El Rancho. As I pick my way along the trail, the sky is now amber-hued with the coming of the sun. I push through the bushes and find myself back on our protected land. I make a beeline for my cabin, closing and securing the door, pausing half a beat before I dare to move.

The first thing I do is snatch up my phone, hitting the auto-dial for my mother. Each unanswered ring is a tiny stab to my heart. I hang up and, bracing myself, scroll through my address book to Olivia's number. As I wait for the call to connect, I pace the length of the room, gritting my teeth for her snarky response. She's the last person I want to call, but as my Mother's Maiden, she should know where she is at all times.

Her voicemail picks up. I spin in frustration, knowing she's seen my call and chosen to ignore it.

I glimpse myself in the mirror as I pass, then stop mid-step.

My eyes have changed. The irises glow—my barn owl eyes. But they're rimmed with black. The eyes of my father. Crested owl eyes.

A knock on my door startles me enough to make me jump. I wait, unsure if I should go to it. A knock again, and then the door swings open. It's Desi.

"Girl, you gotta get your butt up to the main house. Things are happening."

I stand unmoving, tucking the mask behind me. I'm not sure why I don't want him to see it. Is it because of what I did? My spell? Did it go wrong, hurt someone I didn't intend? Do they already know about Èvelyne?

"Desi, something—"

He grabs me by the hand. "Let's go, *chica*! This is what we've been waiting for!"

He pulls me out the door and down the steps. I tuck the mask under my arm to keep it hidden as we cross the lawn.

"I really don't have time for this right now, Des. Something's happened."

"Damn right something's happened."

"You guys know?"

"Know what? Girl, what the hell are you talking about, huh?"

"Oh," I say, picking up voices and excited chatter from the back patio even though we're yards away. "There's been word. From Mexico. Not from…"

Desi does a double-take. "Damn. You really are changing, aren't you?"

"No, I'm not! Wait…what do you mean?"

"Well, either you became psychic overnight, or you picked up on what's going on. Your hearing. It's gotten better, right?"

I nod, but my heightening powers are the least of my concerns. I need to get to a phone. I need to find out what happened to my mother.

"It's only a matter of time now, Val. And it couldn't have come soon enough."

He squeezes my hand before dropping it and turning to the group encircling Esme and Don Vega, who are in quiet conversation. As we gather, seeing everyone has arrived, Esme holds up her hands to quiet the nervous chatter under everything.

"Everyone. We've received word from our brothers and sisters across the border. The Opening of the Flower has come. It's time to journey south to receive our gift, *La Néctar Sagrado*."

A wave of excited celebration rolls through the crowd.

"Tonight, I, along with my Maiden Lidia and those in the coven who shall act as our guardians, will travel to Cancún to meet with our La Lumbre of the south. In two nights, we will collect *La Néctar*. We will bring it back, not only for ourselves, but for our Sisters and Brothers in *El Norte, El Este, y El Oeste*."

Lidia moves beside me so quietly that I don't notice until I feel her breath on my ear.

"This is what I was talking about. Only those with enough experience can go to gather La Néctar."

Can she see in me how I covet? How I wish I were going with them to bring back our life-giving Elixir. If I used my father's feather, I would be one of the lucky ones.

"This is freaking crazy!" Desi says, pulling me to one side.

"So, you're going then, huh?" I say.

He stops, and the smile slips from his face. "Yeah. I mean..."

I nod.

"Look, Val."

I take his hand in mine. "It's fine. Only third-degree witches go with Esme to be there when she opens the Reliquary."

"And Lidia, of course, as Esme's Maiden."

"So, why do you get to go? What do you do?"

He stops, a frown wrinkling his forehead. "You know Esme needs protection. But she also needs us in case something happens, and we need someone else to open the Reliquary."

I nod. "And third-degree witches can stand in for her."

As soon as I say it, I lock eyes with Lidia. She has a smile on her face that is part satisfaction, part challenge. I'm not sure when her attitude turned from camaraderie to competition, but there's an iciness to her now that wasn't there when we first met.

As the group breaks up and everyone scatters to their respective roles, I'm left, as always, waiting on the sidelines.

This is what Lidia meant about acknowledging my potential and others not seeing what I have to offer. But I've been a witch all my life, and I'm still sitting around waiting for others to do the important work. If I were a third-degree witch, I would be on that trip.

"You better go pack then," I say to Desi, leaving him behind before I say something ungracious.

I'm almost to my cabin when there's a shriek overhead. At first, I think it's the same sound from earlier, the tormentor back with Èvelyne's mask to haunt me. When I look up, a flurry of white feathers flies past my head.

I turn to find an owl face down in the grass. I bolt toward it, calling out to the others rushing to the same spot. My stomach drops at the thought. Èvelyne. She's here, after all. She must have gotten away from Los Cazadores.

I throw myself to my knees, leaning over to check the owl. It's still breathing.

I gingerly slip my fingers under its falcon-like wings, carefully contracting them so I can flip the bird over more easily.

When I do, I gasp and drop the mask to the grass.

The white face outlined in black. The spotted head. The barred brown chest. It's not Èvelyne. It's Will.

"Move aside," someone says.

I can't. Panic clutches my chest, my arms. Why is Will here? Was he with Èvelyne when she was attacked? When Los Cazadores took her mask and bone whistle?

"Give him here," Don Vega says, standing over me.

Will's eyes are closed. His chest rises with slow, shallow breaths. His yellow beak is half-opened. Otherwise, he's still.

I lift him to Don Vega, who takes him in both hands, Will's long tail feathers spilling downward. Turning, he moves in double-time to the house.

Desi pulls me up onto my feet and helps me stand. "Damn. A hawk owl, huh? Who is he?"

"Will. My friend."

"Did you know he was coming?"

I can only shake my head. I try not to overreact, but why wouldn't he tell me beforehand? Did he get caught up in the attack? Why isn't Èvelyne with him?

Desi takes me by the arm, and we head to the main house. When we arrive, Esme has cleared the large table in the sitting room. Will, still in owl form, is lying on a large white towel.

"I need an egg. And water. Now," Don Vega says.

Desi drops my hand and rushes past him into the kitchen, gathering the supplies and bringing them to him. Desi hands him a clear glass of water and an egg, which Don Vega accepts hurriedly.

Placing the egg in the glass, Don Vega holds it in his cupped hands. He lifts the glass to his lips and whispers over it. Then, speaking louder now, he continues a prayer in Spanish. He gently removes the egg from the glass and hands the glass back to Desi. Taking the egg in one hand, he starts at Will's head and sweeps the egg down his body to his feet. The egg takes on a pale yellow glow.

"He's sweeping away the negative energies. Making way for healing and balance," Desi explains.

I nod, watching as he moves the egg through the air, paying special attention to Will's wings.

After drawing a cross in the air with the egg, once over his head, then his heart, Don Vega moves in closer. Holding the egg under Will's beak, he waits until Will takes several shallow breaths. The longer he holds it there, the color of the egg brightens, and it glows vibrant orange, thin veins darkening the shell. As they shift and swirl, they form an image.

A crude owl shape flits across the egg's surface, encircling it. It darts around, climbing and then flipping and diving as though it is flying. A second owl appears at the bottom of the egg, and as the first approaches, the egg turns bright red. The second owl dissolves into nothing, and the first owl goes into a tailspin before it seeps into the orange and is gone.

"He was in a chase," Don Vega says. "Our sisters of the north were attacked. But he made it out unscathed."

"Then why isn't he moving?" I ask. "He must be hurt. Something else is wrong with him."

Desi drops my hand and moves to the table. He takes the glass of water and holds it out to Don Vega, who slowly, carefully cracks the egg into the water.

"The egg stays in the water for a time before I read the whites to see what ails him."

When he turns back, Desi is there with a bundle of lavender. Don Vega repeats the process, sweeping Will's body with the herbs, then placing them on the table.

He takes a small glass tumbler from Desi and dips his fingers into the liquid inside, anointing Will on his forehead, above his heart, and on the middle of his chest.

"*Gracias*," Don Vega says, looking skyward.

Desi continues to work, taking the lavender, lighting it, and letting it burn.

When Don Vega waves me over, I edge toward the table, afraid that my being there will harm Will somehow. But when I sit next to him, I feel comforted and place my hand on his head.

Don Vega pats me on the shoulder, then moves to where Desi is working. They whisper, and I keep watch over Will, unable to take my eyes from the rise and fall of his chest. I listen for each breath, but he doesn't seem hurt or injured.

"The egg absorbs the unwanted energies," Desi says beside me. "Don Vega will read the shape of the yolk. The color of the water. The patterns in the whites. It all tells him something different."

Don Vega holds the glass to eye level, studying the yolk floating in the water. I can't tell by his expression whether it is good or bad news. He has that same intensity in his eyes. That same stoicism in his stern jaw. When he moves toward us, he holds the glass out.

"The water. Do you see how it is murky?"

I nod. "What does it mean?"

"The *barrida* has released unwanted energies that were harming him."

"Something someone did to him?"

"It's hard to say. It could be. Or it could be the exhaustion of flying all the way here on his own."

I nod, turning back to Will. He looks peaceful now; his brown and white feathers slightly flutter as he breathes. For now, all we can do is wait for him to wake up.

Before I can breathe, Will sputters, his chest heaving. Blood trickles from the side of his beak.

"The Elixir," Esme says. "He needs it now, Valeria." She snaps her fingers and gestures to a large framed photo on the wall.

I stand unmoving, my feet planted to the ground. It is too much. It's exactly like Gwen. She tried to help me and was killed for her efforts. Now Will has come all this way to find me, and he's just as badly hurt.

Dree pushes past me and moves to the painting, sweeping it open on its hinges attached to the wall. She waves her hands over the lock. It unbolts, and the door behind the frame pops open. Removing a small box from the safe, she turns and rushes past me, bringing the box to Don Vega.

"I...I didn't know," I say. My face burns hot with the guilt of doing nothing, of freezing in front of everyone.

"It's okay, *prima*," Desi says. "This is too much. He's going to be alright."

As Don Vega opens the bottle and lifts the decanter to Will's beak, the severity of the night, the intensity, and the trauma of what I experienced all take their toll. I grasp the edge of the table to steady myself.

Prying Will's beak open, Don Vega deposits a drop of the Elixir onto Will's tongue and gently closes his beak to ensure he swallows it. I don't notice Desi is beside me until he slips his hand into mine.

"Val. You should rest," Desi says.

"No. I can't leave him."

"I'll stay with him, cuz. You go get some rest, huh? This has been a long day."

"I'm not leaving until he's okay!" I shout, shoving Desi away from me. I lunge for Will, but Don Vega catches me by the arm. His touch is instantly soothing, but that doesn't stop the worry from seizing my body and making everything around me shine too brightly.

Don Vega edges me toward the door. As we exit, I notice Dree standing off to the side, holding my mother's mask. I snatch it from her.

"I found it in the grass," she says.

"What are you... Was this you? Did you do this?"

"*Mija*, no," Don Vega says, trying to usher me outside.

"I should stay," I say, glaring at Dree, glancing at Will. Leaving him will make me look that much more inept. Like I can't handle these tense situations. Like I'm a child who needs someone to hold my hand.

"Desi is fine to take care of your friend. Besides, something else is bothering you."

He gets me outside, but I can't shake what I felt when I saw Dree with Èvelyne's mask. The person in the forest was smaller than Nico López. Smaller than any Los Cazadores. Could Dree be my tormentor? To get back at me for how she feels I treat Desi? It's an ugly thing to think that one of our own would hurt a High Priestess. But I can't keep it to myself. Not after what I saw on the egg.

"The other owl in the vision. It was my mother."

"It could have been, yes."

"I know it was her. I went outside the grounds earlier to clear my head, and I heard her calling to me."

"From back home?"

I shake my head. "From the canyon. Her distress call. It was clear. It came from nearby, from her bone key. So I followed the sound."

Don Vega is quiet, studying my face.

"I know I shouldn't have gone out alone after the trouble I brought to us in town tonight. But I couldn't stop myself, not when she called to me. At least, someone did. With her whistle."

"And what did you find?"

"This."

I hold Èvelyne's mask out to him. Upon seeing the blood, his cool expression falters. A glimmer of anger, the darkness lingering under his surface, makes his eyes go dark.

"Her call. You heard it?"

I nod. "Whoever it was had her bone whistle."

I reach for the cord I wear around my neck and pull it out, along with my father's feather. Seeing them there together, as though they are reunited, gives me a chill. If she was hurt, really hurt, if they killed her—

"You would sense if they harmed her that badly, Valeria. You're bound to her by blood. You would know."

"I know already. Something terrible has happened to her. She may not be gone, but she's lost at the very least."

"Then," he says, placing his hand on my shoulder, "we will find her and make those who took her pay for the torment they inflict."

When his face darkens like a cloud crossing over the sun, and his eyes flash bright orange, I remember that same look when he protected me after the attack at his *hacienda* when Los Cazadores killed my *papá*. It's his strength and resolve, instilled with an undercurrent of loyalty, that keeps me from crumbling to pieces.

"You are like your *mamá* and *papá*, Valeria. You can face any darkness. You have the tools you need to channel your deepest energies." He gestures to the grounds of El Rancho, to a small plot of land off the back. "Go to the plants. Call out to them. Listen to them. When you make your intentions known, those who will serve you best will make themselves known, too. Give them your love, your respect, your attention, and they will repay you in your magic. When you heal with them. When you cleanse with them."

I nod and hug him, but healing and cleansing are not my only intentions. My family has been attacked. More than once. Healing and cleansing are well and good, but someone needs to pay.

"Plants, herbs, flowers, water. These things are all important in the work we do, Valeria. But if we fall into the trap of feeling we need them for protection, we end up bringing about more instances where we need that protection. Understand?"

"Kind of like a self-fulfilling prophecy?"

"Yes. Remember to focus on keeping yourself strong. Stress, anxiety, fear—all these things lower our energy vibrations. It is how unwanted things, such as sickness and disease, can take hold."

Not all darkness is unwanted, though. Especially not mine.

As he moves to the house, I glance at the bloodied mask in my hand. My mother's energy has waned since the last time she wore it. I only hope our blood bond hasn't completely severed. I have to find her before it's too late.

Esme and Don Vega exit, talking for a while before they hug. He returns to his truck to drive back to La Hacienda. After Esme retreats to the main house, I go inside my cabin, close the door behind me and stand with my head back, my eyes closed.

There have been so many close calls. Much closer than ever before. I realize living in peace may not be possible with the Hunters continuing to attack. What will it force us to do to protect our coven and the things that matter to us most?

Someone is playing with me. Taunting me. They've made this personal. First, they kill Gwen. Then they attack us on our most sacred night, the same night they make it clear they have my mother and will go after anyone who stands in their way, including Will.

It can't be Nico López. He would have said something, relished seeing my reaction at knowing he had my mother. This was from someone else.

The thing is, they don't know what they have awakened in me. Or what I have awoken in myself. Don Vega was right. It's about motive. If they intend to taunt and torment me, then I won't beg forgiveness for how I respond to these actions. Before, I was worried about the darkness the black witch moths were warning me of. Now I realize they were offering their dark magic to me, instilling in me their power and lighting my path with cinders I will use to burn down anyone and anything that seeks to take one more thing from me.

I have my own intentions. The first is to go to the river and finish my spell, so whoever is after me will pay for what they've tried to take. Then I'll do some taking of my own.

CHAPTER 13

The Fire

When I step out on my porch, the heat of the day is already burning off the morning mist. It lingers like smoke above the trees, the whisper of a promising new day, and the first thing on my mind is finishing what I started. The spell Lidia shared with me to reciprocate the pain Los Cazadores have thrust upon me burns in the back of my brain like a hateful demon I need to exorcise.

Holding the bundle Lidia gave me on my first day in San Diego, I sense the residual darkness coming from within the folds of the fabric. What if keeping these remnants of the trouble I had in Montréal is the very thing bringing that darkness back to me? Maybe casting off their negative energy will make things better. The only way to do that is to end this spell and let the darkness flow away from me, from all of us, for the last time.

I take the bundle of wrapped hair and shove it into my bag before I get dressed. As I'm about to go back outside, I see Will walking toward me, grimacing. I drop everything and rush out, bounding down the steps.

"I need to talk to you about what happened back home," I say.

"Good. Because that's why I was coming to see you."

"Why are you here, Will? Where's my mother?"

"No beating around the bush, huh? You realize I'm injured here, right?"

I pause for a beat and then wrap him in a hug. He grunts, pulling back from me.

"Oh, I'm sorry," I say. "You really should be resting. The Elixir is weak, which means it will take longer for you to heal. It's just nice to see a familiar face."

"It's not like La Lumbre are strangers to you, Val."

"I know. It's…different here."

"Good different, or…?"

"Well, let's just say my problems kind of followed me here."

"Are you saying I'm a problem? Huh?" He elbows me, then cringes, his hand reaching for his bandaged shoulder.

"Not you. Los Cazadores. They've been on us since I first got here."

"Yeah, Desi filled me in on what went down last night. You're all right, though?"

I nod, biting my lower lip.

"Or…not," Will says, taking my hand and leading me back to my porch, where he eases down to sit on the top step. "I hate to pile on when so much has happened."

"So you're trying to soften the blow by beating around the bush," I say. "What is it? Did something else happen back at La Maison? Is everyone all right?"

I already know the answer, but it's too much to ask him directly.

"Mostly. Val… There's no simple way to say this."

"Where's Èvelyne?" I blurt out. "I know she's here somewhere. Why didn't she come with you?"

"What makes you think she's here?" he says.

"I'll show you."

I jump up, taking the steps two at a time and heading inside. I return with the sullied mask. When I hold it out to him, he turns it over to inspect it.

"Where did you get this?" he asks

"Last night, I went out for a walk and heard my mother calling to me."

"You must have been imagining it, Val."

"I wasn't imagining it. This is *her* mask. And I know my mother's call. I've known it since before I was born, Will. It was her. Someone else was in the forest with me. They had her mask. And her bone whistle."

Will draws his breath in sharply. "Are you serious?"

"You think I would joke about this? Something obviously happened. Isn't that why you flew all the way here?"

He pats the spot next to him on the stoop. When I don't sit, he reaches for my hand and tugs me down.

"I don't need you to coddle me. I need answers. So, tell me." I pause, staring at him intently. "Los Cazadores attacked La Maison, didn't they? They took my mother."

He nods. I wish he hadn't.

"How? When?"

"Èvelyne went out for one of her sojourns to the mountains. She—"

"Wait, what? Are you serious? Did she have her guards with her?"

When he shakes his head, I jump up. "Why? How could you guys let her go alone?"

He tilts his head to one side. "*You're* asking *me*?"

"This isn't the time to joke, Will. This is serious," I say, snatching the mask back.

"I realize that. Which is why I came down here."

"How did my mother end up here?"

"I don't know. I didn't even know she was here. I only came to tell you that she disappeared. I didn't think this was something you should learn in a phone call."

"Yeah, well, at least someone had the balls to tell me. I called Olivia, and she ignored me."

"Well, she's the least of your worries if *this*," he says, gesturing to the mask, "is what we're dealing with."

"*We* are not dealing with anything. This is *my* fight."

I hurry up the steps past him and inside, going for the top dresser drawer where I hid my stash of altar tools from Lidia. When I turn around, Will is standing in the doorway.

"Where are you going?" he says.

"I have unfinished business."

"I'm coming with you."

"No, you're not."

I take my coat and head for the door; when he doesn't move, I shove him aside. He cries out as I push past him.

"Look, I didn't mean to—I'm only... Listen, I can't sit around here waiting while Los Cazadores have my mother."

"I'm not telling you to sit around. I'm saying you need to be careful. Smart. Don't go off without thinking about your next move."

"Oh, trust me. I've been thinking about this for days now. It's about time I did something about it."

"Val, wait." He calls after me, but I jump off the porch and start for the driveway where Desi stands, talking to Dree.

"Hey, cousin. What's—"

I hold out my hand to him. "I need your keys."

"What? Why?"

I snap my fingers at him. "Keys. Now."

"Whoa, Val. Hold on," Will says, joining us. "You can't go off on your own. Not after what happened to Èvelyne."

"Something happened to your mom?" Desi asks. "Why didn't you say anything?"

"Look I don't have time to argue with you, Desi. I need to go. So if you won't lend me your car..."

"What happened to her? Is that why you're here?" he asks Will.

"You know what? Forget it," I say. "I'll ask someone else."

I push past them and start for the house, but Desi grabs me by the arm.

"Slow down, *prima*. Dang."

"I can't! I need to do something. Now!"

"What's this about?" Desi asks.

"You want to know so badly? Here!" I pull out the bloody mask and shove it into Desi's hands.

He shrieks and drops it on the grass. "Where did you get that thing?"

"It's my mother's. Something happened to her. Someone called me out to the forest using her bone whistle and left this for me to find."

"Who...who would do that?" he asks.

I glare at Dree, remembering her holding Èvelyne's mask last night. She raises an eyebrow at me, but I don't dare share my suspicion with Desi. There's enough tension between us as it is.

"I'll tell you who. That same animal who's been following me since I got here. The same one who chased me with that possessed coyote by his side."

"Whoa, possessed?" Desi says. "What are you talking about?"

THE BONE KEY

"It doesn't matter. It had to be him. He had the scar. That same one Don Vega gave him the day my father was attacked. It's too bad Don Vega didn't claw his eyes out!" With my fingers clenched into a claw, I drag my nails down his cheek.

Desi shoves my hand away. "*Mierda*, Val! You're freaking me out!"

"Imagine how I felt, seeing him again." I clasp my hands into shaking fists. Hatred surges through me like an electric current. "He was just a kid then, but I'd know that face anywhere."

Picturing his face makes me want to strike out. To scratch, to claw, to bite.

"Damn. I don't know what to say, Val."

"He tried to take everything from me. And now he's back to finish the job. My mom—I don't know if she's here. Or maybe...maybe she's already gone."

I stare at the bloody feathers, grasping them in my hand like I'll be able to feel her somehow or conjure an image of her in my head. But her energy isn't here. It's already dried and faded, dark like the blood on the feathers.

I shove the mask at him and turn away, unable to quell the rising tide of anger. A circle of moths hovers around me in a swarm, ready to attack. I grab his hand, squeezing. "Now that you know, can I please use your car?"

"Val, you can't just take off like this," Will says. "You don't even know where she is."

"He's right, *prima*," Desi says. "We need to tell Esme so she can alert the guards, then we can figure out who took her and where."

"We all know who took her," I say, clenching my hands. "Why do you think Los Cazadores attacked us last night? To keep us occupied."

"Okay, fine. But that doesn't tell us where she is."

"Look," I say, pacing away from him, then stopping mid-stride and turning back. "I don't have time to talk about this. I'm done talking. It's time to do something about it."

I push past them and start up the driveway when a car comes from the back of the grounds and stops out on the road. Lidia is in the driver's seat. I head right for it.

"Val, wait!" Will shouts.

I dart to the passenger side and slam my door to drown out their protests. Both Desi and Will rush toward us. I turn to Lidia with the cigar box in my lap.

"Let's go finish this."

She smirks and takes off, heading from El Rancho toward the main road to the freeway.

I grip the box as Lidia weaves in and out of traffic, heading south toward Hacienda en Las Lomas, eyes forward as though her senses are in tune with every car and truck ahead of us. I will them to move aside; somehow, they comply. Cars change lanes before us, leaving our path free and clear.

My phone rings five minutes into our drive. It's Desi. I can sense his desperation, his fear, as easily as my own, but I don't answer. I need to concentrate.

An incantation escapes my lips as we drive. My face is fiery, my brow sweating. My hands and arms burn like I'm too close to flames. I calm my breathing, sending out a wave of positivity and protective energy. It comes back at me and fizzles out.

My stomach roils with desperation to get there and finish this, with anger at the sheer audacity of Los Cazadores and their invasion of our territory after all these years of living in peace. Their constant persecution. Their relentlessness as they finally did the unthinkable—taking one of our High Priestesses. My mother. I won't let this stand. Staying hidden no longer matters. And channeling my inner fire will help me see this through.

The road leading to Don Vega's feels like home to me now. But we aren't driving out this way for a social visit. There is important work to do. Vengeance takes focus and determination, and I have more than enough of both.

Pulling off the main road onto a rugged dirt path, Lidia parks the car next to a large tree. I am out of the passenger seat before she turns off the engine. I slightly decline and slide down to where the river runs under the bridge. I kneel on the riverbank and take the scarf from the cigar box; I unwrap it and hold it over the current.

Lidia moves soundlessly and sits next to me without speaking. She nods, the determination in her eyes matching my own.

A hot wind rises, as does the pent-up energy of the grass and trees, and the flowers and insects awaken, reminding me of my Earth self, my roots, the power within me—within everything around me—waiting to be harnessed. I'm so in tune to the land I don't even need to look to the horizon. The moment the sun breaks in a hazy pink hue over Viejas Mountain, my skin blushes with warmth. A quick gust makes my father's feather tickle my neck. The wind? Or is he here with me, like Don Vega said? Does his energy remain, even now? I believe it does and that he's here giving me the strength and wisdom to carry out my task.

The current picks up, lapping at the edges of the canal. The sun rises further, bringing heat and intensity to my thoughts. My pulse quickens the way it always does when I practice my Craft. It's when I feel most alive, most like myself.

"Spirits of Water…"

Espíritus de agua.

My words percolate on the water's surface, coming to me in Spanish, voices from beyond space and time. Voices of my ancestors, passing their wisdom to me.

"…and Earth."

Y tierra.

"Of Fire and Air…"

De fuego y aire.

Wind whips my hair around me. When the ashes are picked up and taken away, I sense strength rising within me.

"I request your help so our enemies will pay for the evil caused to our sisters and brothers."

I turn the scarf over so the remaining ashes fall into the water, which carries them downstream.

"May their cruelty forever disappear."

The water greedily laps up the soot, and it dissolves below the surface. In the distance, a sudden screech punctures the silence. It's not the cry of hunger or an attempt to scare away a predator. It's a cry of extreme pain. And everyone knows an injured animal is dangerous.

Back home in Montréal, we survive, but Èvelyne encourages us not to harm other living beings. The spell Lidia gave me is one that protects—but with intent.

All this time, I've only wanted to keep myself and my coven safe. But I'm tired of living in fear with the perpetual shadow of hate lingering over me. I'm taking charge now. Doing to others what they seek to do to me.

When I stand, a sharp pain pierces my temple. I gasp, crying out.

"What happened?" Lidia asks. "Are you all right?"

Somehow, I make it up the incline and stagger to the car. I get inside and slam the door, still holding the bloody mask in one hand.

Electricity spiderwebs across my forehead. "I...I don't know."

"We need to get back to El Rancho," she says.

Another jolt. A deep baritone vibrates my eardrums so viciously it hurts. I get a flash. Black feathers. Bright yellow eyes. Then fire.

"No. We need to get to La Hacienda. Now!"

Lidia nods and then peels off into the mountains. As we speed up, the wind whips through the window. My ears burn with a shrieking call from Don Vega. Each one aching more than the one before it.

I place the mask on my lap and brace myself against the dashboard with both hands, squeezing my eyes closed. When the pain subsides to a dull pulse, I open my eyes again and lock gazes with a coyote on the other side of the river. When I flash my owl eyes at it, the animal turns and bounds away. Los Cazadores thrive on keeping us in fear. The only thing they have to fear is me.

I flashback to when I snuck from my bed and listened at the door while the adults talked about the rivalry between Los Cazadores and the Aquelarre Búho.

"Why would they do this?" my mother asked.

"This is what they have always done, Èvelyne." It's Don Vega. He sits with my mother's hand in his.

"But why now? We have been living separate lives. Aware of one another but vowing not to threaten the other."

"They are of one mind. There is something they want, and when their kind wants something, they will stop at nothing to get it."

My mother was quiet for the longest time. So long, I couldn't help but peek my head around the corner. When I did, I saw her—she didn't cower or cry. There was a fire in her eyes, one that replaced their normally icy blue.

"I will not let them take another thing I love."

Her words strike me now as Lidia races into the mountains, and a jolt of energy zaps me in the middle of my chest. The sky turns a sickly red-black, and in my mind, I picture the *ahuehuete* at Don Vega's hacienda turned black. The garden and all its life-giving flowers singed to dust.

"Hurry," I say through gritted teeth. "Please, Lidia."

The closer we get to the hacienda, the harder it is to stay in my seat. My hand grips the door handle, aching to get out, to run to him. Blood doesn't matter. Don Vega is one of my coven—my chosen family—and he's in danger. When we approach La Hacienda, I can't feel Don Vega anymore. When we turn onto his property, I know why.

Black plumes of smoke swirl in a torrent where La Hacienda used to stand. Flames lick the sky, raining down embers that have already charred the grass and set the firethorn bushes ablaze. I open my door and take off for the house.

The old cypress archway, the *ahuehuete*, sits collapsed on the ground. The baubles are blackened, the feathers and thorns scalded away. Phantom laughter, mine as a child, sounds in the ether. Memories, once vivid, are now scorched, so they are only remnants of themselves.

A gust of wind throws the smoke and fire toward me. Is it threatening me or trying to keep me away? I back off, keeping a wide berth as I skirt around to the side of the blaze.

"Don Vega! It's Valeria! Are you in there?"

Cries scrape from my throat, but the cracking, hissing fire is so loud, it swallows my voice in an endless cavern, silencing me out of spite.

"Tío Silas! Tío!"

Nothing. I go for a water bucket, lying abandoned on the grass next to the house. I have to duck to the side and edge my way forward, the fire is so strong. The acrid air chokes me, so I bring my arm up to shield my mouth and nose. Even if Don Vega is still inside, there is no way he could call out to me.

But that won't stop me. My eyes sting. The fumes are suffocating. From somewhere, there's a call, high and shrill. A blur of brown feathers swoops past my head directly into the burning hacienda.

I back away, then take a few steps forward, helpless, digging my fingernails into my palms, wanting with every fiber of my body to go in after the owl to help save Don Vega. But a gust of wind whips up the flames, and I'm forced back again.

When it dies down again, I start forward, but someone grabs me.

I spin, ready to strike, only to find Lidia behind me.

"Stay away!" she says, coughing. "Don't get too close!"

She pulls me away, but I'm desperate to get inside. Frantic, sick at seeing the hacienda this way. Spotting a rake abandoned in the dirt, I take it and bat down the burning plants, trying to extinguish the flames. Sparks fly at me, pinpricks of fire singeing my arms and legs.

I cry out, and Lidia hauls me back even further.

"No! We can't leave him! Not like this!"

"It's too late, Valeria! There's nothing left to do."

"He could still be in there! He might be—"

"He's not, Valeria! There's no way!"

Something shifts, splintering overhead. The wind lifts dust and ash in the shape of a wing, yanking me back as the arching beams over the patio collapse. I scream, throwing my hands out to protect me. The beams fly across the yard and land an impossible distance away from us, thudding to the blackened ground.

Lidia moves toward me, but not too close. When I catch her gaze, she isn't looking at me. She clasps her hands in front of her, but her eyes are determined and focused, staring at my father's feather. My hand goes to it. My instinct to protect it burns hot. Warning throbs at both of my temples.

She motions for me to move back a safe distance but doesn't touch me. We stand watching, waiting. I'm not sure for what. It's futile. She's right. I don't sense Don Vega any longer. The connection we had is severed.

"It's just a terrible accident," she says eventually, still staring at the billowing smoke.

"This was no accident. *They* did this. They did this, Lidia."

She doesn't respond, which is probably a good thing because after what I find at my feet, I will strike the next person who says the wrong thing. Smothered under ash and splintered wood, Don Vega's ceremonial mask sits scorched black. I lift it in my hand. Its edges break off and blow away.

My breath comes too fast, too hard. I feel like I'm about to pass out. My stomach turns. My mother kidnapped, Don Vega gone. The hacienda and all those memories of my *papá*, my *tío*, of the love we shared here —obliterated.

Smoke swirls overhead in a veil that shifts and carries with the wind, spreading like two blackened wings, threatening to smother us. The shroud divides and disparts into a swarm of moths surging closer. I crouch, protecting myself, but they don't come for me. Instead, they twirl around Lidia, pinging off her face, her arms, her hands. As she swats them away, the black veil around her shimmers, and like an oasis reflecting light, her face shifts into someone else before the swarm dissipates, and she bolts away from the moths.

I tuck the mask under my arm and dash for the car. Lidia calls to me, but my blood rushes through my body, my ears burning with the tortured calls from Don Vega and from my mother ringing in my head, haunting me with knowledge of what's happened and warning me of what's to come.

I'm more like my mother than I ever admitted. I will not let the Hunters take another thing I love. I will not allow it.

CHAPTER 14

After The Fire

Coming down the mountain from Hacienda en Las Lomas, oppressive smoke is an otherworldly hitchhiker following us home. It reminds me of the stories my father told me of the time he spent with Tío Silas, learning and honing his Craft, and how the spirits of those who had come before him were always around, like voices in the mist. It was a nice sentiment at the time, but accepting the spirit of Don Vega as only a memory is too excruciating to bear.

By the time we get to the coast, dark clouds obscure the cobalt sky, infecting the low-hanging sun with a diseased glow that mirrors my inner turmoil. Every inch of my body aches—with fear, with pain, with so much loss—and an image of Mabon, of my mother standing framed in the doorway of La Maison, comes to me unbidden. The promise of the changing seasons feels so far away now; I want nothing more than to surround myself with her white light. But I'm enraged, and the peace of home, of La Maison, is out of my reach. There's no way I'm leaving California now, not with everything we've lost. Not with how we've been pursued by Los Cazadores. They have to answer for what they've done.

Pulling up to El Rancho, the intensity in the air is a barricade that presses against us as we drive through the grounds. When Lidia turns off the ignition, an eerie silence represses all magic and light from this place.

There is no bird song in the lush palms. No lively music percolates from the back patio. Gone are the intermittent lilting songs from the stellar jays who jump from tree to tree. The hedges, once hip-height, have grown ten feet in my absence. Barbed vines encircle the front gate, intertwining with the bone talons of the archway.

The spacious grounds have become a desolate ghost town cast in a dark pallor as though the spirits of Día de Los Muertos still linger. Long shadows draw across the ground like piercing fingernails, silencing the whispered memories of those who came before. Paradise has definitely been lost.

I push through the gate and start for my cabin, leaving Lidia to report to Esme. Footsteps sound behind me, and I spin, prepared to strike, to scratch, and bite.

"Whoa! Val, it's—"

Desi's mouth hangs open. He reaches out, stopping short of touching me. "Where the hell did you go? I've been calling you."

I hold up the remains of Don Vega's mask. Soot discolors the feathers and what remains of the clay face.

"Is that...how did you...?"

"I had a vision. Lidia and I followed it to Hacienda en Las Lomas. We were too late."

"For Don Vega? No. No! This..." he reaches for my charred clothing. "This happened to you there?"

I can only nod. Flashes in bright orange come to me—the smoke swirling in a tornado of heat. La Hacienda in flames. Don Vega's energy gone, the emptiness of his land palpable, all the plants and flowers drooping, their life seeping from them; even the ground and the earth and the skies know he is gone.

"Did he get out? Is he—"

"No. They took him. Like they took everything else." He puts a hand on my arm, but I pull away from him. "I don't need your pity, Desi. I'm done crying."

Before he answers, I push past him, taking the mask with me. I'm halfway across the yard before he catches up. I cross the patio and burst through the back door to see the coven assembled around the kitchen table —some sitting, others pacing or standing around in small groups. All conversation stops when I enter.

"Where's Esme? I need to talk to her." No one answers. "Where is she?"

Desi comes in behind me. He brushes past, moving toward Dree, who stands next to the counter, her arms crossed over her chest, hip hitched to one side.

I gesture with both hands, pleading. "Tell me!"

"Val," Will says from the sitting room. "What happened to you?"

I find him in the sitting room alone. Brushing off the silence from the others, I race toward him.

"Look, I'm sorry about earlier. I'm glad you're alright."

He sits up on the couch, bracing his bandaged arm. "Who cares about me? What happened to you? Where did you go?"

All eyes are on me now. Behind me, Desi whispers to Dree, and when I turn, she glares at me.

"*She* did this. *She* brought them here."

"You forgot I can hear you?" I ask, returning Dree's harsh gaze.

"No, I didn't."

Desi dips his head and avoids looking at me.

I stand and approach them. "If you have something to say—"

"I've got plenty to say." Dree pushes past Desi, flinging away the hand he puts on her arm to stop her.

But I don't back down, even as she steps up to me. "Don't hold back now. We're all family here."

"*We* are," she says, gesturing to those behind her.

"We're all part of the same coven," I say.

"You're a guest. The same with your friend here. Only y'all brought your troubles with you. And now we're the ones paying for them."

"Seriously? Los Cazadores is a problem for all of us—everyone in this coven. I thought we were all supposed to stick together. I thought we were sisters and brothers. Or is that all talk?"

"Val, come on," Will says behind me, taking my hand and trying to pull me back.

"No! I won't take the blame for this. When Los Cazadores attack one of us, they attack all of us."

"Only we're the ones who lost something here!" Dree shouts, lunging at me.

Desi jumps between us.

"You think I didn't lose something? I loved Don Vega, too. He was an uncle to me."

"Just because you finally show up here don't make you one of the family, *Norte Blanco*." Dree emphasizes the last words as if they are an insult.

I stride to the photo wall, pointing to the portrait of my father in his regalia: his majestic jaguar skull headpiece with its fierce, pointed incisors on either side of his cheeks, the mane of feathers giving him a magical aura, and the feather and bone necklaces highlighting his physique.

"I'm already part of this family, in case you forgot. My father was Don Vega's Jaguar Valiente. And my mother," I hold out the bloody, soot-tarnished mask and move next to Dree, "is the High Priestess of L'Assemblée de la Terre. I belong here as much as anyone."

"We haven't had trouble with Los Cazadores for years. Not until you hauled your reckless ass out of protection and let them in," Dree says, jabbing a fingernail into my shoulder.

A flash of that night in the woods with Gwen and the percolating field of protection around La Maison assaults my memory. When I'd glanced back into the forest with all the coyote eyes watching us, the field of protection had moved somehow.

"Now we're all paying for it," Dree continues. "You couldn't have picked a worse time to show what kind of screw-up you really are."

I lunge for her, but before I reach her, Desi shoves his way between us and pries us apart. Instead of coming to my side, he moves beside Dree and speaks to her softly.

The door to the back patio flies open, and Esme rushes in, her dress flinging behind her.

"Stop! No more fighting. We have enough to worry about!"

She is barefooted and paces the room, studying each of us. Ash smudges her face, dried in streaks extending from her eyes down her cheeks. She flexes her hands and then scrunches her fingers into fists before she spins away and retreats.

Lidia follows closely behind to a compact room off the patio, glassed in and filled with candles. A long wooden table adorned with flowers and draped with jewels serves as an altar. Herbs are tucked in between candles gathered in groups, offset by collections of stones and crystals.

Lighting a cone of incense, Esme kneels in front of the altar. She sits that way, unmoving at first. Then, a low chant, glimmering gold, shimmers in a thread above her head and drifts out to the rest of us. She extends her hands in front of her, continuing to chant in Spanish. As she stands, she seems to grow taller, her head tilted back. But she isn't growing. Her feet have left the floor. She hovers half an inch above the black tiles, then an inch, then a foot. Her body flickers so quickly, she is a vibrating still-frame, channeling her powers.

When she comes back down and her incantation subsides, she bows her head and turns, moving toward us.

"There has been a terrible event at La Hacienda, but it was no accident. Those who hunt us are to blame—those who have sought us out for centuries, determined to take those and that which is most important to us."

"High Priestess," Desi says behind me. But she holds up one hand to silence him.

"I went to our Healer's home—what remains of it. The vial of Elixir is gone. This is a tragedy we cannot forget, but it also shows us why Los Cazadores have neglected our pact and why they seek us out after so many years of peace. They want our magic, our Gift. They want our Elixir for their own gain."

Scattered conversation filters throughout those gathered.

"How can we know this?" Desi asks. "Maybe they destroyed it? Or Don Vega hid it? Did he...was he..."

"There was no body. But that fire...the devastation." Esme nods her head. "If any man could survive that fire...Don Vega could."

I can't help but find some comfort in her words despite what I saw. Don Vega survived the lightning. It made him the man he is. I feel it in my bones—he is not gone.

"Why would they come now, though?" Desi asks.

"This pact we made was years ago, after the attack at La Hacienda," she says. "When we lost one of our most valiant witches."

I glance at my father's painting. I swear there's a glimmer in his eyes, his lips moving in a silent lament.

"It became too much, the animosity between us," Esme continues. "Even though we did not start it, we worked with Los Cazadores to bring peace between our families. It seems they have given up that peace and would prefer to take what isn't theirs. That's the thing about coveting—it's a corruption, one that poisons everything. It makes one turn to their inner darkness."

I can't help but think she is talking to me, but I can't absorb her words. The moths are screaming to me from the shadows that have overtaken the grounds of Rancho de las Garras.

"They have taken more than that," I say.

"That is why it is important now more than ever that we travel to Mexico," Esme says, "and rekindle our powers so we can protect the Aquelarre Búho with every skill we have."

"What about...what about Don Vega?" Desi asks.

The question hangs heavily in the room. Esme's expression does not change, but her eyes speak of something more than she has revealed.

"I went to La Hacienda. His aura was weak."

"So not *gone*," Desi asks.

His eyes are red-rimmed, and now I understand why he was so quick to lash out at me. He has been studying under Don Vega for months. Losing him is the same as it was for me to lose my father. Now I feel guilty about brushing him off when he wanted to know about Don Vega, about what happened at the hacienda, and if I knew if he was safe or not. I want to go to him, to pull him in for a hug, but Dree, watching me, slips her arm around Desi's waist and pulls him close.

"For now," Esme says, "we don't know where he is. We don't know if he made it out of the fire and is safeguarding himself somewhere or if he is lost to us for all time."

I feel the wave of hostility at my back from the others, but I don't dare to face them.

"We need to focus on what is most important," Esme says. "And that is traveling south to meet with our *compadres*, attending the Opening of the Flower, obtaining more of the Elixir, and protecting our traditions so we, as a coven, can continue celebrating our Craft. At the same time, we need to be careful. With Èvelyne Leclair taken, I must be the one to bring back the Elixir for us all. Which is why only those vital to the ceremony will travel to Mexico."

"But, High Priestess," Dree says, brushing past me toward her. "You need all of us there to protect you when you're most vulnerable."

Esme places a hand on Dree's arm. "We are all vulnerable, Dree. The Elixir is weak in each of us, not me alone. Only those who are integral to the ceremony shall go. Those of you who are the strongest must remain here and protect our home. You will receive the Elixir when we return."

Dree implores Esme, her hands upturned. "Forget this house. We can build a new one. We should be together to protect one another."

I scoff. "You were ready to throw me to the coyotes a minute ago, and now we all need to be together?"

She spins to face me. "Maybe not *all* of us."

"Enough!" Esme shouts. Her voice is so loud it shakes the foundation. Dree turns away from her, retreating to the comfort of Desi's arms.

"We have more important things than your argument," Esme says. "This animosity is exactly what the Hunters want. To divide us, to make us vulnerable. Weak. I will not allow them another chance to attack us. They have already taken our High Priestess of La Asamblea de la Tierra. They will not take another. Those who are traveling, pack your things. We leave tonight."

Esme spins and leaves the room, Lidia following close behind her. The others retreat to their rooms—all but Desi and Dree, who stand off to one side, talking in hushed tones. Seeing him go to her instead of to me is an insult.

"So much for being family," I say.

He turns to me, hurt in his eyes. "Don't do this, Val."

"Do what? It's obvious what everyone else thinks of me. That I don't belong here. That I'm just 'visiting.' I never thought you were one of them."

"It's not like that, and you know it."

I shake my head, ignoring Will as he tries to pull me away. I shove his hand off my arm and turn back to Desi. "I don't know that. The whole time I've been here, you tell me I'm getting in my way. That I'm lost in my thoughts. But maybe that's because I'm not your hesitant cousin anymore. Maybe you don't want to see me grow. Maybe you're like everyone else— happy to have me stay where I am because you don't have to see what I offer. Maybe it's something different from what you could ever do yourself. Maybe it would have been better for all of you if I never came here."

Dree faces me, her eyes shooting daggers. "You got that right."

Instead of leaving, I stalk toward her, leaning in. My face grows hot, my eyes glowing bright yellow.

"Well, I'm here. And too bad for you, I'm not going anywhere."

I head out of the room, but she can't help getting one last dig in.

"Ain't that the truth! Your ass is gonna be stuck here while we go do what needs to be done."

I race away from them, but it does nothing to stop Dree's jab from echoing in my head. When Will catches up to me, he grabs me by the hand. I spin away from him, forcefully yanking my hand from his. I can't stand to feel the thrum of his pulse, to sense the confusion and shock coming from him. Not with everything else.

"What's going on with you, Val?" Will says. "What's this thing you've become?"

"*Thing?* You think I'm a *thing* now?"

"Oh, come on. You know that's not what I meant."

"Then why don't you tell me what you meant?"

He scratches the back of his neck. "You're not the Val who left Montréal a few weeks ago. You're different here. I've never seen you talk to Desi like that."

"Yeah, well, I'm tired of being the nice one. You see what it got me? My so-called family shunned me. My cousin sides with someone who's not blood. That betrayal…it reminds me that I'm in charge of my destiny. No matter what people think, I'm capable of. Because I'll tell you, it's a hell of a lot more than even I expected."

I leave him there, stunned, and cross the grounds to my cabin. When I get there, I burst inside and pace the room like a caged animal, unable to relax.

Desi is one person who is truly supposed to have my back, and he chooses Dree? Him and all his talk about *familia* and calling me his *prima*… It's all lip service.

Walking away from him feels like I'm shaking off a shroud that's been keeping me grounded. Maybe Lidia was right all along. Maybe sticking with Desi is the very thing holding me back. I've felt most free when I'm with Lidia. I've been able to tap into my dormant talents and felt encouraged, not judged. If that isn't family, I don't know what is.

I'm done. Done being patient. Done waiting for my abilities to show themselves. Done waiting for Gifts given. I'm ready to take.

I go back outside, onto the porch, and look toward Lidia's cabin. She appears in the doorway, a silhouette set against the warm light behind her.

I focus my gaze, and everything drops away. The background blurs, and when she edges out into the light, her face comes into stark focus. Her eyes, hungry, find me. Her mouth drops open, a smile pulling her lips back to expose her teeth. I nod to her and in a hissing on the wind, I call to her. And when she responds with a sharp screech, higher and sharper than usual, it sends electricity up the back of my neck.

No more hiding in the shadows. I am ready to revel in them.

CHAPTER 15

Into Darkness

Behind the main house, weathered iron gates protect a hidden garden. I lift the latch, crossing the threshold between this world and the otherworld, where perfume and poison curlicue in the night air with tang and bite. Taking up a pair of weathered gloves, I pace to a spot in the very back, one that whispers to me with words I don't recognize but tantalizes me all the same, making my skin tingle with anticipation. I kneel on the ground and lean over the delicate plants. With the ethereal chatter of field crickets my only soundtrack, I pluck sunburst flowers of angelica and shiny black berries of belladonna, and gather blackthorn and florets of sunflower. I pluck out a stone and seashells from the border of the garden plot. After taking a small bell from one of the wind chimes, I stand and push my shoulders back, holding my head high.

Lidia stands beside me, staring again, eyeing my father's feather before she locks eyes with me. Her brown eyes glimmer an icy blue in the halflight. This time, she lifts the feather around my neck, sweeping her thumb over the fine barbs. Her fingertips graze my skin with nails sharp as knives. There's a hunger in her eyes, a darkness that lingers beneath her curiosity. It reminds me of how Nico López looked at me in San Diego. How his drive to get what he wanted was oblivious to everything else around him. The thrum of her heartbeat pulses in her neck, and her cheeks flush. There's a flash of something different in her eyes, like she is possessed, before she drops the feather and breaks the connection.

"We each have something the other one wants."

I clasp my hand around the feather and tuck it under my shirt for good measure. "It's obvious what you want. Though I don't know why."

"I just *want* it." The baleful gleam in her eyes sends a rush of adrenaline through me. "If you give it to me, I'll give you this."

She pulls something from her pocket and holds it out, a blackened piece of leather cord poking out from her closed hand. When she opens her fingers, a small object dangles before me.

Pale light filters through the window, but it is enough to see. No longer than a thimble, the object attached to the cord has yellowed since I last saw it. Hairline cracks tinged brown with age discolor the sides. An owl's face carved in bone sits at the top, its center hollow to help the sound travel.

Don Vega's bone key.

"You give me the feather of your Jaguar Valiente and you can have Don Vega's key. I know how much it means to you. What *he* meant to you."

"I imagine he means the same to you?"

She doesn't respond. Her eyes are dark, dull, bearing no emotion for the man who has protected our coven for years and devoted his Craft to teaching them, inspiring them. Seeing her so unaffected by his passing, as though he was a stranger, sends my heartbeat racing, pulsing in my throat so I can barely breathe.

Inside, someone calls for her. She doesn't flinch, only moves closer, dangling the bone key in front of my face. Her fingers graze my skin, and when I look down, the feather is gone from around my neck and in her hand instead.

I cup my hand around the bone key and take it just as she turns. A cold gust of air follows after her as she runs to the waiting van, ready for the journey to the airport.

The bone feels light and vulnerable as I cup my fingers around it. The smokiness of burned wood floods my nostrils as if I am back at his hacienda again. If Don Vega had his key, would he have called out for us? Could we have saved him from the fire if this was the only thing left of him?

Watching Lidia enter the van, I fight the urge to chase her down. To snatch back my father's feather and never let it go again. But I feel the weight of someone else's gaze. Desi stands in the drive with his packed suitcase next to him. We haven't talked since the blow-up with Dree earlier. When he took her side over mine and showed what family means to him. His expression is one of stubborn hostility and stoic pride as I cross the grass to meet him.

"So, I guess we're leaving," he says, shifting his weight from one side to another. "You gonna be alright here?"

"I'm good," I say.

"Look, I know Dree said some things."

I nod, looking past him where Lidia and Esme get their bags into the van. "Things are tense. I get it."

"But you did too, Val. You acted like we don't care about you."

"That's how I feel."

"It's not true, though. You know this, *prima*. Come on."

He takes my hand and I feel the rush of turmoil through his body. Fear in the timbre of his heartbeat. Anger in his breath, each one more harried than the last. Determination is a cloak of red energy that envelops him.

"I've never felt truly at home here," I say. "No matter how many times Esme says it's my home. Even with my father's photo on the wall in there. I've always felt like a guest. I've tried, but—"

"Have you, though?"

His words sting like nettle pricking my neck.

"I mean," he continues. "Since you've been here, you're either alone or with Lidia. You haven't really come up to the main house. We want your time, Val. Your effort. You're part of the family. But you have to act like it."

I drop his hand, and the sting of it shows on his face.

"Now isn't the time to talk about this. You're leaving. Just be safe, all right? I'll be sending all my love and light to you and the others."

"Val, wait—"

But I'm already gone, already halfway to my cabin, the collection of goods from the garden under my arm willing me forward to do what I need to. I don't need their approval. I never did. What matters is how I see myself.

I retreat to the stretch of land behind my cabin, where the trees are thick, and a small patch of grass is soft and worn down. I sense my father as I sit in the small clearing. How many times did he come to this place looking for answers? How many times did he sit in this spot and work to hone his Craft?

I'm no longer content to wait or ask for permission. I'm tired of being polite. I don't intend to hurt anyone, but I will not sit by and let things happen to me. I'll make them happen *for* me.

I spread an altar cloth on the grass and lay out my foraged goods. The stone I place to the north. I reach for my father's feather, and my stomach lurches at the space where it used to hang. Instead, I take the small bell and place it pointing east. The sunflower petals go south, and the seashell rests in the west. Sitting cross-legged, I take Don Vega's bone key in my palm. When I close my eyes, his face comes to the forefront of my mind, sending me back to the time and place I first held the key in my hand.

∿

After the attack at Hacienda en Las Lomas when I was a child, I couldn't sleep. I was crying, sick, and feverish. Don Vega came to me and gathered me in his arms. Out on the ridge, on the stone overlooking the valley, we sat, with me on his lap, my arms encircling his neck.

"*Pequeño pluma*," he said. "It will be okay."

I shook my head and rested it on his shoulder, spotting the cord of leather. When I reached for it, I expected him to tell me not to touch it, as my mother had done so many times with her own. Instead, he lifted it, placing it in my tiny hand. It was lighter than I expected and so curious that I stared at its white marbling with awe.

"This is one of your most powerful tools as a witch, *Pequeñito*. It gives you a voice when yours may falter. It grants you power when yours wanes. And when the time comes, it will unlock the talent your ancestors wished for you before you were born."

When I took it from him, it felt warm in my hand.

"One day, you will have a key of your own. Protect it from all who covet it, Valeria. It holds your power. A power that may fade but will never extinguish."

∿

The memory dissipates on the wind, and I'm back in the present, sitting in the dark near my cottage. I cup the key in my hand, feeling it warm at my touch. I know it's not my power alone that brings it warmth. I believe with everything in me that it still holds Don Vega's lingering power. Because he's not gone. He can't be.

With Don Vega's face in my mind, I focus my thoughts on him, feeling the power dormant within me, waiting for release.

At first, I think it's my breathing. Soft, lilting, like a sigh swirling overhead. But the whisper expands from one to several, then many voices speaking words I can't decipher. Opening my eyes, I look skyward and gasp, reaching out. The stars have been snuffed out. The moon is gone. As sound reverberates around me, I sense the moths—waves undulating like rivers of black silk, so numerous and thick they black out the night sky.

They circle and dive, haphazardly flitting against one another, a massive susurration descending like a cloak from high above.

The wind picks up and carries to me a voice, like a half-remembered thought lilting through the trees—Don Vega at La Hacienda.

These are not imaginings. They are your abilities, showing you the truth you seek if only you will allow yourself to see.

A hunger rumbles within me—I crave them. My mouth opens of its own volition.

Don Vega's voice again. *Not all dark things are terrible. It depends on the intention behind it.*

The darkness ebbs in me, drawing the moths down, down from the sky, until I throw myself onto my back to accept them.

For some of us, the shadows call. Some of us can use those hidden places, those hidden energies. But for others like you, the shadow blocks you. It obscures you from reaching your full truth.

My head flung back and my mouth wide, I extend my neck to open my throat fully.

The only way to move forward is to confront it.

In an unending current, the moths swirl into a singular ribbon threading into my mouth. Their razor-sharp pinions slice and draw blood as they enter. Velvet wings slip across my tongue, tickling as they surge down my throat, distending my belly as their flitting fills my core. Their dancing is an eddy circling inside me.

Your strength comes from within. Only when you free your inner darkness can you access your abilities.

My body shudders with delicious darkness. I sit up and look out over the grounds. The trees, the main house, the cottages—all turn to gray as the color seeps from them. In the air, shimmering energetic spirals encircle the roof, faded auras of those long passed. Glimmering pollen percolates up from the garden like fireflies. Chattering bats dart through the treetops, welcoming me.

I stand and proceed with tentative footsteps like a fawn learning to walk for the first time. Reaching out, I trace my hand in front of me. A trail of purple glides behind it like stardust. Someone advances, their aura a pulsating halo of orange.

"Val, what's going on? Are you hurt?"

His voice shatters the reverie, and I realize I'm still lying on the grass and haven't moved an inch. I look up to find Will standing over me. His forehead is knitted together with concern. He pulls me up, and I see my shadow-self standing in the grass. She comes toward me, and when she slips back into my skin, my entire body is alight with an intensity as rich as black velvet.

I sway and stagger a few steps, the swirling eddy of the moths now a fluttering buzz inside me. I feel lighter. Electricity surges in me, sending blood rushing from my fingertips to my toes. I sense something awakened. Something *other*.

I lurch away from him, drunk on this unfamiliar sensation. He calls out to me, but my other self wills me forward. I take off across the grounds before I stop mid-step. I hunch, crying out as my bones shift. My skin burns as it pulls and stretches, my cells expanding and contracting. I tear away my clothing, letting it fall away from me like leaves. My hairs prickle, pulling as they grow, stretch, elongate, bloom. The hair shaft becomes the spine, tendrils spurting from the center, tiny barbs soft like down growing into feathers.

I extend one arm out to one side. My fingers elongate, and each digit softens and smoothes, growing flat and becoming feathered at the tip. Unfurling from each arm is a spray of feathers, the underside velvet alabaster, the others chocolate brown.

My hair contracts up the side of my head, each strand pushing out into twin tufts like pointed horns on either side of my forehead. I'm suddenly at ground level. The grass is cool under my taloned feet, humming with ants and centipedes and other things lurking unnoticed. Will approaches, looking down at me with his mouth wide, his gaze one of wonder.

He reaches for me, and I cry out, releasing a peal from my throat.

Unfolding my wings, I spread my fingers, the feathers widely extended, splayed, and on full display. When I take a few steps, hesitant at first, each is a wondrous exploration.

I start into a run, hopping with each step, my head down. Determination pushes me forward as I flap my wings, eager to lift off. I waddle, pushing myself up, hoping the momentum will carry me upward.

Leaning and spreading my wings, I pull the air under me. My feet lift from the ground and I rise in a short arc, landing a few feet further in the soft grass. I try again, pushing through the air, my talons digging into the dirt to give me traction. Propelling myself, I flap my wings with everything in me. I rise. Flap again and again. I lift higher. I keep my feet before me to steady myself when I fall.

I hover as long as I can before my wings ache. With a final *shush* of my wings, I land in the grass, slumping onto my side. My feathers contract, and my muscles and tendons lengthen again. My hair sprouts from my head, tumbling down to my shoulders. My legs and arms ache as they grow, stretching out.

I am back to my normal self. I let out a cry of excitement and frustration.

"Val! It happened! You did it!" Will rushes forward. He peels off his coat and drapes it around me as I push myself up, my muscles spent. My arms and legs feel heavy, like I'm anchored to the ground.

But from somewhere nearby, something rustles. I follow it, making it across the grounds before Will can follow. I lunge, my hand pushing through the brush and clutching the animal. I pull it, squirming, from its hiding place. It's a hare, light brown, its eyes wide, its nose wrinkling, pulsing as it sniffs me out. For the first time, I sense that animal instinct in myself. But we are not kin. A hunger like no other washes over me as the hare stares at me, wide-eyed, its heart pulsing a rhythm against my hand before I kneel and release it to bound away.

Disappointment fades into the outer edges of my thoughts. I can move fast—without a sound. I hear things, and I can see them from yards away. I have all the heightened senses I need to hunt, to protect, to seek. I have everything I need.

I'm going to Mexico. And no one can stop me.

I lurch for my cabin with only one thing on my mind.

"What are you doing?" Will asks, following.

"I have somewhere I need to be."

I head for the closet and haul out my bag, shoving a few items of clothing inside before dressing quickly.

Will spins around when he sees I am clothed and tries to get ahead of me, but I'm moving so fast, he can only plead with me from behind.

"I know you're scared. For the coven. For Èvelyne. We all are. But you need to slow down and think about what you're doing."

"Why shouldn't I go? She's my mother, Will," I say, facing him. His pulse is fast; his heart hammers in his chest. So loud. Louder than my own. "I can't sit here and do nothing."

"No one expects you to do nothing. You can help those that are still here. Your other brothers and sisters need you, too."

"You saw me out there. I shifted. It might have only been for a few minutes, but I did it. Aren't you wondering how that's possible? I haven't had the Elixir like the rest of you, but I can shift. *This* is my Gift! The thing I've been searching for all along!"

The weight of this ability is so much more than I expect that it knocks me sideways. I stagger a few steps, but Will is there to catch me; when I look up at him, his eyes glow, reflecting my own owl eyes.

"This changes everything," I say. "This means so much to me. To the coven."

His mouth is a straight line as his eyes fade back to their normal blue.

"What?" I say. "You don't think this isn't monumental?"

"I do, Val. It's just…"

"Just…what? Don't tell me you're like Desi. Like Olivia. Don't tell me you want to keep me down here," I say, gesturing to the floor before pointing skyward, "when I could be up there where I belong!"

"That's the last thing I'm saying, Val. I just want you safe. To think before you go off on your own."

I shake my head. "You're exactly like Olivia. All my life, I've coveted this Gift, to be able to shift. If I can do so without the Elixir, it means so much. And now you want me to stop. To wait. Why? Why shouldn't I have what everyone else has?"

"Because you're not *like* everyone else, Val. This means something, like you said. I want you to be careful as you figure out what it means, not for us, for *you*. I've always felt you had skills you never knew. But that doesn't mean—"

"You can't talk me out of this, Will. If that's why you came here."

"It isn't."

My skin flushes at his response, but I push the feeling aside.

"Good. Then maybe you should be the friend you claim to be and support me. You've been telling me for years not to be so cautious. This time, I don't need to be. I'm going to Mexico."

A flash of disappointment colors his expression. "Why? To prove to everyone you can shift? Why do you feel the need to validate yourself like that, Valeria? What will that give you?"

I close my bag, slinging it over my shoulder and brushing past him.

"I have nothing to prove. Not even to myself. I know what I am."

He follows me out onto the porch. "The last thing we need is you taking off the way you did the last time, especially after what happened to Èvelyne."

He doesn't say it, but I think it. It's my fault. If I'd never left, she wouldn't have put herself in danger. She left the protections to call to me, hoping I would hear her, even though I was so far away.

"She's a grown woman, Valeria. You are, too. You're allowed to make your own decisions."

The way he says it makes me feel small.

"How did it happen?" I ask. "How did they get to her? Take her? Was it like Gwen? Did they injure her?"

He looks past me, not wanting to confirm my guilt. "She went out into the forest to that spot near the river you both love."

My nose fills with the fresh scent of pines and earthy moss. My skin grows cold with the chill of November air rolling in from the Laurentians. I hear the chuff-scrape of deer and moose rubbing their antlers as they head up into the highlands for winter.

"Why was she alone? No guards went with her? Not even her Maiden?"

The thought of Olivia makes my neck grow hot.

"She insisted on going by herself. Taking to the skies and soaring over the river, the pines. You know how she is about autumn in the mountains."

Crackling fire and charred bark waft around me.

"Did they hurt her when they took her?"

The question lingers, unanswered. I glare at him, my eyes glowing hot with an intensity I've never felt before.

"I don't know for sure. But they left something. Someone threw it over the front gate."

He holds it out to me; it's strange to see it here. It's the photo from my wall at home—the one of Èvelyne and I. She's like an angel, the sun filtering through her hair like gold silk, and I'm all surly with attitude, not appreciating what I had at that moment.

I take it from him. Dried blood on the glass obscures my mother's face.

I pull down my sleeve and swipe it across the glass, but it does nothing. I scrub, digging my fingernail through the fabric. Anything to get the blood off. When I do, it's like I hear her voice, her cry in the night—the sound of her shriek coming from the bone whistle. That person in the forest knew what they were doing. It was intended to torture me, to see my reaction.

"This isn't only about taking what we have," I say. "It's about them torturing us. Making us feel unsafe. Why do you think they did this? Why do you think they came here? Brought me my mother's bloody mask? Attacked Don Vega the way they did? To make us cower. To make us hide in the shadows. I've been doing that my entire life. I won't do it anymore. Nobody should have to live that way. Not when we have the power to control it."

"You know the High Priests and Priestesses made this choice a long time ago."

"Of course I do. It was my father's death that forced them to decide that not using our Gift openly was the way to protect it, to protect the coven and stop the Elixir from falling into the wrong hands."

"Right. And for good reason."

"But things have changed. Los Cazadores are actively hunting us. And I won't let that slide. I don't think the rest of the coven will either. Not after what they've done to my mother and Don Vega."

"Val…"

"No. Listen…I get where you're coming from, Will. I love that you came all the way down here to warn me about my mother. That means so much to me."

"That's not the only reason I came, Val."

When he moves in closer, the heat between us amps up so much that I have to back away to feel the cool night air between us.

"I need to focus on getting her back. And the only way to do that is to go to Mexico whether it's proper for me to go or not."

I take the steps two at a time, and I'm across the yard before he catches up to me. This time, he's the one pulling ahead, and he moves to stop me.

"Val, wait. If you're going down there, let me go with you."

"I can't ask you to do that, Will. You've been hurt enough already."

His jaw pulsates. He shakes his head and leans down. "That's the one thing you could never handle. People believing in you. But we do, if you'd only see it."

"You've been hurt enough already. Los Cazadores keep going after those I care about. I won't let them do it to you, too. Not again."

I push him aside and head for the driveway. An intense wave of energy hits me as I move out from the protective cocoon of the grounds. An image of crumbling stone comes to me, of trees and fiery orchids and the ocean beyond. Am I seeing this place or is someone sending it to me? Either way, I'm going there. No matter what I might find.

Like smoke drifting down from the mountains, Don Vega's voice comes to me one last time.

No one is immune from coveting. But to be driven by those dark thoughts, to make that your entire being, can take a toll and doom you to a life you didn't expect. One that is more dangerous. One that makes you lose things you didn't intend to lose.

He meant it as a warning, but I see it as an incentive. I've already lost things I never wanted to lose. I have no intention of losing more.

CHAPTER 16

From Within

Just south of the ancient city of Mayapán, the incantations of long-gone priests waft in a dizzying torrent, willing me, pulling me to the ancient walled city.

As I approach the defense wall and file through the vaulted gate, the ruins of this once-great Mayan capital spread out before me. Temples and altars are aged with deep coffee-colored stains and crumbled into debris on the ground. Shrines and platforms, larger-than-life sized, give the place a palpable aura of power. Oversized murals of war and masks of death linger in the shadows. But I am not here for a history lesson. Neither is my coven. We are here to protect our future. The Elixir is what we seek.

The Observatory—a large, rounded tower—sits atop a stepped platform amidst an ancient tangled forest. Tiny birds flit overhead, calling out a warning that predators are in their midst. A cool dampness perfumes the air with soil and decaying moss.

At the base of the stone steps, Esme stands in the center of the group. Desi shifts from one foot to the other, smoothing down his vibrant pink shirt. Dree spins her hair around her finger as she paces away and then joins him again. Seeing Lidia, how she clutches her hand to her throat, sends a pang of envy through me and makes my half-eaten airplane meal churn in my stomach. She has my father's feather, but not for long. I'm taking it back.

Next to her, Esme is calm. Centered. Holding court over the group, talking in a low voice to them, reassuring them of what's to come.

What I want most is to take off running, to feel the prick and pull of my skin changing, the hairs elongating, sprouting feathers. I long to feel the confines of my human body melt away in a flurry of feathers and air, becoming something softer, stronger, something so much more of this earth. I want to soar around over their heads and drop into the middle of their circle. See the looks on their faces when I reveal myself to them. Watch the wonder when they realize I am one of them, and I didn't need the Elixir to prove it.

All this time I've been focused on how they see me, how I fit into this coven, this family. I've been coveting the things they have, the wonders they can do, and looking down on the abilities I already owned. Even as I stride and feel the pull of my skin shifting over my bones, a voice in the ether comes to me like a forgotten memory. As much as I want to see the look on their faces, I stop myself. Even here, so far from home, Don Vega's voice is with me.

Only when you are free from your inner darkness can you access those abilities.

All this time, I believed the black witch moths were haunting me. And even though I've taken them into me to channel their darkness, it's all about intent. Maybe the darkness I've been afraid of is the shadowed musings I've had about myself. I've looked down on my abilities because they differ from those of my fellow witches.

I stop and will myself back to who I truly am. As I head for the group, even as the faint murmurs of recognition filter toward me, I will not cower or apologize. I have gifts they can only dream of. Everything I am is as vital to the future of this coven as they are.

Desi is the first to turn to me. His eyes go wide, and his mouth drops open. When I'm a few feet from the group, his lips curl into a smile.

"Cuz! I knew it."

"Knew I'd spoil the party? Or that I wouldn't listen and would come anyway?"

"Both! Come here!"

He clumsily staggers toward me and throws his arms around me. I'm thankful for the welcome, but the others don't look happy to see me. The only one I'm interested in is Esme.

But it's Lidia who speaks up. "The Opening of the Flower Ceremony is for higher witches."

An iciness laces her tone, sliding from her lips with precision and bite. I can't respond. I can't find the words. All I can focus on is the cord with the feather looking so at home around her neck. She had no problem taking it from me when she needed it. I realize now that she has what she wants. She doesn't need me any longer.

"My mother's in danger. I won't sit back and wait for anything else to happen to her."

She squares off against me. "You don't have the skills we need. This is for powerful witches. Ones who can protect and fight. Who won't need anyone to hold their hand when things get tough."

Desi squeezes my hand, but I smile, peeling his fingers back and patting his hand. When I turn to her, everything around us fades into obscurity. It is only her and me. My owl vision focuses only on her. She glares at me, stepping up to me. I let out a screech from my throat—the distinct call of a crested owl. It sends her back a step or two.

"Damn, cuz!" Desi says behind me. "You can make your owl call now?"

Esme moves between Lidia and I. She cups her hands on either cheek and stares into my eyes, her own having changed to the dark brown of the crested owl. "Why haven't you told us this, Valeria?"

I blink and my eyes return to normal. "I'm not sure. I guess I didn't want to seem desperate. Like I was trying to go where I didn't belong yet. But I belong here."

"You can't fly," Lidia says behind her. "What good is an owl who can't fly? This is the most important time for our coven. We need those who can protect the Flower. Who will stand and look out for others."

"I don't need to fly to do that. I've been doing that my entire life."

I want nothing more at this moment than to shift, to slap her with my wing as I take off over her head. But I'm done explaining myself to her after she used me to get what she wanted and then discarded me.

"She deserves to be here, High Priestess," Desi says.

"You'd say anything for her," Lidia says. "She's your family."

"We're all family," Esme says, spinning to face Lidia. "Enough of this. We have more important things to do. Come."

Clapping her hands together, Esme ushers us together. When everyone is quiet, she stands before us. The wind swishes through the trees, but when Esme speaks, it falls silent like she has willed it so.

"This is our most important day, the day we have been waiting for the past seven years. As the seasons change and the Wheel of the Year turns, the Flower opens and our powers fade. Our very power is tied to the earth, and it is time for us to renew our dedication to the Gifts our Earth Mother has given us through the First Witch, Lorenza de Salazar."

An image of Lorenza comes to my mind, one that melds every time I've seen her. In the sculpture at La Maison. In the painting at Rancho de Las Garras. In my memory of Don Vega's hacienda with her standing in the shadows, watching the aftermath of the attack from Los Cazadores. Her ebony hair is long and wild; her eyes, dark and curious. Long skirts trail over the ground as she paces. Behind her stands a hut constructed from tree branches. Mud and goat hair, grass, and straw fill the gaps. The roof is hatched and low, and protective sigils are carved into the door. She turns, and it's like she is looking at me. Through me. I remember a face in the forest at Don Vega's hacienda. Not that of an owl or Hunter. Was it Lorenza all along?

Esme's voice pulls me from my memory.

"We are here to gather with our brothers and sisters at the sacred *cenote* where we welcome the Opening of the Flower and collect the life-giving Elixir that will enchant our coven for years to come."

I picture the *cenote*. Lush and green tendrils draping down into the cavern below where cool water beckons. Oh, how I long to dive into the cool water.

"With the threats we have faced, we have to remain alert. We will have our compadres from La Asamblea Sur keeping a continuous watch over the ceremony, patrolling and circling overhead, watching for anyone who seeks to harm us or stop us from securing our future."

The air shifts with unease.

"What about my mother?" I say. "Are we sure they have her? Do we know where she is?"

"Our trackers have been searching for Èvelyne," Esme says, "but they have not located her yet."

"But they must have told someone something. They wouldn't take her without demanding something in return."

"As far as we know, she is safe. I feel in my heart she's still alive."

"I need more than that," I say.

"So do I," Esme says. "We all stand with you, Valeria. Èvelyne means as much to us as she does to you. And we will get her back, along with the Elixir."

With a nod, she leads our group to the base of the platform steps. As she proceeds upward, we file in behind her, moving to the top where the crumbling Observatory looks out across the lush landscape where my ancestors once lived. The air is cool and sweetly damp at ground level, but as we rise, it turns warmer, smokier, as though the remembrances of the past linger somewhere in the ether.

All four assemblies of the Aquelarre Búho usually gather for important milestones like this one, but they aren't here. Without my mother, someone has to stand in for her. As Esme makes it to the top of the platform, I recognize who that someone is.

Olivia's blazing blonde hair is like a spotlight, and when she turns, her gaze burns brightly on me. Burnished steel feathers fashioned into armor peek from beneath her dark green ceremonial robe. On the left breast, the embroidered insignia of our sister covens stands out in stark relief. Overlapping in the center, four feathers form the head of an owl, the quills forming the owl's feet. The feather signifying L'Assemblée de la Terre glimmers in white thread.

Seeing her where Èvelyne should be is a stab to the gut. It burns even deeper when we lock gazes, a smug smirk on her face. I want nothing more than to confront her about everything, but the last thing I want to do is cause a spectacle on this sacred day.

Desi leans into me. "Looks like she elbowed her way to the top while your *mamá* is away."

Facing outward, overlooking the grounds, three other witches remain in a semicircle, each dressed in dark protective gear similar to our owl-feather-shaped armor. Esme greets each of them with a long hug and quick conversation. They are La Asamblea Sur, our Mexican brother and sister owls who were born and live here, making it their duty to keep watch over El Árbol Sagrado, the Sacred Tree—to protect and guard its life-giving flowers year-round in honor of Lorenza, who was one of their own.

Olivia glares at me as I take my position next to Desi, who places a hand on the small of my back to center me. Plastering on a smile, Olivia greets Esme, who nods to the others but doesn't move in too close.

"High Priestess," Olivia says, moving next to Esme. "It's nice to see you again."

"Likewise," Esme says, nodding to her.

The garment Olivia is wearing isn't hers. It's my mother's ceremonial robe.

Desi leans into me, his mouth close to my ear, and whispers, "She didn't waste any time, huh?"

Before I can speak out of turn, she continues.

"It's an honor to be here representing L'Assemblée de la Terre as High Priestess while our High Priest remains home to keep watch over La Maison des Arbres," she says.

"*Acting* High Priestess," Esme says, absorbing the blow for me without missing a beat.

"Of course." Olivia shuffles her feet like she stepped in something.

Desi snorts beside me.

Even if she is only acting High Priestess until my mother returns, I can't help but remember her attitude back home when I showed up for Mabon. It looks like she got what she wanted all along. But I don't have time to worry about my place in Montréal. All I care about is finding my mother and securing the Elixir so the rest of my brothers and sisters will be safe.

Turning to a slender woman—one of La Asamblea Sur—whose eyes remain focused on the horizon, Esme asks, "What can you tell us, Lena?"

She turns, and her eyes flash gold, illuminating her sharp features. "We know she is here. Nearby. Our patrollers have spotted renewed activity in the north, near Merida. We think they have her there."

"La Madera en El Agua," Esme says. "The Wood in the Waters."

"Sí," Lena says.

Desi leans in and whispers, "She's the head of La Asamblea Sur. Another bad-ass witch, like all those who came before her."

A flash comes to my mind—a weathered building in ruins. Three large archways at the top of stone steps. A dark shadow flits in front of the building before I come back to reality.

"They demand the Elixir for themselves," Lena says.

"Why should they want it?" Esme asks. "What power can it give them?"

Lena's eyes darken. "The power to see what we are. Where we go. To be one of our kind."

Memories of the past weeks flit through my mind. How was I able to see myself from their point of view the night of the Día de Los Muertos parade? To see through the eyes of the coyote? It's a magic only we can conjure. And somehow, now Los Cazadores can do just that.

Remember, Valeria. Don Vega's voice makes my chest tighten, he sounds so close. *Remember how you can see. Your talent comes to you in many forms. Your sight is not only about seeing at night because you are an owl. You have an ability that allows you to see the things underneath. Beyond this world.*

"Our sisters in La Asamblea del Aire and La Asamblea del Agua informed us that their members were both tracked by coyotes who seemed to know their moves before they made them," Lena says. "They sent their Seekers to get a better look, and both described their eyes as something decidedly not animal-like."

An image flashes in my mind when I came face-to-face with that coyote in the woods in San Diego. The way his eyes didn't look quite right. Now I know why.

"They can see the way we do because they see as we see," I say, ignoring protocol as the others gaze at me. "When they chased me in the forest on La Día de Los Muertos, I saw one of their coyotes up close. His eyes. They looked almost…human."

"That's impossible," Olivia says.

"No. That's magic. *Our* magic," I say. "How else could they know to find me there, alone?"

"Maybe it's because that's what you do," Olivia says.

I push past her, moving toward Esme. "How else could they find our safe house in the Laurentians? Or track my mother, one of the best of us at staying hidden? They have our magic somehow. And they're using it against us."

"You're jumping to conclusions," Olivia says, moving between Esme and me. "The Elixir is weak in those of us who have had it. That is why the Hunters have been able to track us. Our magic is weak. We are, too. Our camouflage skills are not as strong. This is why we need all the tools we have at our disposal. Why we need the Elixir now more than ever."

Lidia, who has been silent the entire time, stands off to one side, clutching my father's feather. She is unmoving, expressionless, watching Olivia but not speaking or showing any sign of the fiery witch I've grown to know these past weeks.

Esme turns back to Lena. "That is why we must get to the sacred site and finish this. Only then will we have the power to fight off these attacks. What is our plan?"

Lena moves forward, her long hair tied back into a severe ponytail. "Our patrollers are already out and reporting back to us as needed. For now, the path to the site is secure. We should have no trouble getting there. And our sisters listened to your warning not to travel. They've sent what is needed for the ceremony."

"And if there is trouble," Esme says, "our brothers and sisters from La Asamblea Sur already line the procession route. They will remain there to guard us as we undertake this most sacred of ceremonies."

She leans in to give Lena a hug, exchanging a few words before Lena drapes two long pendants around Esme's neck. When Esme faces us, the tightness of her temples makes her eyes seem more focused and determined. But she clasps her hands together, squeezing and massaging her fingers in a nervousness I have never seen in her.

Despite her apparent unease, she gestures to our group, and with Desi on one side and Lidia on her other, she starts back down the staircase. As Lidia passes by me, I stare at my father's feather. I'm screaming in my head that I knew I shouldn't have given it to her. But for whatever reason, I knew I needed Don Vega's bone key. I wasn't sure why. I'm still not sure. But when I reach to make sure it still sits around my neck, I'm thankful I have it.

When Lidia passes by, I try to say something, but she looks right through me. There's something off about her, as if she's only a mirage of herself.

Before I say anything, Olivia brushes past. I follow, hating that I need to go to her. But like Esme said, we are here to work together. Any beef I have with her seems petty given what we are facing.

"Olivia, can I talk to you?"

She continues, not even glancing back at me.

"Olivia, please. I need to know about my mother. How did the Hunters find her?"

"I don't have time to make you feel better about any of this, Valeria. I have more important things to tend to." She continues, picking her way down the steps.

When we get to ground level, I move in front of her to stop her. "Will told me she had taken to flying on her own. Why didn't any of the guards go with her?"

"She's the High Priestess, Valeria. You really think anyone could tell her what to do?"

"No one had to tell her what to do. But maybe if someone had been with her, had treated her with the reverence she deserves—"

"Well, now I'm the one who deserves that same respect."

The wicked gleam in Olivia's eyes forces me back a step. There has always been a darkness in her, but I understand it more starkly now. Maybe it's because I have been away for so long that I see it so clearly.

"You're careless," she says, her words dripping with venom. "It's why Gwen was shot. Why she died. Why the coven is at risk. All because you broke the rules and went out on your own without protection. It's how Èvelyne was captured. Going out on her own the same way you did."

The gleam in her eyes is like a silver glimmer in obsidian crystal. An invisible aura encircles her, and when I try to approach, it repels me and keeps me from being able to move too close to her. Maybe that's a good thing.

"Maybe if she wasn't so willful, she wouldn't have been taken off-guard. I guess that's something that runs in the family though, huh? You. Èvelyne. Even your father, so I've heard. Another one who liked to do his own thing. Too bad it got him killed."

Before I can move closer, she pushes past me and goes to one of the vans.

I can't even respond, I'm so livid. Desi, sensing my anger, approaches me and puts a hand on my arm. "Come on, *prima*. Save your energy for what's coming."

I nod, but I know I saw something there, something I can't quite fathom. Like Olivia let her mask slip for that brief moment and, realizing I'd noticed, she had to insult me to distract me.

When Olivia passes by the group, Lidia seems to blanch, as though Olivia's energy fades all the color and light from her. I blink, trying to make sense of it, but when Olivia moves further away, it's gone.

But Lidia watches me. Something about her makes my skin go cold. She moves in that slinky way, and her lips spread into a slow smile—the one that makes my skin crawl—and it ignites a tiny flame of recognition in me. Before I can move closer and see what it's trying to show me, Lidia moves into the procession, her back to me.

Desi slides closer and nudges me with his elbow. "What's up with that? I thought you two were hella close now?"

"I thought we were too."

I sense the lingering power of my father's feather and chastise myself again for giving in to her. She has power over me. At least, she did. One way or another, I'm getting that feather back. Lidia's animosity seethes around her. I could shut her up with one transformation, one quick change to show her what I'm made of. But the more I think about it, the more convinced I am not to do it. I'm tired of trying to prove myself to everyone.

"Well, I'm glad you're here. To be honest, I felt like a real jerk leaving you behind the way I did. You're not still pissed, are you?"

I nudge him. "We're good."

"Good. Because we got enough to worry about without all that drama. Tomorrow's huge. I'm glad you're here to watch my back."

"Oh, I will."

"Sounds like you got something up your sleeve. You been cooking up a new spell or something?"

"Or something," I smile slyly, and he laughs.

"All right! I knew sassy Val was back. What are you up to?"

I can't stop myself any longer. I close my eyes and will forth my power. When my skin tingles, when my entire body flushes with a surge of black energy, I open my eyes.

Everything is sharper and more vibrant. Feathers sprout across my cheeks, the spray of black across the top of my white head like my mother. The chocolate brown around my neck like my father. I let out a low trill, and he shivers, shaking his head like he can't believe what he's seeing.

"But...no, wait. Val! You haven't...I mean, you're still...you didn't—"

"I haven't had the Elixir yet."

"Uh, yeah. But...how? How is this possible?"

I hesitate. Do I want to tell him about the moths? How they've been haunting me since I was a child? How they've lingered in the periphery for so long, and now, instead of running away, I've invited them in and accepted their darkness? Maybe it wasn't a threat. Maybe after all this time, they were the power I needed.

He's one of the few people I can fully trust. If not him, then who?

Instead of telling him, I hold out one hand, cupped and facing skyward. Leaning in, I purse my lips and blow. From my breath, a black witch moth sprouts, looking at first like a small cocoon in my hand. Then it transforms and grows, unfolding itself with a burst of black dust. It flutters its wings and lifts off, spinning wildly around his head until it dissipates on the wind.

"Well, that's new," he says, doing a double take. "What the hell, Val? When did this happen?"

"Just before I came."

"I get why you've got your sass back. Damn girl!"

I smile, but in the back of my head, I'm tempted to come clean. To tell him I took in the same darkness Don Vega warned me about. But it's too late. The others have come up from the beach, and I don't want everyone to hear. There will be plenty of time to explain. For now, I can only focus on one thing: getting my mother back safely and surviving the most important day for our coven.

When I move in behind the others, and we start away from the Observatory, a swirling chill envelops me. My entire body tenses. I imagine Lidia somehow slipping outside of herself and sneaking up behind me. Wrapping her hands around my throat, tightening her grip. I clutch my neck and fight to calm my breathing. Desi glances at me and raises his eyebrows at me, but I nod to placate him. The last thing I want is for him to think I'm too weak to have his back. Because now more than ever, family means everything to me.

But the vibe in the procession isn't one of jubilation as we set off for the most important ceremony of our lives.

CHAPTER 17
La Primera

When we arrive at the forest, the thick overgrowth of feathery ferns drape across the floor, and as we proceed, grasp at my ankles like a warning. Overhead, turquoise motmot birds flit around the canopy: some watching with accusing eyes, others calling out a shrill song to ward us off. Spider monkeys screech, but when we continue without heeding their call, they fall silent and witness our hallowed procession.

Woodsy smoke lures us down a rough-hewn path into the rainforest. Near the *cenote*, the air grows fragrant and cools as though we've traversed an invisible barrier, slipping into a liminal space between the living world and that of the dead. Every trill of the birds above us is a magical intonation meant only for us. Each rustle of mahogany leaves and the *pitter-patter* of condensation on the palms is a heartbeat of the past, of our ancestors, and the very life within us all.

Ahead of us, an older gentleman dressed in simple white linen clothing and wearing a feather and bone necklace draped down his chest tends to earthen clay pots cooking on an open fire set in the middle of a circle of stones. Steam rises, encircling him in a cocoon, and we gather quietly, watching him lay out stewed meat, corn, and water into which he spoons sugar, each placed at one of the four cardinal points on the makeshift altar set to one side.

As the prayer lilts from his mouth, he fills a small gourd with the corn sugar drink and holds it out to Esme. She bows her head, takes it from him, and continues leading the group toward the opening ahead.

We draw up to an outcropping where the tangled roots of strangler fig trees stretch over a yawning opening in the limestone. Below us, a deep pool throws shimmering reflections on the walls.

The spider monkeys bark one final warning and cease their noise. Overhead, a cry alerts us to a circling parliament of owls arriving to keep watch. Some are pale brown and white Mexican wood owls, like Esme. Others, the deep brown crested owls like my father, cast their orange eyes down upon us. My breath catches in my throat at the sight of the almost-black feathers of a Stygian owl, and for the briefest moment, it's like Don Vega has returned to us.

Some roost high in the trees. Others swoop overhead, their gazes trained on the outskirts. They are our escorts, our protectors, the southern assembly of Aquelarre Búho. La Asamblea Sur. The ones who will keep watch with Desi, Dree, and the others as we gather our most sacred Elixir.

The owls in my midst shift with the soft flicking of wings and feathers. Esme nods to me, inviting me to follow as she swoops into the cenote with Olivia following behind her. Desi gives me a tilt of the head and winks before he and Dree soar up into the treetops to join Lena and La Asamblea Sur in keeping guard.

Above ground, I remain alone, wanting nothing more than to follow them down into the *cenote*. Do I try to shift? What if it goes horribly wrong? What if it doesn't stick like the last time, and I'm trapped down there with no way to get back out?

But that longing within me is strong and wills me forward. All my life, I've been allowing the "what ifs" to stop me. I won't do that any longer.

Encircling the tree, criss-crossing roots from the strangler fig make a lattice of branches and vines that feed on the tree inside. Long strands of fig vines snake through the grass at my feet. I scoop them up in my hand and twirl them around to give me something to hold, but as I edge toward the lip of the opening, the vines cinch tight, sliding through my hand and growing up my arm until I am covered.

The water seems so far away, but echoed voices lure me closer until I grip the vines in my hands, my heels hanging over the expanse below. Easing one foot and then the other down, I allow the vines to take my weight.

When I am confident it will hold, I push off with my toes and let some slip through my fingers.

Past the lip of the opening, I hang suspended between massive stalactites like the incisors from countless ancient underwater beasts protruding from the ceiling. Beads of condensation on the rocky formations caught in the half-light glisten like gemstones.

I spot the assembly on a limestone platform jutting from the water like an island where an enormous tree, studded with spiky growths, sits in the center. I lower myself, and when my feet touch down, I find them gathered, chanting. Singing, stomping, their feet create a rhythm that reverberates up and around the bowl of the *cenote* in a dizzying rhythm, intertwining one voice with the next so they become one.

There's a familiarity here and it slowly dawns on me that this place is similar to the *cenote* Don Vega had painted on the wall of his hut for cleansing rituals.

All at once, a screech from above pierces the air, zapping away all light and sound. My night vision takes over, and in the darkness, Esme's owl eyes blaze bright orange. Next to her, Olivia's pale yellow eyes beam. Each has their arms outstretched and held to the sky with their faces turned upward.

A gust of wind lashes over my head so close I feel something brush my forehead. I drop to my knees, my arms outstretched in front of me, my head tucked between them for protection.

Another screech. This comes not from our Mexican brothers and sister owls. This is one voice, one entity. Lorenza. The First Witch of Aquelarre Búho, of L'Assemblée des Chouettes.

La Primera.

Radiant light penetrates the shadowed cavern in shafts that pierce and warm the interior like a sacred womb. Olive green pods hang ripened from the tree branches, and as she arrives, they pulse before splitting open. Inside, downy white fibers bloom into fragrant white flowers, the orange seed pods jutting out from within. When she stops to land, her talons scratch on the stone and it feels as though the entire *cenote* shifts under the weight of her.

La Lechuza.

Her dark feathers shift and shrink, and her bill contracts into a slender nose. Lorenza, the First Witch who came into being centuries ago, the woman who sacrificed her very being to become what she is, to create what she gave to us, somehow stands before us.

The air in the *cenote* goes still, all sounds snuffed silent. No one breathes. No one moves. And yet there's a vibration encircling her, encircling us. The bejeweled stalagmites release their pent-up moisture, and the droplets fall into the water around her, creating a musical symphony percolating with the laughter and song of our ancestors. Her face is radiant and dark at the same time, her eyes piercing the darkness with such resplendence that tears dampen my cheeks. I fall on my hands to hold myself up from being under the weight of her magnificent gaze.

She brushes dark tendrils of hair away from her face, revealing thin lines tattooed into her skin, decorating her lips like the teeth of a *calavera*. Sunbursts emanate around her eyes, a cross sits in the center of her forehead, and plumeria petals delineate her neck. Faded but indelible, they are an imprint of centuries passed.

"Sisters."

Her voice is commanding, deep, but with a thread of golden magic that slips around me, warming my skin and tantalizing me with her every breath. She glances at each of us, and when we lock gazes, electricity zaps through my body. Her face is the same face I saw in my vision of the treebranch hut. The same long, wild hair that shifts in the light, throwing eggplant hues around her like a crown of galaxies. That same penetrating gaze, curious and piercing.

She wears a woven *rebozo* wrapped around her shoulders. It flows down her back, draping softly over a dark, ankle-length skirt that wavers as she reaches into the folds and reveals a weathered object the size of a music box in her cupped hands. The outside is a lattice of darker wood entwined around the paler wood of the box like the strangler fig vines overhead. The others shift around me, but I don't dare to move.

"The core of our Gift lies within. But we must protect it," she says, holding the box out. "As the outer wood grows, it encircles the Reliquary to safeguard it from those who seek our magic."

As she speaks, the darker wood contracts, pulling back and shrinking like limbs extracting. As they do, it exposes the front panel of the box, revealing a small door with four narrow keyholes.

Esme removes her bone key from the chain around her neck. She inserts it into one of the slots, then takes the pendants given to her by Lena, the keys sent ahead by the High Priestesses of the east and west, and places them in their appropriate slots. When she moves aside, Olivia places her own key in the Reliquary to represent our house from the north. With the last key secure, the latch to the Reliquary pops open. Lorenza trails her fingertips along the panel before she lifts it to expose what the Reliquary protects inside.

A glass vial, set into a pair of wings carved from bone, is nestled in the center. Luminous liquid swirls and sparkles bright purple in the center. Four smaller vials sit empty, surrounding it.

"We must continue to protect that which we hold most sacred," Lorenza says. "To replenish this magic every seven years. If we don't, the Elixir will be lost to us forever, and so too will our Gifts diminish."

Removing the larger vial and the stopper, she pours a portion of the Elixir into a small earthen bowl. She holds the bowl out to Esme, who steps forward and drinks. Esme passes it to Olivia, the next to drink, before returning the bowl to Lorenza. The air shifts with each imbibing, their energy revitalizing as the Elixir flows through their bodies at full power once again.

What does it taste like? Is it sweet or sour? Is it cold to the touch, or does it burn? My yearning is from curiosity, not desire. My entire existence had been about coming here and one day getting the Elixir to advance my skills, but knowing I don't need it to shift has diminished the desperation I felt for so long. The only thing I want now is the bond of drinking it with the others. Yet, I already feel that bond. I feel their collective energy, the same energy I have within me.

Removing the smaller vials from the Reliquary, Lorenza disperses the remaining Elixir into portions for each Assembly. As the Elixir fills the vials, the liquid is at first clear, but then it glimmers like stardust—white like snow for La Asamblea de la Tierra, red for La Asamblea El Aire, black diamond for La Asamblea De Agua, and in Esme's vial, bright yellow for La Lumbre.

The larger vial never empties, not until she fills the last of the smaller ones. Finished, Esme moves to the front of the group and gathers water to create the new Elixir, but overhead, a call interrupts the ceremony, shattering the reverence.

Lorenza returns the vials to the Reliquary before she can distribute them. After closing the latch, the darker wood grows outward again. Thin branches spring from the original wood and intertwine in an elaborate latticework that overtakes the other wood, securing it from the threat.

Just as she does, snarls invade the *cenote*, swirling down in a hostile wave that sends me back a few steps. A flurry of arrows propels through the *cenote's* opening. Esme cries out and pushes me behind her before closing the circle again.

Lorenza cries out, a long peal that sends jagged shards of limestone falling around us, deafening me momentarily. The others around me crouch low to the ground. Esme is the first to shift, but having only had the Elixir, Olivia struggles. When the others have transformed, they encircle Lorenza to protect her.

Pressed against Lorenza, I can barely breathe within her radiant energy, but she clasps my hand. Towering over me, she speaks.

"You only need to look within to see your truth."

Her voice sets off a firestorm in my mind. A slideshow of images plays in reverse: my father, then his mother—my *abuela*—and her mother, who I'd only seen in grainy black and white photographs. She shows me various women, each shifting backward in time from one to the next until the face transforms into hers. Lorenza's. From beneath their feet, long, flowing hair encircles them and grows like vines, connecting them all. I see her face, the way she looked when she became the First.

Younger than she is now, she kneels in the mud near a river bank and a grove of thick-knotted trees behind her. She scoops up the water, gathering it into her hands, wonder in her eyes as she creates. A tangle of words in rhythmic Spanish tumbles from her lips and floats around her like butterflies. As her voice rises, her magic imbues the air around her, and the butterflies darken, but they don't fall. Instead, they rise higher, fly farther, swirling in an endless, dizzying loop up around her until they come fluttering down around her, falling like ash, settling on her shoulders like dark blessings. Others drop into the water, dissolving on contact, obscuring it with her dark conjuring.

Lifting her hands to her mouth, she drinks the concoction. After ingesting it, her hair lifts around her, swirling into an intricate mass in the shape of an owl perched on her head.

The wings soften and smooth down the sides of her face. She turns to me, and I see my eyes in hers. The way her mouth turns up at the side like mine does. I recognize myself in her and she in me. She is my ancestor. I'm made of her blood, her bone, her magic, and her purpose. The rest of the scene drops away, and the moths come, silencing everything and everyone around us so it is only us in blackness. She holds her hands out to me, and when we join hands, the intense surge of her energy takes my breath. I see through her eyes now—everything she has been and wills me to be. Every ounce of her energy—her power, her Gift—seeps from her hands into mine, drawing us together, making us one. One family. I am a witch born of her, of my father, of many generations of Salcedos. She is the source of our Gift. Of mine.

She turns, and her lips move, about to say something, but the sound of barking, ragged and violent, filters down the limestone walls.

Coyotes.

Lorenza shifts into her owl form. Her face is wide and round, like a barn owl, but her feathers are darker, a rich chocolate brown. She soars to the highest perch she can find. Standing under her with their hands joined, Olivia and Esme chant, sending a pillar of light up and out of the *cenote*. It drives the coyotes back for a moment, but above ground, screeches and snarls crash together in a violent confrontation.

I hear a growl behind me and turn to look. A beam of light illuminates an entrance, a tributary that feeds into a deeper part of the cave system, dark like a groaning mouth. Two pairs of glowing eyes stare back at me.

The coyotes dart from the darkness. Before they can get to me, an owl with an eggplant-hued streak of feathers on one side swoops down and swipes at them with her talons. Dree.

One of the animals lunges for her, but her back is turned. I let out a warning call from deep in my throat. She turns with enough time to flap her wings and rise above the coyote's head, but it lurches, teeth bared and snarling. It snaps its mouth shut, empty. She pounces, her talons puncturing its back. The animal yelps and scrambles back into the cavern from where it emerged.

The second one comes at me, and again, Dree sends it flying back into the cavern, but the first returns and leaps for her. It swipes at her belly. Dree goes careening to one side, hitting the wall of the cavern and landing with a dull thud on the limestone floor.

I spin and throw my hands out in front of me. A surge of energy, like when I argued with Olivia in Montréal at La Maison, flows from my fingers and sends the coyote crashing into the cavern wall. With a final yelp, it slumps to the floor and stops moving.

Dree lays to one side, her pain lingering above her like a cloud of hornets. I run to her, afraid to pick her up for fear of hurting her.

A harsh screech overhead shatters the chaos. I glance up to find Desi diving into the *cenote*. When I turn back to Dree, a cry catches in my throat. I reach out for her, stroking her feathers, placing my hand on her chest. She's still.

I turn away, the guilt rushing through my body with a sickening flush of adrenaline. Dree protected me. Like family does. We may have butted heads, but she didn't deserve this. None of us do. I am tired of them coming for us, tired of these attacks and how they always know where we are. I'm ready to take that away from them.

Esme circles the *cenote* with Olivia, but seeing Dree, she descends and settles near her, shifting back to her human form. Olivia lands away from the group. Lorenza flies down, coming to roost on one of the ledges overhead.

Desi shifts back to human form and crawls beside Dree, collapsing against her to sob into her dark feathers. I want to pull him into me, to help him, but I know nothing I say will help him with this loss. I need to do something else.

Next to Dree's body, there's a sheet of tree bark lying to one side. I take the husk and lay it in front of me. I slip out Don Vega's bone key from under my collar and reach for the coyote. Lifting the leather collar around the coyote's neck, I allow the metal pendant to sit against my palm. The coyote insignia of Los Cazadores is a brand I want to slash in half. Instead, I drop it and grip the coyote's still-warm hide in my hand. I swipe my palm across the thick, bristly fur, then clench my fingers around the bundle of flesh. I wish the animal were alive; I want it to cry out in agony like Dree did. I want it to yelp, knowing it's caught and vulnerable. But it's unmoving and silent, its life force spent.

I hold my hand out, comparing it to the animal's paw. I press down with all my weight until its claws extend. Using the sharpest part of the bone, I slice until I cut the talon free. I shove the claw into my pocket, then turn back to the animal, slicing under its hide, tearing a large patch of skin and fur-free, which I lay across the bark.

Above me, Lorenza waits. Her voice sounds in my head the same way I hear Don Vega's voice.

Look inside to see your truth.

I jab the bone into the hide, making two-golf-ball-sized holes where Dree's talons injured the animal. I shove the pointed end of the bone through at the corners of the skin to make four holes. Tendrils from the strangler fig tree drape down, tickling my shoulder. I grab them and yank, and they come away in my hand, thick and writhing like snakes. I encircle the vines around the bark, threading them through the holes at the corners and tying them off to secure them to the fur. Once secure, I lay my creation down and turn back to the animal.

Desi is sitting up now, watching with a glazed look in his eyes. I don't know if he understands what I'm doing when I take the bone, grasp the coyote's ear in my fist, and slice across the skin with a sawing motion. It takes some effort, but the ear lifts away from the animal's head, coming away in my hand when I have cut free the last bit of fur and cartilage. I do the same to the other ear, then take another length of strangler fig vine and sew them onto the fur and bark, using the bone as my needle. My hands work fast, with purpose, and when it's finished, I turn my creation over and hold the makeshift mask to my face.

Nothing happens.

I close my eyes and breathe in, willing my Gift to the surface, calling upon my inner eye to connect with the animal's spirit.

Nothing.

Lorenza calls to me again. *Look within to see your truth.*

The musk of the animal invades my senses. The prickle of coarse fur tickles my skin. I am the coyote. I see through its eyes.

The ravaged animal lies with its eyes half-open and lifeless. If Los Cazadores used this coyote to hunt us, to see us through its eyes and find us, can I do the same to find them?

Placing the mask down, I reach out and hold my hands, palms down, over the coyote's head.

"Second sight, I will you to come to me by this light. I conjure you to open my psychic mind as I speak this charm."

The wetness of skin splitting, the sound of tendons stretching and plucking, fills the cavern. Something warm and gelatinous touches my hands. I open my eyes, and when I turn my palms upright, the coyote's eyes are in my hands.

I place the eyes in the gaps where I've fashioned the eye holes. The veins extend from the eyeballs, suspending them in the sockets.

Lifting the mask, I turn it so the eyes are facing out and hold it up to my face again.

The vines grow and stretch, encircling my head and pulling the mask tight to my face so it cinches against my skull. At first, there is nothing but darkness. The mask feels claustrophobic, like I am smothering in the rotting husk of this dead creature. I take a deep breath, and then, like rousing from a deep sleep, I open my eyes, and I'm more conscious than I've ever been.

My perspective shifts. I breathe in the dankness of the jungle at night. The sun is setting, and the honeyed flowers exhale as they slumber. Everything stretches out before me in a sepia tone, the greenery around me now tinged yellow. The sky is a deep shade of blue, even as the sun dims on the horizon.

I blink, and all at once, I'm seeing myself from behind, from inside the cavern, somehow, even though the coyote is dead. A person steps forward, his bow drawn—it's him. Vicente López.

Heat flushes my body. I tear the mask off, sickened at being able to see myself through his eyes. From the gaping maw of the cavern, he moves toward me, and the light coming from the *cenote* underwater reflects in his eyes like a tarnished mirror. Dull and milky, his irises are devoid of all color.

"You thought that taking my coyote, my sight, would stop me," he says. "But I still see. Magic isn't only yours—it's ours for the taking."

"This magic isn't yours," I say, squaring off against him. "I know how your people stole the Gift from our sister, Lorenza. How they poisoned her, took the thing she held most precious, all to satiate your greed and bloodlust."

"Aquelarre Búho isn't special," he says. "Why should you be the only creatures who have this Gift? Our ancestors had their own magic. They used it to fight as warriors. We'll soon reclaim this Gift and use it to see those dark things hiding in plain sight."

He lunges for me, but a whipping tornado of feathers flies between us and flings its body into him, forcing him back. I dart in the opposite direction, falling onto my knees and skinning them on the limestone. The owl retreats, allowing Vicente to pull out a long, double-edged blade. He lunges for me, but I dodge his advance. When he swings his arm back in a wide arc to attack me again, I lunge for the mask I'd thrown to the ground. Somehow, touching it imbibes me with a ravenous hunger I've never felt before, and when I slip it back on, I turn to him and bare my teeth. A snarling growl escapes my lips, stopping him.

Drunk on the residual hunger of the animal whose fur I wear, I slash at him with one hand. My fingernails have grown into unfathomable claws. He lets out a yelp as they catch his arm and careens away from me. I launch an attack with my other arm, but he catches me before I touch him. Clamping his hand around my wrist, he pulls me to him. Through the coyote's eyes, I feel a sickening desire to obey. He, the master of this animal, holds an otherworldly influence over me. I fight off his influence with every ounce of Salcedo blood within me, growling, gnashing my teeth, butting my chest against his.

"Stand down," he says, smirking with a mad look in his milky eyes, devoid of color now that his coyote hunter is dead.

Before I can move, a flurry of feathers swoops down from overhead. The owls of La Asamblea Sur descend on the remaining snarling coyote, teeth, and talons flashing and lunging in kind. The owls swipe and slice at Vicente's coyote, yelps and screeches filling the air with earth-shattering cacophony until both Vicente and the animal retreat down the dark passage leading from the cavern. Even as they run away, our guard owls chase after them.

The others, including Desi and Esme, surround me as I peel the mask away from my face.

"They've gone too far!" Desi says. "They murdered Dree! Murdered our Mexican brother and sister owls! We can't let them get away with this!"

"I know that, Desi," I say, but as I step toward him, he turns away from me.

"No, *prima*. I can't look at you with that thing. Not after what that animal did to Dree."

He moves away from me, and it pains me to my core to repel him in this way. He's the only family I have left right now. But as much as I want him by my side, the sickening hatred within me squelches any pain I have. I can do more than just stand here. I can help to give us an advantage.

I hold the mask out in front of me and slip it over my head. It takes a moment for the veins to grow and connect again, but when I blink a few times, the crumbling building I saw before comes to me: Vicente's memories of racing up a staircase, darting through the ruins to the top floor. The back of the building is blown out to show the landscape of Cancún in the distance.

"I see a hacienda," I say. "Crumbling stone, sweeping staircases in the front. In the distance, the ocean." I turn my head, and the scene shifts with me, giving me a view of the surroundings. "Across a deserted road, there's another building. Weather-beaten and sunken in. A stone cross on top."

"A church," Esme says. "We have to tell La Asamblea Sur. They will know this place. Come. Bring our sister with us."

Beside me, Desi kneels beside Dree and gathers her in both hands, contracting her wings to lift her into his lap. I stop him with a hand on his arm.

"I'll take her," I say, gesturing to him.

He holds her out to me, trying not to break down, but the gravity of the events makes his body shake with the intensity of holding back.

Taking out a wide swath of fabric from my bag, I lay it down and wait for Desi to place Dree inside it. He brushes and smoothes her feathers, watching as I wrap her securely, then shifts and flies up out of the *cenote*.

I slip Dree into my pack, careful not to jostle her too much. After I secure her, I wrap the vines around my hand. It takes a moment, but they spring to life, lifting me from the ground and helping me ascend to the surface. When I get to the top, Desi is waiting. I hold out the bundle containing Dree, and he draws her to his chest. He closes his eyes and lowers his head, his shoulders heaving with each sob.

"I'm so sorry, Desi. I wish I could have done more."

He nods and brushes away a tear, taking the bundle and turning away.

Outside, the members of La Asamblea Sur who remain shift back to owl form. They gather in a semi-circle around the bodies of those who didn't survive the attack, their broken and bloodied wings splayed out around them. Esme whispers a silent prayer, kneeling over her fallen sisters. When she is finished, the members of La Asamblea Sur take the bodies with them, and in procession, they carry them through the woods toward the ancient city where we first met. High overhead, the motmots are quiet. The spider monkeys are still. The wind is silent. Even the moon and stars dim in honor of our loss.

With Desi at my side, we follow the procession. When we arrive at the clearing where the promise of hope for our renewed Gift shone so brightly earlier that evening, the forest swells with shadows deeper and darker, absorbing our sorrow.

Just before we go, I glance up to the strangler fig stretching into the starless sky. High in its branches, Lorenza sits perched, looking down on us; instead of coming to join us, she lifts off, taking the remaining Elixir with her and leaving us.

The night fades in around us like a soundless curtain drawn across the sky. Seeing Lorenza grow smaller as she flies away, I fight the urge to follow where she leads. It feels like the thread between us is being pulled the farther away she gets; when I can no longer see her for the darkness, it's plucked loose and tumbles down around my feet, my last connection to my father severed. I don't know if I'll ever have the honor of seeing her again. It fills me with an emptiness that swarms through me, funereal moths in mourning.

Instead of drowning in my sorrow, I let it stew. I relish how it feels to let it fester. I will need that darkness, that despair, to fuel me for what comes next. Because there is a showdown coming. My fate waits for me on the horizon—the fate of all of our Aquelarre Búho. I will face it now, come what may.

CHAPTER 18

Second Sight

Skeletal remains of burned-out buildings litter the road to Merida, the capital of Yucatán. Our approach toward the decrepit hacienda heightens my senses as we draw closer.

The coyote mask sitting beside me pulses with intensity: it's like having another entity in the van with us. Desi, who has been catatonic the entire ride, glares at it from the corner of his eye when he thinks I'm not looking. I pull it to me, covering it with my arm, which only makes him glare harder. Disgust curls his lip; his wide-eyed look of someone breaking from a fever dream makes the back of my neck crawl. When he catches my eye, he juts his chin toward my creation.

"Since when you been into arts and crafts, *prima*?"

I tuck it closer to my body.

"Don't you dare hide that thing from me." He glances at the compact bundle at the front of the van in Esme's lap; his chest heaves as he sucks in a breath and blows it out with force. His voice cracks, dripping with pain. "I wanna look at that hideous thing. I wanna see it in front of me. I want to remember the animal that took Dree from me. I want to see how you sliced its skin off. How you shoved the bone under its fur and tore it free from its miserable body. Whatever it takes to get payback for what they did to Dree is fine by me."

I reach out and clasp my hand over his; he bows his head and cries silently, sniffling.

Hearing our discussion, Esme turns in the passenger seat. "This is not about retaliation. This is about protecting ourselves, our sisters and brothers, our Gift, and getting our High Priestess back where she belongs. Remember what our sister Lorenza said—only those who are pure of heart survive. Los Cazadores have made their reasons clear for pursuing us now after being at peace for so long. They *covet*."

Her eyes glimmer, at first a pale glow that blazes bright amber as she continues. "They want our Gift. And they will do anything to get it, even use it against us. But we have something they do not."

She holds her hand out to Desi, who clasps it in his, then holds his other hand out to me so we are all connected. "Our sisterhood. Our brotherhood. Together, we can face any challenge—stare down any foe. They are the ones who act out of fear and spite. They shall never win over us, as long as we stick together."

I hold my hand out to Lidia. When she takes it, my pulse rises, racing at the dark energy coming from her. Her eyes are calm, not giving anything away, but her mouth curls at the edges, covering my skin in goosebumps. It stays that way long after she pulls her hand away.

Outside, the forest thins as we draw closer to the city. Gone is the lush, ambrosial air, replaced by the sound of engines and harsh lights. And under the din of the city, a deep, monotone droning lurks like a guttural growl, making my scalp prickle with anticipation.

We are nearing houses, neighborhoods. Old cars exhale exhaust on their way home from the workday. A vibrantly colored bus sputters past. Birds roost high in the flamboyant trees, their deep orange-red flowers like sunset, with the occasional bat flitting overhead. I feel both at home here and ready for this to be over so I can go north again. But how far will I go? Should I stay in California with my newfound family after everything we have been through together? Even if some of them may not want me to stick around? What if, goddess forbid, something drastic happens to my mother? Will they need me in the north?

Without turning my head, I try to sense Lidia again. She's been silent the entire ride, but her aura has gone dark. She has transformed into an unfamiliar person, and I can't understand why. What happened to her fire?

Where did her spirit go? Why does she feel so foreign now, yet somehow familiar? Why did she turn so cold?

As we near the city center, we're plunged into darkness as the divided highway ends with a desolate road. I wait for the pavement to crumble to gravel. Not far into the journey, our driver kills the headlights and eases forward. My heart races, anxiety and excitement at war within me. Every inch of my skin tingles with longing to find my mother. Desi's mouth hangs agape, watching me as I lift the mask to my face. The tendons and nerves extend and elongate, an endless tangle that snakes around my head and pulls tight.

My surroundings shift to shadowy gray, but the yellow lights on the dashboard glow with blinding intensity. Honing my focus, the skeletal outline of a building lingers ahead of us like a phantom, and I see a crumbling parsonage sitting amongst dry brush and rotting plants. From above, a calming, cool aura of pure white blazes down like moonlight on fresh winter snow. My mother. I'm where she is, seeing through the coyote's eyes from Vicente López's point of view.

Huddled in a corner, she has a white cloth stuffed in her mouth and cinched around the back of her head. Her cheeks are dirty, her hands scraped, and blood is caked under her fingernails. But her eyes are open. She's breathing.

"She's alive," I say. "She looks…tired. Cold. But…" I wait until I see her chest move. Her head lifts. Her eyes open. She stares at Vicente, at me, as though she can sense that I'm looking through his eyes.

"But what? Is she all right?" Desi asks, squeezing my hand.

I nod and turn my head, and with it, my focus shifts, seeing men dressed in dark, bulky tactical gear. Some wear helmets that only expose their faces. Others are in tunics over dark pants that glimmer like black diamonds in the darkness. I slip off the mask, holding it in front of me. "Los Cazadores are in full-body armor. They're dressed for a fight."

"So are we," Desi says, nodding to Esme in the front seat; her low voice drones in a hypnotic incantation that swirls over our heads in blinding vibrancy.

The van slows to a stop, and Esme is out like a shot. She lets out a long, drawn-out call, and after a few moments, a similar call, lower than hers, responds. As we scramble to follow her, an owl coasts over our heads like a sweeping breath. It lands in the center of the group, shifting into a tall, slender man, his ebony hair tied in a low ponytail. Esme leans in to hug him, handing him a bundle of clothing.

"This is my cousin," Esme says. "Lalo."

He nods, but his gaze is solely on my latest fashion statement, designed for the discerning witch tired of not seeing things as they are. I smooth down the fur with both hands, catching his gaze when he nods his approval of my secret weapon against Los Cazadores.

They speak quickly before Esme motions to us. "They will guard us from above. Lalo will show us a hidden path to the hacienda."

She follows him off the main road. Olivia and the others in the first van have already shifted and are flying overhead. I turn to Lidia, but she, too, has flown off without saying a word.

Low stone walls, crumbling into dust, separate the single-lane road from a culvert below ground level. We continue down into the culvert until the trees open up to a wide expanse of land on either side, dotted by burned-out houses, the last remnants of a time long past. The trees are sparse here, providing no cover as we make our way closer to where Vicente is holding my mother.

Lalo leads us into a compact brick building. The back half of the walls crumbled decades ago, and look out over Cancún. At the front, the remnants of a stone cross sit perched atop a threshold that somehow remains standing. It's the cross from my vision in the *cenote*.

We gather near the window, and in the dusky light, three owls linger in silhouette atop a decrepit headstone outside. Lalo darts toward them, taking the object Esme had given him earlier. In the darkness, the mask allows me to see him with reversed colors, like a photo negative. The glimmer of the Elixir shines for a few moments as he disperses it to the owls before he joins us inside.

Desi elbows me. "Do you see them?"

I nod, turning my head toward the hacienda from Vicente's perspective. The brush and *jacaranda* plants have taken over this place. Nature is trying to reclaim it. "About half a dozen stand gathered just inside," I say.

"There are more than a dozen," Lalo says. "Our guards are watching another team at the rear of the property, surrounding the perimeter."

"Do we call out to them? Negotiate?" Desi asks.

"Vicente López will not negotiate," Esme says, clenching her hands into fists. "He is too proud for that."

"He won't stop until he takes everything from us," I say.

"How do you know?" Desi asks.

"Èvelyne believed that living in hiding and not using our magic against them would keep the truce intact," Esme says. "It seems they have taken our silence as an invitation to hunt us down as they did in the past."

Esme turns to me, and that's when Desi gasps.

"He's the one, isn't he? The one who killed *tu papá*?"

I slip the mask over my face. With each step, the mask allows me to connect to Vicente, the master of this creature. I can smell the tang of his sweat, feel the rise and fall of his chest as he breathes, hear the deep timbre of his voice as he confers with his fellow Hunters. I experience everything as though I'm him.

A twig snaps, and we stop. My breath hitches in my throat, mirroring Vicente's reaction. I feel dizzy as he spins his head from one side to the other, trying to pinpoint what he senses in the shadows that spread beyond the hacienda. The connection the mask has forged gives us away to him, even if he doesn't recognize what he's tapped into.

I nod, still wearing the mask and keeping my gaze trained on Èvelyne. The way he watches her like a salivating predator is all the motivation I need.

Perhaps sensing my determination, Desi crouches, preparing to shift. "So what are we waiting for? We can't let them hunt us and kill us. We can't let them get away with thinking they can take whatever they want and eradicate us like we are some kind of pest."

"We will take them in two waves," Lalo says. "The first is waiting to move in for cover. The rest will cycle through in groups of three, fighting them off until we free Èvelyne."

Esme nods, her face serious. "Be cautious. They will do anything to separate us."

The others shift and prepare to take flight. I am alone on the ground with Desi flying above me on the right. My guardian owl. My protector. I glance up at him, and he bows his head ever so slightly, taking my lead as I use Vicente's vision as a weapon against him.

Through the brush, the husk of the hacienda comes into view. Three arched doorways sit atop a double staircase. It's dark within, but the faintest hint of light emanates from beyond the hacienda—the residue of a fire recently snuffed out. The scent of charred ash lingers smoky in the air.

Instead of taking the main staircase, I move past the stone wall to find a place where it sinks into the brush and plants overtake the structure. An arrow whizzes at me; I duck before it makes contact. Desi peels off, narrowly avoiding the projectile. I'm left alone but undeterred. I force my way inside, skulking along the floor. Somehow, I can sense them better this way. I proceed, using my hands like two feet to propel me forward.

Inside, I weave past a half wall and locate a set of stairs leading up to the back of the house. I stand and wait, listening, and lift my head to smell the air. Voices rise from beyond.

I peer out through the fragments of a shattered window, the glass time-stained and milky. Beyond the driveway, lanterns illuminate the woods. A dozen or more figures spread across the treeline in battle formation. One of them paces, stopping when he is a few yards away. He looks directly at me. But I see him in split-screen—him looking at me from the forest and me peering out at him. Vicente López. The man bound to this coyote whose eyes I use to see. The man whose throat I want to slash with my talons.

"We know you're in there," he booms, looking up at me. "And we aren't going anywhere until we deal with you."

Before I can respond, a cloud descends from above. The Asamblea Sur guard owls swoop over Los Cazadores, flying over their heads, some soaring sideways to avoid the poisoned arrow assault from the Hunters. Desi lands on the beam above me.

In my mind's eye, Vicente commands the men. His own thoughts give him away when he glances up at a shattered window over my head. Èvelyne. She's directly above me.

But it isn't only his perspective of me that I see. I see his thoughts, his memories of their travels here. Then I see other memories of someone else, a shadow I can't make out with an aura of dark red that turns black the longer I watch.

I see flashes of Montréal, of the woods outside La Maison, first from the night of Mabon with Gwen. They're perspectives I never had from places I never went. Then, another image—the leaves have turned from crimson and gold to brown, and the first frost glazes the landscape like sugar. This is from a time when I was gone, already exploring my new life in California. I don't know those moments. The memories aren't my own. They belong to someone else.

His gaze snaps to me as if he can sense I see inside his head. When he lifts his arrow and points it at me, it's like I am five years old again. Terror fills me.

I yank the mask away from my face to sever his connection to me and cry out in my owl voice. My mother responds. Her call is a choked screech, but she's still alive. I spin and scramble through the debris, tripping over it to get to the crumbling stairs. I clamber up and move into an open doorway.

Èvelyne is in the corner of the room. She shakes her head, her eyes aglow. Before I can react, a powerful blast of energy from the corner knocks me sideways. I land with a thud, kicking up dust that obscures my vision. I flip over onto my side to find a shadowy figure standing over me.

Èvelyne whistles to me, the melody only she and I know. Just a few notes in an unending loop, enough to conjure an invisible connection between my thoughts and hers. Instead of seeing through the coyote's eyes, the vision changes. Cold replaces the heat of this place. My skin prickles at the vision, my breath escaping in mist. Èvelyne is showing me her flight over the trees back home, her wings spread out as she soars across the impressive expanse of the icy river below. But a sharp impact, a piercing blow, takes her down. When she lands, crying out, she looks up to find a Hunter standing over her alongside someone with a soft, lilting voice. The voices are harried, their tone impatient and guilt-ridden. A cloaked figure pauses, looking over at her for a moment. As the figure turns away again, the moonlight catches her face. Olivia's almond eyes peer back at her.

Blinking, the vision dissipates like smoke. Olivia smiles down at me as if she has seen the vision play over in her mind at the same time. She radiates dark red, the same way she did in Evelyne's vision: the same as when she taunted me in the forest with my mother's mask. The shadow envelops her, absorbing the grim pall of the malevolence fueling her, a disturbing shroud that swallows any light left within her.

"I only took what I deserved. I should have been rewarded for my loyalty long ago," she says, taking Èvelyne by her hair and slamming her head against the wall, where she falls limp. "Èvelyne only held out on appointing her Maiden because she was waiting for you. But when she realized you would never step up, she still didn't want to admit it. So I made her see. Showed her that you were never the right one for the job. I took that last step, and it was exactly what she needed to see."

Her words burn like acid in my brain. Every muscle in my body cries out to attack her, but I keep my breathing calm, controlling my anger.

"That's the problem with you, Olivia," I say, sitting up on my elbows. "You've always felt like you *deserved* things. Even if you didn't earn them."

She kicks me onto my back, pressing my shoulder to the floor with her boot.

"Only a traitor would use what these men have to see," she says. "That you use their vision proves you aren't meant to lead this coven."

"Me? I'm the traitor? Only the worst kind of person would betray their coven for their own gain." I struggle and kick, but she kneels over me, her eyes blazing bright red.

Pressing me down so I can't move, she tears Don Vega's bone key from around my neck. "It's not like I'm taking something away from you, Valeria. You never wanted it. Otherwise, you wouldn't have left the coven to practice on your own. You wouldn't have bailed to join another coven when things got tough."

"That's the thing," I say, glancing at my mother, who has roused and struggles to free herself. "You see us as something different, but we are *all* family."

She laughs. "We might all be owls, but that doesn't make us family."

"Without my bloodline, there would be no Aquelarre Búho."

She shrugs. "It doesn't matter who started this magic or our Craft. It matters what we do with it. And I wouldn't trust some impulsive, indecisive half-breed to run our house."

My memory flashes to the crudely spray-painted insult on my door back in Montréal.

"Of course it was you," I say, lunging for her and grabbing her by the throat. "Who else would do something so disgusting?"

She tears my hands away. "I'm only telling it like it is. You're so conflicted, so blinded by how you keep failing at both sides of yourself. How the hell do you think you can lead our coven?"

I swipe at her, my nails raking across her forearm, but she sidesteps my attack. "At least I didn't sell out my sisters for something I don't deserve!"

Behind her, Lidia appears in the doorway, but she makes no move to help me. Instead, she smirks, watching our confrontation with cold amusement before she saunters into the room to stand beside Olivia.

"Oh, I'll get what I deserve," Lidia says, moving closer like a stalking predator. "And so will you."

Her voice gives me chills. It's Lidia speaking, but Olivia's voice comes from her.

I kick and claw, throwing my weight against her, but she is freakishly strong and pins me to the floor. When I try again, I throw all my energy into her and buck Lidia off. I scramble to pull the mask down again. Olivia looks normal, but Lidia is a shadow of herself, a transparent, ghost-like apparition standing over me. She shimmers in my animal vision. But when she moves in front of Olivia, Lidia seeps into her, and the two, Olivia and Lidia, merge into one person.

Olivia bursts out laughing. I charge at her and wrap my hands around her throat. I tear the pendant from her neck, and an explosion like black ink propels them apart, with Olivia careening to one side and Lidia, now herself again, falling to her knees.

Her eyelids flutter as though she's waking from a dream. Glancing at me, her brow furrows as though I'm a stranger. There's a moment of recognition when she sees Èvelyne, but her body is seized by panic, and she falls to the floor, scurrying away from me.

"Wh-what is this? Where am I?" Lidia says.

I frown and rush at her. "What do you mean? Why the hell would you attack me, Lidia?"

"It...it wasn't me!" she says, skittering away from me. "I don't understand! I...I've done none of this!"

"Don't act like you're innocent," I say, reaching out to grab her by the arm.

Lidia studies Olivia's face, and then the look of realization slides onto her face. "Olivia? From the northern assembly?"

"Oh, please," I say. "Don't act like you don't know her."

Lidia wraps her arms around herself, eyeing Olivia, who stands with her hands propped on her hips.

"I do. But only from the time she came to visit the coven. Said she was there for advice on becoming Èvelyne's Maiden. She wanted to know how I serve Esme, the magic I use."

Stepping toward Lidia, Olivia tosses her hair over her shoulder and reaches out for Lidia, dragging one finger along Lidia's jawline. Her hand comes to rest at Lidia's throat, where my father's feather glows bright orange. Olivia tears it from her. Lidia shudders and pushes away from her.

"All it took," Olivia says, her sickening smile making my pulse surge, "was one meeting. Just a little snip from her head, a few things she holds near and dear, and I had what I needed. It was so easy. As easy as it was to take this worthless memento from you, with a little help from our friend here."

She tosses the feather to the floor, stomping on it before she pulls out a small, carved owl wrapped in purple thread from her pocket. She holds it out, waggling it in Lidia's face, cackling.

"You've been possessing her?" I say.

"All this time, I thought you were clueless," Olivia says. "I guess all it took was a little magic for you to understand what was right in front of you."

She produces a photograph bound in a black string that has unraveled. In the picture, Lidia is sitting on the stoop of her cabin at Rancho Des Las Garras, a wide smile on her face.

"All I needed was a tiny window," Olivia says, taking the loose end of the string and rewinding it around the photograph once. "Lidia's vulnerability was exactly what I needed to gain control of her."

Olivia wraps the binding again. As she does, Lidia's breathing becomes more labored.

"And when I did," Olivia says, completing her binding, "it gave me everything I needed to take what I deserved."

"You could have been Èvelyne's Maiden without torturing her," I say, starting toward Lidia, who clutches at her throat.

"Being Maiden is a stepping stone to getting control over the Elixir," Olivia says. "And let's face it, your mother is powerful, but she's no Primera."

Èvelyne glares up at her.

"You can't think that you would ever be as powerful and worthy as Lorenza," I say.

Lidia gasps, her face going bright red as she struggles to breathe. When I step between them, Olivia shoves me aside.

"We won't find out until I try."

With a sharp pull, Olivia cinches the black binding on the photograph. Lidia staggers backward. I scramble to catch her, but Olivia thrusts her hands out at me. The force of her power sends me skidding past my mother across the concrete floor. With a swift kick, Olivia sends Lidia flying out the window to the ground below.

I hit the wall, sending crumbling mortar raining down on my face. Before I can retaliate, a screech sounds above me. Desi swoops down, his talons extended. He flaps wildly, his talons scraping over Olivia's head, drawing blood from her scalp and above her eyes. Throwing her head back, she bends back at an impossible angle to avoid his attack.

When he comes at her again, she grabs him, tossing him aside, then races toward me. I yank the mask from where it hangs around my neck and clamp it to my face as she tries to snatch it away. I pull it away though as something in the corner of my eye moves. Olivia shrieks and flies through the crumbling windowpane, falling to the ground, her screams ending with a final thud.

Spinning, I find my mother has freed herself. She lies on her belly, her arms extended in front of her; she used up her strength to protect me.

Abruptly, my point of view shifts to Vicente's, who has heard the crash and watched Olivia fly out the back of the building. He stands shoulder to shoulder with his troops, the house looming behind him. Flames dance in the soot-darkened glass of their lanterns.

Outside, Los Cazadores let out a series of shouts, and Vicente glances skyward. Overhead, Lalo and La Asamblea Sur bombard them, diving and slicing at their faces and throats. The men fling themselves to the ground. Feathers tipped with tiny razors draw blood from their arms, their hands, and their eyes.

I scramble to my mother's side and place both hands on her head, whispering a healing incantation feverishly, focusing all my energy on her. At first, she lays still, her breathing shallow; when she stirs and slides her hand out to touch my leg, I feel like I can breathe again for the first time.

She glances up at me, clutching my father's feather. Seeing her through this mask allows me to witness the magic and light and everything wondrous within her. Even as the confrontation rages outside, she tries to sit up.

"Be still," I say, helping her. "The others will fight for us."

"We don't cower. Not after what they've done."

"We face them together then," I say, pushing the mask up onto the top of my head. "As we always have done and always will do."

From outside, a shrill scream punctuates the darkness. I scramble to my feet, and after helping my mother up, we move to the window. Only a handful of the Hunters remain, but Vicente is holding an owl by both wings. Olivia.

She thrashes, but he holds her pinned in his arms.

"We were promised The Elixir," he says, forcing her wings open as far as they can go. "We won't leave until we get it, or we kill every one of you."

"What about the truce between our people?" I say.

"That pact served my people...for a time. But why should such magic be reserved for so few?"

"You promised peace, but you've betrayed that promise. You hunt us. Torture us. Force us into hiding."

A low laugh rumbled in his chest. "Only cowards hide. How does it feel knowing your sisters don't even feel you're worth protecting?"

My gaze darts toward the tree line. I search for the silhouette or shape of an owl in the shadows, but there are none. Did they leave us here? Do they expect Èvelyne and me to fight our way out alone?

The men move together, talking fast and low. When they break apart and fall into line again, Vicente hands Olivia to Nico, who stands next to him. Vicente pulls an arrow from Nico's quiver and draws his bow, training it on us.

When I lock eyes with him, the rest of the world drops away. The forest fades into a blur of shadows, like charcoal smeared across gray paper. Leaves flutter silently in the breeze. The flicker of lantern light makes his face appear gaunt, the way it looks in my memories. His eyes, devoid of all color, find me. Vicente López has led his Hunters to kill us.

"We never agreed to that deal," I say.

"Your sister witch did. I suppose we should thank her," he says. "If it wasn't for her ambition, we wouldn't have found you as you hid right under our noses using the magic we've been seeking for centuries."

As he speaks, the visions I had during my spiritual cleansing with Don Vega play out in my mind. The warriors gathered on the outskirts of the village, their ambush where they burned the huts, spoiled the food and hunted down Lorenza as if she was an animal to tame. The anguish she faced watching her child suffer. Despite that, she hid away the Elixir and faced every punishment they gave her. In the end, when she was battered and bruised when she had everything she ever cared about stripped from her, she steeled herself, picked herself up, and went to the river to conjure the very thing that would protect her and future generations from persecution. Through it all, the black witch moths came to her to comfort her and heal her wounds, acting as her protectors and warning her when any animal or human should threaten her again.

"For generations, we have hunted your kind to take what we should have possessed a long time ago. But to find you vermin living amongst us all this time, with your candles and talismans giving you the Gift to transform? To be higher beings? Why should you be the only ones to benefit?"

His words stoke the fire in me. I stand, no longer hiding from him, and move to where the wall has crumbled away so he can get a good look at me.

"You hunt us for using the very magic you want for your own purposes," I say. "We live away from this conflict and hurt no one. All you do—all you have done—is take. Destroy. Kill. How does that make you better than us?"

"At least we don't hide what we are," he says.

"Neither do we!" I crouch down, and willing every ounce of power within me, I explode upward.

In an instant, my arms contract and bloom in full feather. My nose elongates into my pointed beak as my body narrows and shortens, growing plump and full of plumes. The mask falls to the floor beside me. My mother gasps.

I dive from the top floor and swoop toward Vicente. When I make it to the ground, he has snatched Olivia back from Nico. He pulls her wings to their full spread, and with two large railroad nails, he stakes her to the tree to display her like a prized kill.

I screech, diving for Vicente when overhead, a great gray cloud sweeps over the homestead. At first, it is a silent phantom, and then it descends into an undulating mass with distinct shapes. All around is a chorus of calls: the twittering trill and wail of screech owls, the forceful shriek of barn owls, the trumpet drop of barred owls. All zooming around, dive-bombing, slicing into skin with talons. But another voice, another call, deep and harrowed from centuries of persecution, sends the men flat onto their bellies in the dirt.

Lorenza, in owl form, swoops down from above and needs only to screech to send him lurching backward, but dodging gives him enough time to get in one more attack. Pulling his arm back, he gets off one shot before he falls onto his back in the brush.

The arrow whizzes past me. I swerve to dodge it and go careening onto the dry grass, transforming back to my human form. But the arrow strikes someone with a thick, wet thud. Lorenza cries out and falls to the ground, her wings splayed out around her. Blood blooms from her chest, dark veins stretch across her body as the poison snakes through her.

I screech so loud it deafens me, but from my mouth, a twirling torrent of black moths spews and attacks the remaining Hunters. They scream as the moths overtake them, transitioning into large bats that rise in a mushroom cloud. The bats attack, puncturing with their fangs, smothering with their massive beating wings without remorse.

The men scramble, retreating to the old road as the bats continue pushing them back with their wings and teeth. They fling their bodies into the men until they stagger; some fall only to be seized and drained of their blood. The lucky ones, like Vicente and Nico, escape, tearing through the forest with a dark cloud of bats and the members of La Asamblea Sur hunting them down.

I dart to where Lorenza has fallen. Her body seizes from the poison, her beak opening and closing as she gasps for air. Her eyes, once bright, turn black with infection. Beside me, Desi falls to his knees while Esme drapes my clothing over me.

Lorenza is alive but losing blood. Where the arrow extends from her body, her pain manifests as a cloud of bright red smoke.

"She needs the Elixir," Esme says. "She didn't drink earlier."

But in her owl form, the Reliquary is absent.

Lalo, having swooped down from above, transforms and drops to his knees in the grass with Lena beside him. His angular jaw pulses with worry.

"The coyotes interrupted our ceremony," Esme says as she shrugs into the clothing she discarded earlier. "We need to go back to the *cenote* to finish or our Gift will be lost to those who have yet to drink."

"It's too far," Lalo says, placing his palm over Lorenza's chest. "But there is another *cenote* nearby."

Lena shakes her head, her hair a dark halo. "Lalo, we cannot go there. It's the cursed place."

He glances up at her, his eyes dark with worry. "She does not have time. It's the only way."

Without further discussion, he lifts Lorenza in his cupped hands. She blinks a few times before closing her eyes; her chest rises and falls in erratic breaths. At least she's still breathing. He takes off for a path leading through the forest.

A few feet away, Lidia is on her back in the grass, lying motionless. Her eyes are closed, and her breathing is shallow as I approach. I want nothing more than to grab her and shake her, ask her how she could let Olivia control her in this way. But there's no time for that. Lorenza is fading, and our Gift along with her.

I pause at the tree where Vicente so callously pinned Olivia to the trunk. Blood stains her wings where the nails have pierced them. Her chest barely moves. Edging beside me, Esme reaches for her, cupping her head, which has fallen limply to one side. After a moment, Esme grasps the nails and yanks them free from the tree. She takes Olivia and holds her out to Desi. He hesitates, his chest heaving, hatred coloring his gaze. When he still refuses to take her, Lena, having transformed, steps forward and takes her as the other members of La Asamblea Sur gather the injured and the dead.

As we start through the trees, no one dares to utter a word. The weight of our task to save the Aquelarre Búho, to save everything we've built, is an ominous task that lingers as we traverse the road through the shadows of the forest.

CHAPTER 19

Blackness Approaching

The journey from the old hacienda through the ruins of the ancient city takes every ounce of strength left within me. My legs burn, and I move as though I am wading through drying concrete. My arms feel like elastic that's been stretched out. But I cannot shift. I don't have the strength, and someone needs to help my mother.

With her arm around my shoulder and mine encircling her waist, we trudge along the once-worn trail, now overgrown with roots attempting to trip us. Esme leads the way, with Desi on Èvelyne's other side. The owls of La Asamblea Sur are overhead, some flying out and then circling back to give us cover. The others move from tree to tree, stopping long enough to make sure we are not being followed before they fly to the next tree to do the same all over again.

We reach a crumbling stone wall, darkened by age and time, that separates us from what lies beyond. Recognition blooms in the back of my mind—the ancient carvings of pumas and jaguars, of suns and moons, stir up a story in my mind, a memory of my *papá* telling me stories of the old city and the forbidden *cenote*. Our ancestors deliberately left it out of the city boundaries. It is a dismal place, one that entices us with cool air and whispers of comfort as we approach. But dark things lie beneath, ancient creatures that scared the locals so much they forbade anyone from visiting. I have seen this place before, even though I have never been here in my physical body before.

It's the same *cenote* painted on Don Vega's walls—the sacred *cenote* from my vision of Lorenza. I've been here, at least in spirit. This is where I came during the *platica*, the spiritual cleansing Don Vega performed for me. My vision wasn't a dream after all. This place is real.

Èvelyne stumbles, and it takes both Desi and me to keep her from falling.

"You should rest, Mom," I say, stopping.

"We can't stop. Lorenza needs our help."

"But—"

"No, Valeria. We have to keep moving," she says, taking a tentative step. "She needs the Elixir. I do, too. But you don't. You shifted. Did you drink earlier?"

"No," Desi says, helping to steady her as we move. "Val did that with her own magic."

She glances at me, her eyes filled with wonder. "Like your father."

Hearing her say it brings me to a stop. I pitch forward, the exhaustion, the fear, and the insanity of the situation suddenly too much to bear. But my mother squeezes her arm around me and bears some of my weight so we can press on.

Lalo is already at the opening of the *cenote* ahead of us, his body tense and poised to strike if any of Los Cazadores make an appearance. Overhead, La Asamblea Sur has perched in the treetops. Only then do I notice the nodules—it's another Sacred Tree. A flash of standing on the riverside in the ancient past blinds me—the Sacred Tree, burning from the inside after the attack on Lorenza's village. This is the same place, somehow thriving. But the owl guards don't come with us this time.

Moving down a crude staircase made from the intertwined roots of the tree, we descend into the belly of the *cenote*. There is no limestone paving to walk on. Only a few scattered torches set into the walls for light. Inside, it's ancient and dark, untouched and misty, with dust motes and tiny insects swarming us the moment we step near. This is the darkly whispering place where Lorenza first drew the sacred water to create her Elixir, the sacred womb where she breathed the first spark of life that became the Gift we all share.

Unlike the other *cenote*, this one has an aura that makes my skin go cold.

It isn't the temperature. There's a shadowy feeling in the air, like the whispered memories of our ancient ones have been caught down here, forgotten by time and clamoring for us to hear them, to acknowledge them. To remember them.

Taking a lantern from its crevice, Esme lights the path for us to follow. Once at the bottom of the *cenote*, Desi and I help Èvelyne to a wide slab of smooth limestone so she can sit and rest. Lalo has already placed Lorenza at the base of the tree, where the limestone slopes beneath the water's surface. Too weak to remain changed, she has shifted back to human form. My stomach lurches at the sight of such a noble woman reduced to such weakness. I have to fight the urge to lunge at Olivia, who Lena helps sit at a smaller stone. She's back to her human form, a seeping wound on each hand where Vicente pinned her to the tree. I want to conjure up some withering incantation that will curse her on the spot. Instead, I bite my tongue, a true testament to Don Vega's teachings, to the influence of my mother's strength, and to Desi's hurt and Esme's guidance. I want to be a witch they are proud to stand beside. I want to be worthy of my Gifts.

When Desi sees her, he spins and starts toward her. "She doesn't deserve to be here. Not after what she did."

"Desi, no!" I say, going after him.

But Lorenza stops him by raising her hand, her voice coming out in harsh rasps. "Our sister who came to this circle is not pure of heart. She is one who seeks to take without giving. One who seeks this power for her own gain."

Olivia cups her hands together, wincing at the pain of the seeping wounds, eyeing Desi as she speaks to La Primera. "Sister, please. I—"

It only takes a withering glance for Lorenza to silence her. "One who uses this Gift for her own advantage instead of protecting her sisters does not deserve to benefit from all that I have sacrificed, all that we have endured centuries over. This Gift, if not respected, shall stay with me. Only those who would sacrifice for another before themselves shall receive the honor of my Gift. One who seizes without first earning her place is not fit to remain."

Shadows encroach, and the *cenote* grows darker as Lorenza's anger seethes in a whirlwind around us.

Olivia edges forward, wincing with every step, toward an invisible line where the others stand. I flashback to Mabon, to La Maison. When my mother asked for the one to step forward who should bear the responsibility of the coven with her, I froze. The opportunity to rule by my mother's side, at her right hand, slipped from my grasp when Olivia took it for herself.

Lorenza sees my vision, too and she shifts her focus from my memory to Olivia, her face harsh and unyielding. Olivia shudders beneath her gaze.

"Blood rife with ambition," Lorenza says, the torch flames shimmering as her voice rises, "and disregard for our hierarchy taints this Elixir, and it shall not regenerate unless those who are true help to create it."

She raises one hand and points to Olivia. "You are not the High Priestess of the north. You remain within the coven where our sister Èvelyne Leclair rules. You have not been elevated, not by initiation or election. You are not the rightful Maiden. You have taken the place of another."

When Lorenza looks in my direction, I feel the weight of her gaze. Where I would normally retreat or make excuses, I allow myself to truly consider the idea of standing beside my mother. All my life, I knew I would one day take over for her. Practice beside her. I never considered taking her place because I felt she was always the perfect person to rule L'Assemblée de la Terre. Now I feel that pull in me—not to take her place, but to stand with her.

"Sister Lorenza, please," Olivia says, but I move between them.

"In the forest," I say. "At the safe house. When I arrived in California. On our most cherished days in Asamblea de La Lumbre. All of these times, our enemies found us."

"The Elixir is weak in all of us," Olivia says. "It's not up to me to keep us all hidden. Even Èvelyne couldn't do so."

"No, she couldn't. Not when the person she trusted to be her right hand gave away our secrets," I say. "Sold out her own sisters and brothers for the thrill of power."

Behind me, Desi steps up. "Val, what are you saying?"

"I know what she's saying." Esme moves closer. "Our enemies have been on our heels this entire time, but not through the fault of our own. Instead, they have followed us because of Olivia's desire to take what is not rightfully hers."

"High Priestess," Olivia says to Esme. "Valeria has never liked me. If she had done the work and put in the effort, Èvelyne would have chosen her as her Maiden. But she did not. She left us and chose to practice on her own.

Why should her disregard for the sanctity of our coven be rewarded over the dedication from those of us who have been there all along?"

A vision from La Maison comes back to me—Olivia and Èvelyne together in the parlor after we brought Gwen back from the safe house. The vision continues long after I left the conversation, this time from someone else's perspective.

"I am not sure she will ever advance to be the witch she could be with this guilt haunting her."

In the vision, Olivia stands out of sight. When she leans in, she touches Èvelyne's arm and speaks.

"You have held out long enough for her, High Priestess. It's time for you to look for the true one, a Maiden who will honor what you have built."

Instead of leaving, Olivia remains behind Èvelyne, and for the briefest moment, she shifts. Her eyes determined, hair dark like Lidia's, she leans into my mother once more, whispering into her ear. Poisonous words wrapped in a red aura, a hidden incantation that planted the seed in my mother's mind. It sprouts from Olivia's mouth and intertwines around Èvelyne's head like strangler fig vines. They encircle her, tiny tendrils infiltrating her ears, dark roots poisoning her thoughts.

I snap back to the present and lunge for Olivia. She tries to pull back, but I keep her firmly planted. She kicks at me and pushes me back a few steps, but I refuse to let her go. With both of my hands pressed to her temples, I see through her eyes. She is back at La Maison in her room. She is sitting on the floor, a map of the grounds around La Maison in front of her, with two candles burning—two tiny embers flickering above the map, moving to the old tree where Gwen and I sat before the Hunters found us.

"You did something," I say. "You called Los Cazadores to our location. You removed the protective barrier. You did it on purpose—you put the entire coven at risk for your own ambition."

"I stepped up," she says, shivering. "I took the initiative."

"You pitted my mother against me."

"You did that yourself," she says, her eyes flashing gold. "She used her love for you to blind her, to disregard what you were. What you would never be."

"She only wanted me to be the witch I wanted to be. And I am. This time away has shown me who I am meant to be—the person I had held back. I didn't need your help to do so. I didn't even need the Elixir. But you helped, didn't you?"

I lurch away from her, afraid of the rush of blood lust coursing through my body.

"Want to know where you failed?" I ask, my eyes alight, glowing so fiercely amber like my father's that everyone takes a step back. "Your magic may have held me down, but it didn't matter. I found my way. My calling."

My face shifts. My skin pricks as feathers grow around my face in a resplendent, downy crown.

She spins and, with both hands out, drives me back with bright energy, using her anger against me. It propels from her fingertips like a projectile, coming toward me like a lightning bolt. Before it can hit me, Èvelyne jumps up and steps in the way. The impact reverberates off her body and catapults at Olivia, sending her skidding across the stone until she plunges into the water. When she surfaces, she claws at the rocks, reaching for the edge, but I sweep my hands around again, and a cloud of moths comes soaring from above. They intertwine in a tornado of shadows, surging for Olivia. Threading through her lips, they course into her mouth and down her throat, smothering her until she sinks underwater. She thrashes, kicking up a dark red torrent beneath her, but more moths swarm her—a cloud of darkness enveloping her, smothering her, stifling her screams until they force her down to the depths of the *cenote* and out of view.

I fall to my knees, heaving at the surge of power as it leaves me. Desi drops down beside me, pulling me into his arms.

"Are you okay?"

I nod, but beside me, Lorenza slumps to one side. The ground shakes beneath us, the walls crumbling as a shadow crosses over her face, clouding her eyes.

"Our time is ending," she says, her voice scraping through parched vocal cords. "We must finish the Elixir before we lose our Gift once and for all."

As she speaks, her skin fades and turns gray. Her flowing hair flattens into stringy vines lying limp on her shoulders. Around me, the others gasp. Esme falls to her knees, praying at the sight of the ancient witch fading before us. She starts an incantation, willing Lorenza back to her once-vibrant self. My mother moves beside us, kneeling beside Esme and taking her hand. With the two High Priestesses leading us in a chant, we each speak an ancient spell to aid Lorenza as she fades.

When she reaches up to touch her fingertip to her face, her skin sinks in, exposing her skeletal cheekbones, the hollows of her cheeks. Around her eyes, the tattoos etched into her skin, inking the dark circles around her eyes. The *calavera* teeth around her lips darken her skin, exposing pointed teeth, crumbling and black. The cross in the center of her forehead singes a bright red and then sizzles to black, while the sunbursts around her eyes etch deeper into her skin, leaving raw marks that bruise purple. Her very breath is gone, and with it, her life force. She is nothing more than a skeletal remnant of the vibrant witch she once was.

I move beside Desi, who clamps his hand around mine. As Lorenza continues to fade, tears blind me. I close my eyes, thankful for the momentary reprieve from seeing her die this way, turning her into a living *calavera*.

The thought of it makes me collapse. Centuries of this Gift, a bloodline that flows back through time—eradicated. In my mind, they come to me, the Salazar women. Starting with Lorenza, their faces appear, etched with pain, their skin sinking in and their beauty withering away until they are old and twisted trees, left to dry and desiccate in the desert.

But a final tendril remains—a vein running through me, with a hint of lifeblood still coursing within it.

From within the folds of her *rebozo*, Lorenza retrieves the Reliquary. The wood ages with her, turning black, but when she blows on it, the roots come to life and retract, revealing the interior.

The four vials are full, but the larger one, the source of our Gift, is empty. Unless we fill it and allow Lorenza to take it with her, there will be no Elixir ever again.

Jumping into action, Esme scrambles for a discarded palm leaf, and kneeling, she sweeps it through the water to gather enough for the Elixir. She takes it to Lorenza. From behind us, Lalo appears with a large earthen bowl, the exterior etched with protective symbols, and places it at Lorenza's feet. Esme fills the bowl with water while Desi searches for anything that will burn. He works furiously to light a fire, then takes a cutting from the Sacred Tree. Opening the pod with the talon of his bone whistle, he squeezes the nectar from within and adds it to the water. Esme brings a cone of roughly hewn incense and places it at Lorenza's feet. When she steps back, Èvelyne struggles to stand; she brings forth a sachet and, untying the hemp string, upends the salt inside into the water.

Lorenza looks down at the items and, without a word, nods her head in acceptance. The air shifts around us as everyone takes a collective breath and holds it for a moment.

Èvelyne and Esme flank Lorenza, and each hold out both hands. They lift their bone whistles, poising the pointed talons at the end over the fleshy pad on the heel of their hands. With a decisive slash, each cuts open their skin.

The blood spurts and drops in rivulets in the bowl Desi holds out to them. When it has soiled the flower petals and seeped into the salt and incense, Esme takes the smaller bowl and pours the sacred water from the *cenote*, submerging everything.

The water grows murky and turns black before it swirls and circles the bowl on its own. As Lorenza kneels to lift the bowl, the faintest hint of amethyst light percolates in the water like glitter. As she lifts it, the concoction takes on an ethereal glow that illuminates the *cenote*. The light blinds for only a moment, then extinguishes and plunges the cavern into near-total darkness.

No one speaks. No one breathes or moves.

"The blood is too weak. Without our Fourth, our circle is incomplete," Lorenza says. "The Elixir within us has depleted too much. We are too late."

My heart sinks. This cannot be the end.

And yet it reminds me: my ability to shift without the Elixir means something. I hold within me a special ability, one that does not belong only to me.

A whirlwind of images spins in my head—the vision I had when I was deep in the trance Don Vega put me in during the *platica*. Lorenza kneels at the riverbank, her village burning behind her. She has gathered the tree cutting and the water from the river. The other women join her, and they each offer their blood for the bowl. As Lorenza mixes them together, she adds her blood to the water.

I snap out of the vision and produce the feather, holding it out to Lorenza.

"I am a Salcedo, descended from Las Salazares."

The others turn to Lorenza, who, with a single nod, affirms it.

"I am of this blood, of *your* blood," I say, "and with my sacrifice, we make this Elixir anew."

She takes the bowl and holds it out. With the feather's quill, I slice my palm. A droplet of blood hits the surface. The last remnants of shimmering light fade, and the *cenote* darkens further; the Elixir swirls with a golden thread in the bowl. When the blood and water, the sacred plant and the salt, bind it and intertwine completely, Lorenza drinks down the remaining droplets of Elixir from the vial.

Once she is done, she stands still, and as the Elixir courses through her body, she seizes and rises a foot off the ground. As she hovers there in the throes of agony, she cries out, the anguish scratching from her throat so harshly that it sends each of us to our knees. I lean forward, pressing my forehead to the stone before me, but I can't stop myself from looking. Peering through my fingers, I watch as light shoots from her mouth, from her eyes, like a poisoned laser. It projects around her, filling the entire cavern with dark smoke so everyone and everything is obscured.

A terrible screeching shreds her voice, and for a moment, I go deaf. I squeeze my eyes closed at the piercing in my eardrums. Only when she stops does my hearing return, and I dare to look up at her.

The poisoned cloud surges back to her, streaming into her mouth as a swarm of black moths; with every winged creature, Lorenza's body fills back out again, like they are the very breath she breathes, unending life returning to her.

When she lowers enough that her feet touch the stone before me, I reach out, sliding my hands across the cold stone to touch her, if only to make sure she is real. Her skin is warm, coursing with renewed magic, the magic that has sustained her for centuries as our First.

"Stand with me, sisters, brother," she says, her voice as strong and as unwavering as the warrior she is. "Stand with me and take this Gift we have created."

I obey, wiping away tears, unable to hide my awe at her resilience, and as I rise to meet her, Èvelyne, Esme, and Desi do the same. In return for our respect, she kneels to gather the Elixir. Holding out the Reliquary, she fills the central vial, the one that she will keep guard over while we wait for it to ferment. She hands the other vials to Desi. He cups them in both hands, nodding to her as he accepts the sacred offering, the one Don Vega would have distributed to our sister houses to sustain our Gift in the coming years.

"You are the bestower now, brother," Lorenza says. "Do so wisely and with honor."

Closing the Reliquary, whose black wood seals over the exterior of the box, Lorenza takes it. Now able to move on her own, she stands and regards us each.

"Our pact endures for another seven years. I trust that you, my sisters and brothers, will remain steadfast in your journey."

I bow to her, and when I stand upright again, she nods to me; at that moment, her approval is like a weight lifted from my very core.

Transforming back into her owl form, Lorenza lets out a call. A flap of her wings lifts her over our heads, and beneath her, the moths circle her until they, too, soar overhead, trailing after her in a wavering cloud that takes to the skies before they disappear.

No one speaks. When Desi moves beside me and puts a hand on my arm, I can't feel his touch for the electricity spiking through my veins.

"You're more than just La Tierra, *prima*," he says, his eyebrows arched high and his eyes wide. "More than La Lumbre. You're descended from the First Witch."

I smile and nod, looking away from him for a moment to understand what those words mean. Magic and darkness are within me: the ability and talent to be everything Lorenza is. Not only because I am her descendent but because I am more than blood and bone, more than feather and fire, more than earth, water, and air. I am all those things, but I am also made of dreams, desires, and a love and luminosity that can shine even in the dark.

As I turn to rejoin the group, I spot something small and dark on the floor of the *cenote*. Kneeling, I reach and tenderly lift a tiny moth that has fallen and no longer has enough energy to go on. I lift it to my mouth and blow. It singes bright white, folds and unfolds its wings for a moment, showing me that even in death, there is beauty. Even in darkness, there is light, and that is the hope we must cling to so we can survive the dark times that come.

I stand and tuck the moth into the folds of my coat, patting my pocket before I turn to where my mother stands, watching me. As I move to join her, she wraps an arm around me, and we follow the others from the darkness of the *cenote* into the growing light of dawn.

Ahead of us, Desi and Esme lead the way up the rough incline to higher ground. Trailing behind them, I look down into the water. Somewhere in the depths, Olivia lies after losing at her own game. Torn between wanting to leave her there for what she did and the pull to bring her home, even if she is no longer welcome, makes every step away from her more difficult.

When I get to the top of the *cenote*, La Asamblea Sur has congregated, and they lead Èvelyne and the others to a safe place to rest. Laying in the dirt where I discarded it, the coyote mask is a hollow shell. I lift it, turning it over in my hand. Seeing it stirs my hatred for what the Hunters did to all of us.

The group falls into lively chatter, but below the laughter and conversation, something stirs.

I frown, scanning the tree line, but there's no movement. Again, an undercurrent of darkness comes for me, so I lift the mask and hold it to my face. The unmistakable outline of a man beyond the entrance to the forest startles me.

I call out a warning cry. Someone shouts, and then everything slows. It's Vicente. His arm pulls back, and he flings a six-foot-long spear at us. I dodge it and spin away. The obsidian-tipped spear soars past me and lands in the trunk of the Sacred Tree with a thunk. Vicente López turns and retreats, with the owls of La Asamblea Sur chasing after him.

Darkness explodes from the trunk in a toxic cloud. The poison from the spear seeps from the tree's wound, sending a sour scent into the air. Plagued tendrils radiate out from the impact, down the trunk, and through the branches. A memory of Gwen flashes in my mind—an image of her writhing in pain at La Maison after the attack in the woods, her body riddled with thin black veins filled with the Hunter's poison. The same veins infect the tree throughout its trunk and expand to every branch. It's the same horror from my vision of the attack on Lorenza's village when the same Sacred Tree was set ablaze. I fall to my knees, pain shooting through my limbs. Beside me, my fellow witches do the same. We are bound to this tree: what is done to it is done to us. The pods shrivel, taking with them the life-giving sap needed for our Elixir.

"We have to save the tree!" Esme shouts.

Desi jumps into action, fighting his way to the tree. Taking the vials from him, Esme pours the Elixir into her hands, smearing it over the bark. It glimmers as it seeps into the wood.

Beside her, Desi stands with his eyes closed, his hands turned palms up to the sky as he chants. A swirling, glimmering incantation escapes his lips, and he lifts a few feet off the ground the way Don Vega did during my cleansing ritual. At the lip of the *cenote*, darkness approaches. It scorches the tree from its core outward, infecting it with disease, shriveling its fruit, and moldering its roots.

Time is running out. My blood courses swiftly, willing me forward. I know what I have to do. I must do what Lorenza did to complete the Elixir when she first created it, when she used a rock sharpened to a point to chip away a piece of her broken bone and added it to the mixture, setting it alight in a dazzling display of dark magic. We are made of magic, and that magic can heal. I have to stop the infection with the power I hold within me.

Gripping my bone key tight, I jab the taloned end into the fleshy part of my palm. Pain shoots across my hand where blood spurts from the wound. Then, willing forth my power, I dive into the *cenote*, transforming as I freefall into the cool water below. It envelops me, pulling me to the bottom where the Sacred Tree takes root.

Time-settled sand obscures the water when I use my beak to dig, but I work until I feel the roots deep in the bottom of the pool. I push my wounded wing into the hole, allowing my blood to seep into the sediment, nourishing the roots before I cover them again.

Spinning and pushing off from the cave floor, I scream. A cloud of shadows, the black witch moths, course from my mouth. Like a torrent, they swirl around me, pushing me up until I break the surface.

Sputtering, I transform fully back to my human self and gasp for air, choking, letting out a scream at the pain searing through my arm. Someone grabs me under my armpits, drags me up onto the limestone slab, and drapes a cloak over me.

I flip over onto my back, gasping for breath with Desi kneeling over me. Behind him, the disease in the Sacred Tree moves in reverse, traveling back up to the top, but the tree is changed. Her olive leaves are shriveled and black. Her fragrant flowers disintegrate, and the orange seed pods turn dark crimson and harden on the vine. The etchings in the bark deepen and blacken and shimmer a diseased shade of gold.

Desi hauls me up and wraps a length of cloth around my hand to protect the wound while I steady myself.

"I think you've done enough good for one day, Val," he says. "Let someone else do something for a change, huh?"

He helps me up, but when he pauses, I look down to the water. For a moment, an ancient broken mask with a crudely fashioned beak floats on the surface. One eye peers at us, and in my head, an unending chant set to the music of our Mayan ancestors comes to me as Lorenza shows me an ancient scene of a time when the *cenote* was not underwater and the ancient ones left sacrifices for the gods.

From behind them, a slender man in an owl feather headdress approaches. Lorenza holds the bowl out to him, and as he speaks, his voice encircles them in a magical loop, a blessing for their offering. The warmth of his voice brings tears to my eyes. It's foreign, yet so familiar. The women join in, and their shared voices help Lorenza as she gathers her strength. She holds her free hand over the bowl. From inside, pale white light glimmers and grows until it rises to encircle the women in its radiance. As it does, her mouth drops open, and her eyes go wide, seeing her magic transform into dazzling radiance.

As the scene fades into the water and the waves lap around us, the moths swirl, coming together in a cloud that encircles the ancient mask. I reach for it, almost slipping back into the water. My fingertips graze the ancient wood, breaking off a portion around the eye before it slips beneath the surface and sinks back to the bottom of the ancient cavern for protection.

Before everyone moves away, I turn to where I discarded the coyote mask earlier. Lifting it into the fading light of the dying fire, the sight of it brings heaviness to the air. Its fur is matted with dirt and blood, and the vines have dried to thin strips. The vacant eyes are a haunting reminder of what it took to grasp the truth: something I am thankful for but scarred by just the same.

Stepping forward, I hold the coyote mask over the fire. For a moment, flames light up the eyes, and it is as if the animal lives again, here to take what it wants. I toss it in the fire. The impact sends sparks skyward, the fire consuming the animal's remains and cleansing my soul. This offering is not an ending. It's a vow that I won't stop protecting my coven from those who seek to take the things we hold most dear. Even if they should one day take our magic, I'll share my own so we don't have to rely on anyone or anything to keep us safe as we practice our Craft.

    Above, voices call out to us, and for once, I let Desi carry me without fighting him. For once, I lean on someone else as we climb from the underworld, crossing the threshold into our coming future.

CHAPTER 20

Beginning Again

A few weeks later, I'm back in Montréal, back in the woods outside La Maison des Arbres. Lit hollow gourds line a pathway carpeted with fiery sunflower petals and marigolds that bring a warmth to me I had forgotten. In the clearing, my mother has assembled Andres Beauchêne and half a dozen longstanding members of Assemblée de la Terre. We encircle a bonfire, its ashes perfuming the air with acrid smoke while embers set the forest aglow. Seeing my mother and Andres together fills me with gratitude to be back with my northern sisters and brothers of L'Assemblée des Chouettes again. Esme and Desi also stand among us, having flown north to join us for this act of renewal.

The wind whips through white birches, stark without their leaves, carrying with it the whispers of those who come back to us on Samhain. The snow has come early this winter, and for that, I'm grateful. Like a homecoming, the fresh air enlivens my spirit and offers me a bright backdrop compared to the darkness I faced in Mexico.

The dying sunset throws plum and crimson light across crisp fallen leaves, and the deep scent of burning logs seeps through the cold air around us. As my mother, dressed in her ceremonial robe, finishes the last of her blessings, Desi strikes a wood match and uses it to light a tablet of charcoal sitting in the bottom of a shallow clay bowl with feet fashioned from ivory owl talons. Taking a cone of incense, he offers it to the burning charcoal.

When the flame extinguishes, and the smoke draws up in a long, undulating tendril, Desi lifts the clawed bowl and swirls it toward each of the four corners so the smoke intertwines amongst those of us gathered.

Behind him, rapid, monotonous drumming starts, a strong tempo that resonates like a shared heartbeat. As the rite continues, Desi places the bowl down and turns to the bonfire behind him. Set to one side, a small table holds the tools he needs. Salt goes into the bowl first, followed by a splash of rubbing alcohol that sends a sizzling spark of glimmering ashes into the air. Basil, rosemary, and mint add a fragrance that is crisp and biting. Before holding the bowl out to us, he lights another match and throws it in.

"To those gathered, I ask that you release into the fire the things that no longer serve you."

Èvelyne is the first to do so. Taking a slip of paper, she turns to Desi. The white feathers encircling her neck like a boa wave in the breeze as she drops the paper into the bowl, where it ignites and then turns to ash. Handing her a handful of palo santo from a small dish, he offers her the fragrant wood.

"Feed the fire with your offerings."

She takes it, tosses it into the bowl, and then nods to me.

The paper burns warm in my palm from my desire to let go of the ills of these past months and my need to leave behind the influences that worked to hold me down.

When I, too, throw my intentions into the fire, the warmth across my face is both comforting and inspiring. I have every element within me, but my fiery spirit, my Salcedo side, burns deep and passionate within me. It always has, but for so long, it only smoldered. My experiences down south helped me to reignite the magic that burns within my soul and showed me that the darkness I was afraid of didn't need to be something evil. That it could be channeled in the right way.

As I toss my paper in, I hold it over the flame for a moment. Written in dark script, my declaration burns golden as the flames take it.

Seeing it turn ash gives me a renewed hope that I will remember how I am more than capable of doing what it takes to further my Craft and use my Gift to protect my coven so we may continue to thrive.

"May the divine beings who watch over us," Desi says, "assist us on this path."

Standing back, I watch Desi upend the bowl so the ashes float away on the breeze. I slip my hand into the pocket of my cloak, finding a smooth, mottled brown stone I've been carrying with me since we left Mexico. My father's voice comes on the wind.

Pequeña pluma...

Smiling, I brush my fingers across the surface, tracing the definitive v-shaped point in the center to highlight the owl's face etched into it. In my other pocket, a dark brown stone with deep-set, vibrant orange eyes brings to mind Don Vega's gravelly laugh. Somehow, I believe he will come back to us, even if it is only through our magic. He survived the lightning that day in the desert when he was a young man and the ancestors tested him. In my bones, I know he is a force unto himself, one that will always be with us.

Cradling both stones, I set them on a slab at the edge of the bonfire, a remembrance of those who helped make me who I am. Keeping my hand there for a moment, I feel their heat, their life, warmed by the bonfire as if they were here for a moment.

One by one, the others lay their mementos. Desi places a purple-gray owl down to honor Dree. Though his mask obscures his face, tears shimmer in his eyes. I take his hand and squeeze as he steps back into the circle.

Next, Esme lays out four small tan stones, one of each member of La Asamblea Sur who lost their lives protecting us.

When the tribute is complete, we stand in solemn silence, with only the crackling of the fiery logs, the wind whistling through the trees, and the clean crispness of the snow to witness our eulogy for the spirits of those we have lost.

As the remembrance breaks up, I peel off my mask, and holding it in front of me, I smooth the feathers. Stark white feathers on the cheeks to honor the Leclairs; dark brown across the top of the head with two tufts of white represent the Salcedos. At last, the mask is no longer something to hide behind. It's something to show and honor both parts of my true self.

I turn to the others gathered with us, some of whom warm themselves by the fire, and some of whom move to the long banquet table laden with a feast of apples and pumpkins, succulent roasted hens with pears, root vegetables, and jugs of cider. Seeing both sides of my family here together is all I ever needed. It gives me a sense of home, showing me that no matter where I go, I have a place.

But I can't help but think about the encroaching shadows as the season of darkness arrives. What lingers in those shadows for me and for the four houses of Aquelarre Búho? Vicente López and Los Cazadores are not gone, only retreating as they have done before. What is their next plan? I've seen their determination firsthand now. They won't hide with their tails between their legs for long. Not after what we did to them, not after they've seen what our Gift can do. Their attacks, their ability to infiltrate our coven, are warning enough that our existence is at risk if we don't protect ourselves from their ravenous envy.

The shadows encroach as we stand around the bonfire; instead of ignoring them or willing them away, I open myself to them and welcome their lessons. The tiny pinprick of moth wings flickering against my bare skin awakens me to the lingering warning. They shimmer in blue-purple shadows in the forest, percolating in the trees until I notice them, and when I do, they take off, coming to me. As they swirl around me, I tilt my head back and watch their dizzying dance. This time, though, Desi does the same, and when he sees them, he lets out one of his characteristic cackles. Beside me, Esme lifts one hand to catch a moth on her fingertip. I laugh for the first time in a long time, thrilled to see their joy after so much pain. When I catch Èvelyne's gaze, she's smiling, but it's a sad, melancholic smile, and her eyes give off a hint of warning. The smile slips from my face as I sense it, too. Even though I'm elated that the others can see the moths now, they swirl around us, darkening as their wings blacken and they multiply, flying around in a tornado that swirls around la Maison and swallows it whole. I reach up to where I've fastened my father's feather in my hair, a touchstone to his fire and to mine.

A warm hand touches me on the arm, pulling me from the vision. I find Esme standing beside me, her black curls tousled by the wind. She holds out a hand to me, and when she opens it, a black witch moth sits unmoving in her palm. The fire light picks up the iridescent thread lining each wing, and the black eye spots peer up at me like a curious visitor waiting to disclose her secrets.

"She carried out her days of protection and now deserves a place of honor." Gesturing to my mask, she tucks the moth, wings splayed to show off her spots in the center of the forehead. She places a hand on my shoulder. "*Pequeña pluma*, I am proud of you. *Tu papá tambien.*"

Slipping her arm through mine, we move to where Desi stands, chatting with Èvelyne. Seeing my mask, Desi nods.

"Love the fresh look, *prima*. Suits you."

"Thanks, cousin."

Behind him, music swells, and laughter percolates in the air. As he turns to leave, I stop him.

"I have something for you."

Turning to a compact bundle beside the fire, I hold it out to him. Watching his smile shift from curious to nostalgic, he holds the object up.

Most of the wood is charred away, but the wide opening for the eyes remains. As he holds it up to study it, the firelight flickers from behind the mask—Don Vega's mask—and it's like he's here with us.

Without saying a word, Desi tucks it under his arm and pulls me in for a long hug.

"*Gracias, prima.*"

"*De nada,*" I say.

Letting out a sly chuckle, Desi squeezes me and then pulls away, pausing only to glance over his shoulder. "Looks like things are ramping up. You coming?"

I nod and move to find somewhere to put my mask, but Èvelyne holds out her hands.

"I'll take excellent care of it. You go."

"You're not coming?"

She smiles as Esme leans into her, hugging her with one arm. "Someone needs to keep the fires burning. You go have fun. Let us crones have some alone time."

I laugh and hand the mask to Èvelyne, then brush past her, unbuttoning my robe as I go.

By the time I return to the fire, everyone is in various states of undress. The music swells, and bodies sway to the beat, silhouettes against a blazing backdrop. With the flames leaping skyward, I drop my robe and slip from my gown, delighting in the chill on my skin.

Voices and music intertwine, swirling around in a dizzying atmosphere that instills electricity in the air. The celebration after so much turmoil sends a thrill coursing through my veins. Moonlight filters through the trees, making the shadows contrast more starkly with the brilliant white of the snow. Aromatic ash and incense comfort and tantalize me, and the connection to the Earth, as we stand on the precipice of one season changing into the next, fills me with such promise.

Nestled within the thick reserve of silver maple and red ash, La Maison is protected on all sides. Their bare branches reach skyward like gnarled fingers, ever-vigilant over the estate, our land, and the entire coven the same way they have for decades.

In the back garden, milkweed casts downy fibers into the air like tendrils of smoke as the wind rises. The bonfire throws shards of light that illuminate the goldenrod and choke cherries like fine jewels.

The revelry makes the past suffering fade from thought. My doubts and trepidation drop away from me like falling leaves as I spin and twirl, allowing the smoke and heat, the laughter and cries of delight from the others, to carry me, lifting me from the forest floor. My toes graze the ground, and as I rise, my legs narrow and shorten. My bones shorten, and my plumage blooms, first like flowerets and then full feathers. With each swish, I ascend higher until my wings skim the treetops.

Overhead, a crested owl cries out, and Desi circles back to join me. Picking up my pace, I rise to meet him, and we race to join the others, fanning out beneath the moonlight over the valley below.

Glancing down, La Maison sits cradled, protected amidst the pines. Even as shadows encroach on the outskirts, I proceed, determined to meet them head-on. As we soar out over the river, the stark freshness of the snow glimmers in the moonlight. Looking down at the houses, at the pines and birches of the woods spread out around La Maison Des Arbres, tiny pinpricks of light pierce the shadows, a reminder that no matter how fearful we are, promise and hope always linger on the periphery, to inspire us to use our Gifts, and to uphold the vow to protect that which we hold most sacred. They remind us of the things we sacrificed and the sacrifices made before us so we could live this life.

Soaring higher to meet the others, a glimpse of my wings surprises me. There, amongst the snowy feathers and the mottled brown ones, iridescent stripes decorate some of my feathers, where small black spots appear like the black witch moths who guided me all these months and who linger deep within me, waiting for release. As I race to meet the others, an intense rush of air propels me forward as the moths stream past me. At first, they move in a haphazard dance, but then they merge in a swirling mass, swooping and diving in unison. When they come together, the black cloud becomes the pointed face and large ears of a coyote. As the wind whips through the murmuration, the moths somehow yip and snarl, their cries a high-pitched, howl-like warning.

Instead of peeling off to safety or hanging back to avoid them, I dip my head and rise ever closer, even as the coyote cloud opens its mouth. With my sister and brother owls descending to fly alongside me, we soar into the coyote's mouth as it closes around us, and we burst through the other side with a determination to face any darkness. This warning only stokes a flame of inspiration within me, a reminder to honor my true self and allow my other abilities to flourish from my soul—rooted to this earth, my blood like ice, my spirit like fire.

Acknowledgments

The Bone Key would not exist without a core group of family, friends, and fellow authors.

Firstly, my heartfelt thanks, to Chris for all those late-night brainstorming sessions, and most importantly for your unwavering support of me. I love you!

To my family, near and far, for encouraging me in all my pursuits.

To my Midnight Society family—Amy, Brian, Erica, Jenna, Jolene, Kathy, Vicki—for always being there in spooky spirit, even when we're far from one another.

To Richard Thomas, who convinced me I had the talent to take a tiny seed of a short story and turn it into a fully-fledged manuscript. And to my fellow Novel In A Year classmates—Bryan, Jeremy, Lisa, Roni, Starlene, Scott 1 & Scott 2—the connections me made through our year of book creation together have truly enriched my life.

To Quill & Crow's head mistress Cassandra L. Thompson, for making my publishing dream come true.

To the entire murder at Quill & Crow Publishing House, for their enthusiasm, as well as Tiffany Putenis, Lisa Morris, and Mathew L Reyes, whose keen eyes helped me shape my debut novel into the book I envisioned it could be.

To Fay Lane, for designing a cover that truly captures the wonder, magic, and haunting beauty of my witchy world.

And to everyone who reads The Bone Key. All I've ever wanted was to share my writing with others. Your interest in this book means everything to me!

~M~

About the Author

Canadian author Mary Rajotte has a penchant for penning nightmarish tales of Gothic folk horror, which have been published in a number of anthologies. In 2022, she launched Frightmarish: a quarterly Gothic LitZine for devotees of dark fiction that explores the creative macabre through prose, poetry, artwork, and activity pages. When Mary isn't writing, you can find her standing on her tiptoes at concerts or conjuring ideas by moonlight. Sometimes camera-elusive but always coffee-fueled, Mary lives in Toronto, Canada, with her fiancé.

𝕏 ⦿ ❊

Glossary

A
Ahuehuete (Spanish): cypress wood, National Tree of Mexico
Aquelarre Búho (Spanish): Owl Coven
Asamblea del Agua (Spanish): Water Assembly
Asamblea del Aire (Spanish): Air Assembly
Asamblea Sur (Spanish): Southern Assembly
Asamblea de la Lumbre (aka Las Lumbres) (Spanish): Fire Assembly
Assemblée des Chouettes (French): Owl Coven
Assemblée de la Terre (French): Earth Assembly

B
barrida (Spanish): ritual "sweeping" to clear away negative, dense, or unhealthy energies

C
calavera (Spanish): skull
Los Cazadores (Spanish): The Hunters
Curandera/Curandero (Spanish): Latin American shamanic healer

D

GLOSSARY

Día de los Muertos (Spanish): Day of the Dead, to honor the deceased and celebrate their memory

E
El Árbol Sagrado (Spanish): the sacred tree, whose flowers are used to create the Elixir for Aquelarre Búho
los espíritus y los muertos (Spanish): spirits and the dead
El Este (Spanish): The East

F
flor de vitalidad (Spanish): flower of vitality, used to create the Elixir for the Aquelarre Búho

G
grito (Spanish): a shout, often of joy, excitement or pride
Los Guardias (Spanish): The Guards, specially trained protector owl-witches

H
Hacienda en las Lomas (Spanish): House in the Hills, the home of the Curandero for the Aquelarre Búho

L
La Lechuza (Spanish): The Witch-Owl, from Latin American folklore
Limpia (Spanish): cleansing rite/ritual

M
La Maison des Arbes (French): The House in the Trees, the coven house for Assemblée de la Terre
La Mariposa de la Muerte (Spanish): The Butterfly of Death, aka the Black Witch Moth
el mercado (Spanish): the market

N
La Néctar Sagrado (Spanish): The Sacred Nectar, used to create the Elixir
El Norte (Spanish): The North
Norte Blanco (Spanish): White North

GLOSSARY

O
El Oeste (Spanish): The East
ofrenda (Spanish): offering, usually placed during Day of the Dead celebrations

P
palapa (Spanish): palm roof
Pequeña Pluma (Spanish): Little Feather, Valeria's nickname, given to her by her father
platica (Spanish): a talk, usually of spiritual counseling
La Primera (Spanish): The First Witch of Aquelarre Búho, Lorenza de Salazar,

Q
"Que sus almas descansen en paz" (Spanish): "May their souls rest in peace"

R
Rancho de las Garras (Spanish): House of Claws, the coven house for Asamblea de La Lumbre

S
sarape (Spanish): poncho
Seekers (English): specially trained protector owl-witches from the Assemblée de la Terre of the Aquelarre Búho

Thank You For Reading

Thank you for reading *The Bone Key*. We deeply appreciate our readers, and are grateful for everyone who takes the time to leave us a review. If you're interested, please visit our website to find review links. Your reviews help small presses and indie authors thrive, and we appreciate your support.

More Books from Quill & Crow

Her Dark Enchantments, Rosalyn Briar

The Famine Witch, Stephen Black

Song of the Sea, Sabrina Voerman

Milton Keynes UK
Ingram Content Group UK Ltd.
UKHW042153111024
2112UKWH00021B/90/J